Only for Christmas

Tracy Corbett started writing in her late twenties. As well as writing novels, she's written several short stories, pantomime sketches and magazine articles. Tracy describes her writing style as modern tales of romance, with engaging quirky characters, who overcome adversity, grow as people and conclude in satisfying optimistic endings. When she's not writing, she enjoys amateur dramatics, gardening and music. She works part-time for a local charity.

Only for Christmas

TRACY CORBETT

CANELO

First published in the United Kingdom in 2023 by

Canelo
Unit 9, 5th Floor
Cargo Works, 1–2 Hatfields
London SE1 9PG
United Kingdom

A CIP catalogue record for this book is available from the British Library.

Print ISBN 978 1 80436 500 7
Ebook ISBN 978 1 80436 501 4

Cover design by Rose Cooper

Cover images © Shutterstock

Look for more great books at www.canelo.co

Printed and bound in Great Britain by Clays Ltd, Elcograf S.p.A.

1

MIX
Paper from
responsible sources
FSC® C018072

For Mum,

Love you x

Chapter One

Sarah Haynes was faced with one of those excruciating moments in life. A man was looking at her expectantly, waiting to be told how wonderful he was, when in reality all she wanted to do was punch him on the nose and wipe the smug smile from his face.

'I've done what you asked,' he said, nodding towards the newly cemented wheelchair ramp. 'And two days ahead of time. Finished before the weekend. Just like you wanted.'

Only so he could have Friday off, she mused. They wouldn't have worked that hard simply for her benefit. His idea of hard graft differed significantly from hers.

This must have been how her granny had felt when one of her bruiser cats had dragged the bloody carcass of a squirrel into her pastel living room, deposited the dead animal by her feet, and gazed up at her with an *Aren't I clever?* look. A look that switched to confusion when her grandmother started screaming about the cost of removing splattered blood stains from her blue satin curtains.

Sarah knew that screaming on this occasion wouldn't be appropriate, however much she wanted to. Partly because it would be unprofessional, but mostly because men like Knob the Builder would only see it as proof that

1

women were 'too emotional for the workplace', as she'd overheard him saying to his motley crew.

Restraint was called for. 'The design I signed off had a flat section at the top,' she said, resting her hands on her hips, making her navy suit jacket gape at the front. 'And yet you've taken the ramp right up to the door. May I ask why you did that?'

'There weren't enough space for a flat section,' he said, sniffing and making a horrible snorting sound. '*Regulations* state we need to leave enough room for pedestrians to use the pavement. Your design wouldn't have worked.' He seemed pleased with himself, like he'd got one up on her, throwing her need to conform to 'regulations' back in her face.

'Your design won't work either,' she replied, tapping her foot impatiently.

He frowned. 'Nothing wrong with our work, love. This is quality workmanship.'

Sarah sucked in a breath. 'Firstly, I'm not your "love". My title is Head of Human Resources. Secondly, any design change should've been run past me first.' She raised her hand when he attempted to interrupt. 'And thirdly, far from completing the project ahead of schedule, the ramp will now need to be removed and redesigned, exceeding the budget, and delaying providing disability access to the rear of the hospital even longer. We have members of staff requiring immediate wheelchair access to this section of the building, so this is far from ideal, wouldn't you agree?'

'Why would it need removing?' He walked up the ramp and yanked open the wide glass door. 'See? It's fine.'

Sarah supressed a sigh. Goodness, the man was dim. 'The door opens outwards.'

He glared at her. 'Yeah... So?'

'You've failed to include a flat section at the top of the ramp. Which means, anyone in a wheelchair will be rolling backwards down the ramp while trying to open the door.'

He stared at the ramp, frowning. 'Shit.'

Lord, give her strength. 'Exactly.'

He scratched his head. 'But the doors are automatic; you don't have to pull them open. You just press the button. See?' He actually demonstrated the action for her, as if she wouldn't know how to press a button. Seriously?

'In order to set off the sensor,' she said, speaking really slowly so he could keep up, 'they'd need to approach the door, which means they'd then have to rapidly reverse down the ramp to avoid being hit by the opening door.' Honestly, it wasn't rocket science.

He stared at the door, and then the ramp, as if he didn't quite understand. Which, sadly, didn't surprise her. But it did depress her. After all, she had to work with the man. Whoever had appointed him maintenance manager had a lot to answer for. It wouldn't have happened on her watch, but he'd been hired before her promotion.

She glanced at her watch; it was gone five p.m. and dark. The temperature was rapidly dropping and she was starting to shiver. 'Pack up for tonight, but I expect your team back here first thing tomorrow. I want this ramp dismantled and rebuilt within the week.'

'A week?' He snorted again. 'That's impossible, love.'

She narrowed her eyes in what she hoped was an intimidating fashion.

'Er... I mean, *boss*. We'll need to hire a hydraulic hammer to break up the concrete. And there's still the issue of leaving enough space for pedestrians. *Regulations*, and all that.'

And there it was, the not-so-subtle dig that this was somehow her fault. 'Regulations that require us to ensure the building is DDA compliant. Please revert to the original design and create a flat section at the top. You can then build the ramp at a right angle adjacent to the building, rather than coming up straight from the pavement. That way we satisfy both sets of regulations.'

He gave a half-hearted shrug. 'I suppose that'll work.'

She rolled her eyes. 'Something I could've told you if you'd come to me when you realised the original design wasn't going to work. Next time, don't change the design without getting my sign-off first. Got it?'

'Whatever.' His petulant nod was accompanied by a disdainful sneer.

Like she cared what he thought. Any man, for that matter. She was tired of being walked over. Well, she wasn't putting up with it any longer. Her career was at stake. She might have allowed a man to ruin her personal life, but she was damned if she was going to let anyone scupper her professional reputation. She'd worked too hard to let that happen.

Marching up the ramp, she pulled open the door, making a point of having to step backwards out of the way, before disappearing inside and letting the door swing shut behind her. Sometimes a dramatic exit was called for. And this was one such occasion.

She could well imagine the unsavoury names Knob the Builder was mouthing at her departing back. They were no worse than what she privately called him. She was past worrying about what other people thought. Gaining a man's approval was not something to aspire to; making a success of her job was far more important. Sometimes that meant making tough decisions.

As she headed through the open-plan canteen, with its contemporary white furniture and jade accents, it was easy to forget she was working in a hospital. That was the private sector for you. Anything messy or treatment-related was hidden from view. The board of directors wanted their 'guests' to feel like they were in a plush hotel, with five-star cuisine, and concierge service. The staff wore navy uniforms, with a jade tie for the men and a neckerchief for the women; shoes had to be black, shirts a crisp white, and minimal make-up and jewellery. It was all very classy, tasteful, and a far cry from her days working in the NHS, where the focus had been on how to deal with the onslaught of patients filling the waiting rooms, rather than the need for toilet roll edges to be folded into an exact point. She'd nearly fallen off her chair the first time she'd seen that as an agenda item at their monthly management meetings. Talk about contrasting priorities.

As she approached her office, she could see her team had packed up for the day. Unsurprising. That was another thing about the private sector: no one worked overtime. There was no need. Operations were scheduled, clinics ran during office hours, and the consultants fitted in their sessions around playing golf and attending lavish lunches. It was amazing how calm a medical environment could be when you didn't have to deal with heart attacks, car crashes, or a man inserting a vacuum cleaner pipe up his backside. It was an X-ray image that would haunt her eternally.

Deciding she'd had enough for the day, she collected her coat and bag from her office and was just about to switch off the light, when she noticed a well-dressed man smiling at her from the doorway.

'I was hoping to catch you before you leave; I wanted to introduce myself. Stephen Stokes.' He extended his hand with a confidence that matched his potent aftershave. 'New medical director.'

Ah, the rumours were true, it seemed. 'Welcome to the Queen Adelaide Hospital,' she said, shaking his warm hand. 'How was your first day?'

'Good, thanks. It seems like a well-run place.' He was handsome, she'd give him that. His brown eyes were so dark they looked almost black, which might have been appealing, if they hadn't lingered ever so slightly on her breasts as he checked her out. 'I have some questions about staff contracts I'd like to discuss with you.'

Sarah withdrew her hand. Making instant judgements about people wasn't her thing, but she'd met enough senior managers in her time to know which ones were modern-thinking, respectful and decent, and those whose attitudes dated back to the 1950s. Sadly, this man, dressed in his sharp Savile Row suit, with his fashionably styled haircut, suggested the latter.

The best way to deal with men like Stephen Stokes was to set clear boundaries.

'As you can see, I'm on my way out, but feel free to contact my colleague Georgia, and set up an introductory meeting. My diary is pretty clear next week. We can discuss the contracts then and any other issues you'd like to raise.'

He gave a slow nod, as if vaguely amused by her dismissal of him. 'I'm not one for formal meetings; I prefer the more casual approach. Do you have time for a quick drink? I hear there's a great wine bar on the Fulham Road.'

She hooked the strap of her bag over her head. 'I'm afraid not.'

'Another time, maybe?'

'Maybe.' Eager to escape, she moved towards the door, swerving around him when he refused to move out of her way. 'I prefer to conduct work meetings on the hospital premises and during office hours,' she said, praying one of the cleaners would miraculously appear and save her.

'Ah, a woman who knows her mind. I can respect that.' A response that might have been more reassuring if his arm hadn't brushed against her breast as he moved past. 'I'll ask my secretary to set up a meeting. Have a great night,' he said, sauntering off.

Waiting until she was sure he'd left, she locked her office door and almost ran for the exit. Her first assessment of Stephen Stokes wasn't a great one. It might turn out to be a mild case of sexism, rather than full-on misogyny, but anyone who still referred to the role of personal assistant as 'secretary' clearly wasn't going to be joining the hospital's Equality, Diversity and Inclusion panel any time soon.

Shivering from equal parts disdain and cold weather, she skipped across the hospital forecourt, slowing to a reasonable pace when she was sure she wasn't being followed. Paranoia wasn't a welcome characteristic, and neither was constantly suspecting the worst from people. But that was what happened when life had let you down. More specifically, men. Or rather, one man in particular.

Breathing in a blast of cold air, she headed away from the hospital towards Putney Bridge, admiring the way the dark December night was lit up by an array of coloured lights. Most of the shops already had their festive decorations up, a cascade of flashing fairy lights that twinkled away as she walked down the street, shivering beneath her padded coat.

Above her, a set of stars twinkled brightly, glowing and cheerful, making her fellow pedestrians gaze up and smile in awe. Sarah kept her eyes down. It would take more than a few sparkling lights to ease her aversion towards anything Christmassy, which was a shame, as she used to enjoy the festive period.

Christmases at her childhood home in Cheam, Surrey, had been fun. Nothing elaborate or expensive, just time spent with family playing games, opening stocking presents, and pretending to enjoy the huge turkey dinner her mum would inevitably ruin and then get flustered over, before resorting to cooking oven chips, and vowing never to repeat the experience the following year. The memories made her smile.

Her parents had relocated to Devon following their retirement, and her brother was married with kids of his own, so Christmases in her twenties had been disjointed affairs, screeching to an abrupt halt five years ago when her life had imploded and killed any desire to celebrate 'the most wonderful time of the year'. She'd avoided it ever since, turning down invitations and spending the day alone in her pyjamas eating cheesy beans on toast. And that's exactly how she liked it. She'd rather stick pins in her eyes than join in with the festivities.

As much as she hated the festive lights, seeing Putney Bridge illuminated against the purply-black sky was another experience entirely. It was a view she'd never tire of. Warm white lights ran the length of the bridge, bleeding onto the Thames, making a gentle rippling effect as the water ebbed and flowed below. Ornate Victorian street lanterns lined the length of the bridge, their brass carvings from centuries past and beautifully eccentric. You didn't see street lights like that on modern roads.

She was so busy admiring the lanterns, she almost didn't see the bundle of matted fur curled against the bridge wall. Only a small yelp caused her to glance down, otherwise she might have walked straight by. Huddled against the brickwork was a dog. The poor thing was shivering and quietly whimpering. Turning full circle, she couldn't see any signs of an owner. Cars sped by, along with a few red double-decker buses, but there were no other pedestrians in sight.

'Hey there, fella.' She crouched down. She had no idea if he was a 'he', but he looked male. Maybe it was the bushy eyebrows, or the large doleful eyes, pleading with her to take pity on him. It seemed cruel to punish a dog for the behaviour of all males. After all, he could be the exception.

She edged closer. 'What's your name, eh?' He recoiled when she extended her hand, trying to see if he was wearing a collar. His matted fur and sorrowful state indicated that if he did have an owner, they hadn't looked after him very well. She was just wondering whether to call the RSPCA, when he scurried forwards and rested his head on her knee. He looked up at her as if he'd decided she could be trusted.

Sighing, she patted his head. 'Well, I can't just leave you here, can I?'

When he appeared to shake his head, she blinked, before deciding it must have been a trick of the light. He was a dog. Dogs didn't speak human.

Removing her coat, she wrapped it around him and picked him up, struggling under his weight. 'You're heavier than you look. Someone's been feeding you, but not for a while, I'm guessing.'

He snuggled into her arms. Talk about manipulative. She'd been here before, succumbing to a male who toyed with her affections. She needed to stay strong.

'Don't get too comfy; I'm not allowed pets where I live. This will be a short-term arrangement. One night only, you understand? And that's not something I usually do. I'm not a one-night stand kind of girl. Not that I'm a commitment kind of girl, either. I don't do relationships, so count yourself lucky. You've caught me in a weak moment.'

His eyes never left hers, and he seemed to nod in understanding as she rambled away, rapidly getting more out of breath as she headed across the bridge, her arms aching from the dog's weight.

She half expected his owner to appear at any moment and accuse her of dognapping, but no one did. Poor thing, no one wanted him. She knew the feeling.

By the time she reached Oxford Road, where she lived, she was panting.

'You know, this is not how I envisaged spending the night,' she said, climbing the concrete steps from the street level up to the three-storey Victorian semi. Once a grand dwelling, the building was now converted into three flats. 'I'm regretting living on the top floor.'

Before she could escape from view, the basement door flew open and Diana Kelsey appeared like an angry demon, her fleece kaftan and slippers no match for the cold, but her neighbourhood watch instincts defying the weather.

'Who are you talking to?' she demanded, her husky voice cutting through the icy air as she held on to the doorframe, a cigarette burning away in her hand. Even in the dim light, her dyed blonde hair was visible, glowing under the weak street lights. 'Have you been drinking?' Which was ironic, seeing as Diana's recycling bin was overflowing with empty wine bottles.

'Just talking to myself, Mrs Kelsey.'

'What's that you're carrying in your arms?'

Oh, hell. 'Er... my dinner.' She almost felt the dog flinch. He wasn't the only one panicking. Diana was not the type of neighbour to turn a blind eye. 'I stopped off at the shops to get myself a few provisions. You know what it's like, you go in for one thing, you end up buying half the shop.' She was rambling.

'You're rambling.'

'You're right, I'm rambling. Sorry, it's been a long day.' She gave a self-deprecating laugh. 'Anyway, best get going. Dinner to prepare. Have a good evening, Diana.'

'It's Mrs Kelsey to you,' the woman yelled after her.

'Right, sorry. My mistake. I don't want to keep you outside in the cold, Mrs Kelsey. Why don't you head inside.' Her legs felt heavy as she climbed the steps.

'I'll go inside when I'm good and ready. I don't need you dictating what I can and can't do. I'm seventy-five, not ninety-five.'

Sarah nearly dropped the dog. Diana was only seventy-five? She'd thought her neighbour was older. A lot older. Thank goodness she'd never said anything. 'Night, Mrs Kelsey.'

Far from heading inside, Diana watched her, a suspicious expression on her face as Sarah tried to open the door without revealing the dog or dropping him. Thankfully, he stayed quiet, as if sensing discovery would result in him being shipped off to Battersea Dogs & Cats Home.

Once inside, Sarah kicked the door shut and took a deep breath before heading up the next flight of stairs.

A faint light seeped from under the doorway of the first-floor flat, indicating someone was staying there. She didn't have much in common with her grumpy downstairs neighbour, but their shared annoyance when the owner of Flat 2 moved out and advertised the place as an Airbnb momentarily bonded them. They'd been subjected to all manner of tenants, from loud stag parties to members of an unusual religious order, to drunken Oxbridge students wanting to cheer on their team at the famous boat race. Whoever the latest visitor was, she hoped their stay was of short duration, and they refrained from chanting, smoking weed and all-night partying. Her patience was wearing thin.

Her arms were numb by the time she fell through her flat door and lowered the dog to the floor. He shook out his fur and cowered on her prized oriental rug.

'Don't you dare pee,' she said, flicking on the overhead light to get a better look at him. Shortish legs, long body, floppy ears, and brown and white patchy fur. 'Well, hello there, Fred.'

He cocked his head, as if intrigued by her choice of name.

'You remind me of a cartoon strip my granny used to like. Fred Basset.' She pointed to her bathroom. 'It's hard to tell under all that dirt. Bath time.'

He started backing away.

'I hate to break it to you, Fred… but you stink.'

Ignoring his indignant whining, she picked him up and carried him into the bathroom. 'You know, this is the first time I've had a male in my flat since moving in.' As if sensing this was a significant turning point in her life, he licked her cheek. Grimacing, she pinned him with a steely look. 'Don't get too comfy. This is a temporary situation.

You hear me? I cannot have a dog. It's against tenancy rules.'

If she wasn't mistaken, his expression said, *We'll see about that*, and Sarah was left wondering if it was too early in the evening to follow Diana's lead and open a large bottle of something very alcoholic.

She had a feeling she was going to need it.

Chapter Two

Having spent his first twenty-four hours in the UK trying to recover from jetlag and a bad aeroplane meal that had left him feeling nauseous and fearful of contracting campylobacter, Lucas Moore was ready to see his family.

He could have taken the advice of the travel agent and used public transport to head across town, experiencing a ride on one of London's famous double-decker buses, or venturing underground to catch the Tube, but he was equally excited to hail a black cab. It was like being in a movie. Besides, he was still sleepy from jetlag, so a cab journey was safer. Falling asleep on a bus and ending up stranded in a remote area of England wasn't the kind of adventure he was looking for.

He rubbed condensation away from the window so he could admire the view. London was just as he'd imagined. Centuries-old buildings, narrow streets and a veil of grey fog hanging down from the sky like a net curtain. A contrast between the old and new. The roads were crammed full of cars, trucks and more people with umbrellas than he'd seen in his life.

The cab driver blasted his horn and shook a fist at another driver who'd pulled out of a side turning. '*Wanker!*' he shouted out the window, his insult resulting in a V-sign from the other driver. Lucas grinned. Yep, he was definitely in the UK.

When the cab pulled up at his sister's address, he paid the driver, smiling when the cabbie saw the size of his tip. 'Cheers, mate,' he said, lifting his cap. 'You gotta love the Americans.'

Exiting the cab, Lucas looked up and down the street. Nice area. Big houses, fancy front yards and expensive-looking vehicles in the driveways. Harper had done well for herself.

Walking up the long driveway, he admired the clipped hedges and landscaped borders, all dusted with a thin layer of white frost, like something from a Dickens novel.

He hadn't seen his sister and nephews since they'd visited him in the States last fall, and he was excited to see them. His decision to take an extended vacation and spend some quality time in the UK wasn't something he'd planned, but once he'd discovered Harper's marriage was heading south, he'd booked a flight. The timing had worked out perfectly. His new position at the Lyndon B. Johnson Hospital in Houston didn't start until the new year, and although he could have gone travelling, or lazed about in London for the month, he'd applied for a licence to practise medicine in the UK. It would be cool to see how treatments differed between the countries. Besides, he'd go stir-crazy if he didn't have something to do other than sightsee.

Despite ringing the bell three times, it took a while before anyone came to the door. Strange, as they knew he was coming.

When the door finally swung open, he was greeted by his eight-year-old nephew, Max, taller than he'd remembered, but still a bag of bones and with a mop of blonde curly hair.

'Uncle Lucas!' The kid launched himself at him, jumping up and clocking his uncle on the chin.

He hugged his nephew tight, drawing in the scent of crayons. 'Hey, there, buddy. How you doing?'

Footsteps thudded across the wooden flooring and another blonde bullet smacked into him with a thud. Seven-year-old Elliot had joined the party, a mirror image of his older brother, but with a cheekier grin. A grin currently covered in chocolate spread, which quickly transferred onto the sleeve of Lucas's cream sports jacket.

Among a huddle of hugging, kissing and both kids talking over each other at rapid speed, Lucas became aware of raised voices. He assumed it was the TV on too loud, but as the noise level of his nephews lowered, he could make out his sister and brother-in-law arguing. That wasn't good.

Thankfully, the boys seemed oblivious. Or maybe they were just used to it. By all accounts, arguing had become commonplace in the Evans household lately. Another reason for him booking a flight. His sister needed an ally.

'Do you want to see our bedrooms?' Elliot looked up at him with a pair of huge blue eyes. 'I have dinosaur wallpaper and new Lego to play with.'

'And I have a drawing board,' Max chipped in, swinging on his arm.

'Sounds cool. But I'd better say hi to your mom first.'

Max's eyes dropped to the floor. 'Mummy's arguing with Daddy. They told us to go to our rooms. We're supposed to go to Daddy's for the weekend, but I don't think Mummy wants us to go.'

Elliot flinched when a door slammed down the hallway. There was a moment's silence before the shouting started up again. The poor kid looked traumatised. They both did. His nephews weren't as oblivious as he'd imagined.

Lucas dropped to his knees. At six foot, he towered over them. 'How about this? You head up to your rooms, and I'll go and speak to your mom and dad. Maybe I can find out what the problem is. How does that sound?'

'Can you ask them to stop shouting?' Elliot blinked away tears.

'Sure thing, buddy.' Lucas kissed his nephew's forehead. 'Head on up. This'll be sorted in no time. Adults argue all the time. I'm sure it's no big deal.'

The kid didn't look convinced.

Hugging them both, he waited until his nephews had disappeared upstairs, before heading towards the shouting. He wasn't overly enthusiastic at the idea of intruding on a domestic situation, but what else could he do? It wasn't like he could walk away now he was here.

Slowly pushing open the hallway door leading to the kitchen, he could see Harper's back. She was wearing oversized loungewear, with her hands raised and gripping her long wavy hair. On the other side of the kitchen island was her husband, Paul. He was wearing a work suit, looking irritated and angry. It wasn't behaviour Lucas had seen before; his brother-in-law was usually a mild-mannered guy.

'Sorry to interrupt, but you might want to keep the shouting down.'

The sound of his voice cut through the yelling and both parties swung around to face him.

'Lucas!' Harper flew across the kitchen and fell into his arms, sobbing so hard he struggled to hold her upright. 'Thank God you're here!'

Over the top of her blonde head, Lucas met Paul's pained expression and offered him a sympathetic smile. 'Timing was never my forte,' he said, hoping to lighten the moment. 'Your sons were pretty distressed hearing you two yelling at each other. I figured you'd want to know. I can't imagine upsetting your kids is what either of you wants.'

Lucas braced himself for being told this was none of his business, but his sister just sagged against him, and his brother-in-law looked contrite. 'You're right. We're out of line,' Paul said, rubbing his face. 'We should know better.'

Harper's head shot up, clocking Lucas on the chin, which was still sore from his nephew's headbutt. 'Don't you blame me for this, you son of a bitch! This is your doing!'

'I'm not the one being unreasonable,' Paul sighed, loosening his tie.

'You don't call screwing your PA unreasonable?'

Lucas flinched. Paul was having an affair? That was a new development.

Breaking eye contact, Paul turned away, a sure sign of guilt. 'She's not my PA and this has nothing to do with Laura.'

Harper pushed away from Lucas, slapping her hands down on the kitchen island. 'Like hell it doesn't! If it wasn't for her, you wouldn't be leaving me!'

Lucas stepped between them. 'Hey, hey, guys, calm down. This isn't helping.' He had to raise his voice to be heard over the shouting. Ironic, seeing as he was trying to lower the temperature, not add to it. 'Take a breath. Both of you.' He turned to Paul. 'The kids said something about you taking them away for the weekend?'

He glanced at Harper. 'That's right. I've rented a place across town.'

'Yeah, so you can continue screwing your PA! How convenient for you!'

His sister never lost her temper, so things must be bad for her to be losing control like this.

Paul raised his hand. 'I can't deal with this right now. I'm done arguing, Harper. I'm taking the kids to mine for the weekend, as we agreed. Hopefully, by the time I bring them back on Sunday, you'll have calmed down.'

Harper's response was to throw a metal colander at her husband's head.

Thankfully, it missed.

'Asshole!' she screamed, before collapsing onto a barstool and wailing like someone had died. Her marriage certainly seemed dead.

Lucas waited for Paul to leave, before rubbing Harper's back and making soothing comments about 'staying strong', and 'hanging in there'. He had no idea what he should say or do at a time like this, but saying nothing felt wrong.

As he stroked his sister's back, he wondered when she'd lost so much weight. He could feel every vertebra in her back, and what was with the jogging suit? Harper was normally a fan of the latest trends and having her nails and eyelashes done. It was disconcerting to see her looking so dishevelled.

He heard footsteps on the stairs. 'Do you want to say goodbye to the kids before they leave?'

Harper shook her head. 'I don't want them to see me like this.'

'Fair enough.' When he heard the front door shut and the house descended into silence, he pulled Harper into his arms. 'I had no idea things were so bad, sis. What do you need? What can I get you? Wine? Vodka? Chocolate ice cream? Run you a bath? Just tell me. I'm here for you, okay?'

'I just want to sleep,' she said, straightening. 'I need to go upstairs.'

'Sure, whatever you need. You head up. I'll be right down here. Call when you need me.'

She shook her head. 'Go home, Lucas. I'll be fine.'

'Are you kidding me? There's no way I'm leaving you like this.'

'I'm not going to do anything crazy, if that's what you're worried about.' She reached up on tiptoes and kissed his cheek. 'But you might have noticed I'm not quite myself tonight. I'm so glad you're here, you have no idea. But right now, I need to be alone. Come back tomorrow morning, okay?'

'Are you sure? I'm happy to crash on the couch?'

'I need to vent, and I can't do that with you here.' Her smile was weak. 'It involves more yelling. There will be crying. And no doubt the destruction of Paul's expensive suits. He hasn't collected his clothes yet. I have a window of opportunity, as they say, and I don't want you implicated in my crimes.'

Lucas didn't like the sound of that. Revenge never ended well. 'No scissors. Or sharp knives. You hear me?'

She nodded. 'Loud and clear. I'll stick to ripping.'

He squeezed her hand. 'And don't go yelling too much, or the neighbours will call the cops.'

'I'll use a pillow,' she said, removing a large tub of chocolate ice cream from the freezer. 'I'm a cliché, I know. But I really would rather be alone.' She fetched a large spoon from the drawer. 'Please, Lucas.'

'Okay, but I'll be back first thing in the morning. You and I need to talk.'

She flipped off the lid and scooped up a spoonful of ice cream. 'We do.'

'And if the kids are away then I'll be staying the weekend. I don't want you being on your own. Not like this.' He gestured to her tearful state. 'I'm worried about you.'

'Don't be.' She threw a set of car keys at him. 'Take the Bentley. Come back tomorrow.'

He fumbled over the keys. 'I can't take your car; I've never driven in the UK. I'll crash for sure.'

'Good. It's one of Paul's cars. It'll teach him a lesson. Just don't injure yourself.' She kissed his cheek and disappeared from the kitchen. 'Love you!' she called back.

'Love you too!' he yelled after her, staring at the set of Bentley car keys. Seriously?

At least it would save him the cab fare.

Ten minutes later, having set off the car alarm and climbed into the passenger seat – before remembering the UK was left-hand drive – he was good to go. How hard could it be?

He hadn't driven a stick-shift since college, and he needed to drive on the opposite side of the road. Apart from that, not much difference, right?

Okay, so they had things called roundabouts, which made no sense, and the London traffic was hectic as hell, but he wasn't one to dwell on the negatives. He was about to drive a four-litre, electric-blue Bentayga EWB SUV, with a V8 engine. Holy cow, this was the stuff of his childhood dreams.

He was like James Bond's American cousin – tasked with masterminding a car chase around London, beating up the bad guys and saving the girl. Except there was no girl, sadly. And there were no bad guys. And certainly no chance of a car chase – not when the traffic prevented him travelling above ten miles an hour. And James Bond never had to rely on a satnav to find his way home. Still, it was exciting just the same.

The slow traffic turned out to be a good thing as it gave him more time to work out which side of the road he was supposed to be on. The fog didn't help, and neither did the agitation of his fellow drivers. Somehow, he managed to reach Putney Bridge without stalling, getting slammed with a road violation or hitting anything.

By the time he'd circled Oxford Road three times searching for a parking space, and contemplated returning the car to his sister so he could catch a cab, he was sweating like a racehorse. London driving was not good for the soul.

His parking effort wasn't great. One wheel was bumped up on the sidewalk, but he couldn't face trying again. Seven attempts at parking a Bentley, with a group of teenagers shouting 'Tosser!' at him from across the road, was humiliating enough.

Pressing the key fob several times to ensure the car was locked, he skipped up the concrete steps leading to his rental apartment. He was hungry. He had planned to eat with his family, but that wasn't to be. So much for a nice evening catching up: it was like a warzone at his sister's place. Maybe he'd head out for fish and chips later; he was eager to sample the UK's famous cuisine.

'*Oi*, you can't leave that parked there,' a woman yelled at him.

In his thirty-five years on the planet, Lucas had never been yelled at so much in one day. What was it with this place?

It took him a moment to work out where the woman was. He looked over the side of the steps and realised she was below him, standing at the doorway of the basement apartment. 'Hey there, neighbour.'

'Don't you "hey there" me, young man.' She looked like a character from a Roald Dahl novel. Her dyed hair was fixed in curlers, and she was leaning on a walking stick, her long dressing gown bright green like a lettuce leaf. 'You ain't left enough room for my walking frame. I've had enough of you visitors, turning up here, thinking you own the place, blocking the pavement. Selfish, the lot of you.'

He jogged down the steps and walked around to her doorway. The last thing he needed was to fall foul of his neighbours.

'Hey! Don't come any closer.' She pointed her walking stick at him. 'Not if you know what's good for you.'

He lifted his hands in surrender. 'I'm harmless, I promise.' He tried for a smile. 'I just thought I'd introduce myself. Lucas Moore. I'm staying in the apartment above.'

Her eyes narrowed as she studied him. 'You American?'

'That I am, ma'am.' He mock saluted her.

'I'm not the bleeding queen,' she said, leaning heavily on her stick when she began coughing.

'Apologies, I'm still getting used to the culture change. What should I call you?'

'You don't call me anything, you cheeky blighter.' She banged her chest when she wheezed. Her breathing didn't sound good. 'Just move your ruddy car.'

Dread settled in his stomach. 'Here's the thing, I'm not used to driving in the UK. It took me an age to get into that space; I don't fancy my chances moving it. I'll be gone first thing tomorrow, so would it be okay if I moved it then, ma'am?'

Another poke of the walking stick. 'Like I said, I ain't no ma'am.'

'Then how should I address you? Where I'm from we like to show old folk some respect.'

'*Oi*, less of the "old", matey.' She patted the side of her curlers. 'And you can call me Mrs Kelsey.'

He extended a hand. 'A pleasure to meet you, Mrs Kelsey.'

'I doubt that,' she said, sneering. 'I'm not known for being neighbourly.'

'That's a shame. I'm new to town and I don't know many people.'

'Yeah, well, that's not my problem.' She waved her hand about. 'Now, what you doing about that car?'

'I'm going to move it first thing in the morning. If that's okay with you, Mrs Kelsey?'

'You make sure you do. First thing, mind, no taking liberties.' She shuffled back indoors. He wanted to check on her breathing, but he suspected she might wallop him with her stick if he suggested it, so he thought better of it.

'You have my word!' he called after her. 'I hope to see you around, Mrs Kelsey.'

'Not if I have anything to do with it.' The door slammed shut.

'Night then.'

Silence.

Okay, so not a great first interaction with his neighbour.

Maybe he'd have better luck with the tenant in the other apartment. The light was on upstairs, so he figured someone was home. Hopefully whoever lived there would be less volatile than Mrs Kelsey.

He took the two flights of steps up to the top of the building and knocked on the door of number three. No answer.

He could hear movement inside, so he tried again. This time he heard a faint bark, followed by a load of hushing. There was a pause before the door cracked open a fraction.

'Yes, what do you want?' A pair of deep brown eyes peered at him through the gap. Pretty eyes. *Well, hello there.* Things might be looking up.

'Hey there, I'm Lucas, your new neighbour.' He held out his hand, hoping for a warm response, but the door remained only partially open. 'How y'doing?'

Her brown eyes flickered over him. And then she frowned. Frowning was never a good sign. 'Did you need something?'

He tilted his head. 'Something?'

'A cup of sugar, or something? Isn't that why most people knock on a neighbour's door?'

'Er… no, ma'am. I'm good for sugar. Just thought I'd be polite and say hi.'

'That's it?'

'Yep, that's it.' Anyone would think a neighbour being friendly was unusual.

She disappeared inside, and for a moment he thought she was going to shut the door. He wasn't expecting a dinner invitation, but would it hurt her to say hi and shake his hand?

Turning for the stairs, he was resigned to striking out with both his neighbours, when the door opened again.

'Sorry about that.' Her face was more visible now between the gap. And boy, what a face. If Mrs Kelsey was a Roald Dahl character, then this woman was a contender for a Disney princess. Long glossy dark hair, a heart-shaped face and a set of pouty lips that made him a little dizzy. 'I'm sorry, you've caught me at a bad time,' she said, glancing behind her.

'No worries. You own a dog?'

'A dog?' Her head shot around to face him. 'Why would you think I owned a dog? That's absurd, of course I don't own a dog. I've never heard of anything so stupid. No dog here. Nope, nothing of the sort. No pets in this apartment.'

Why was she so flustered? 'I thought I heard a bark.'

'You must be mistaken. No barking. Only...' She blinked furiously, as if trying to figure something out. 'The TV! Yes, that's it. It must be the TV. Or maybe an echo. Battersea Dogs Home isn't far from here. Perhaps a bark caught on the wind and travelled here. You know, on the breeze.'

Okay, so his neighbour was cute as hell, but also batshit crazy. Maybe she had more in common with Mrs Kelsey than he'd thought. Shame, as she really was extremely pretty.

'If there's nothing else?' Her fingers tapped impatiently on the door.

He backed away. 'No, nothing else, just wanted to say hi.'

'Well... hello to you too, but I need to go... and do chores. Yes, that's it. I have... chores. Very important chores. Time-critical chores.' She started closing the door. 'Goodbye.'

'You have a name?'

She stilled. 'Sorry?'

'Your name? You know, in case we bump into each other again.'

'Oh… Sarah.'

'Great to meet you, Sarah. Maybe see you around?'

'Maybe.' The door slammed shut.

Well, that told him.

Letting out a long whistle, he rubbed the back of his neck. What the hell? He'd only been here a day, and so far he'd been caught in the middle of a domestic, yelled at by one neighbour, and annoyed another… who had then offered him sugar. Was sugar a euphemism for something? Drugs? Sex? Was she a hooker? Oh, hell, maybe sugar was code for something in England. He'd best do some research.

Either way, it wasn't a great start to his trip.

Welcome to the UK.

Chapter Three

Sarah could think of a dozen other things she'd rather be doing on a Monday afternoon than being stuck inside the new medical director's office getting grilled about staffing contracts. Even pulling her teeth out with a pair of rusty pliers would be preferable, especially when there was nothing really to discuss. The staff contracts adhered to current employment legislation and were reviewed annually, but Stephen Stokes had insisted on a meeting. He wanted an opportunity to meet with the team and find out more about them, which was the last thing Sarah wanted. The less people knew about her, the better.

'That's the boring stuff dealt with,' Stephen said, rocking back in his large leather wing chair and smiling. He looked pleased with himself, like they were playing some kind of mind game and he was winning. 'Now for a more informal chat. Tell me a little about yourself, Sarah.'

It was an innocuous enough question, but one she hated. Talking about herself wasn't something she felt comfortable doing. Still, if she stuck to details about her work life, she'd be fine.

Clearing her throat, she crossed her legs and tried to look composed. 'As you know, I'm head of human resources. It's a position I've held for over four years. Prior to that, I had various positions in payroll, finance and HR support. I have a degree in business psychology, and I'm involved in various hospital committees, including the Equality, Diversity and Inclusion working group.'

'Impressive.' He tapped a cream folder lying on his big leather-topped desk, something he must have had recently delivered, as the previous medical director hadn't owned anything so grand. 'But all of that I could've found out by reading your personnel file. I'm interested in who you are away from work, Sarah.'

She tried to keep her expression neutral, unnerved by the way he'd said her name; it sounded far too intimate.

He came around to her side of the desk. 'I like to know what makes my team tick. What motivates them, what are they passionate about?' He perched on the edge of the desk, his leg brushing against hers. 'For instance, are you married? I don't see a ring.'

Instinct made her touch her ring finger. A diamond engagement ring had once sat so proudly there, and even though the dent in her flesh had long since faded, the humiliation hadn't.

'I don't see that my personal situation is relevant to my ability to carry out my role,' she replied defensively. Her tone was prickly, but he'd touched a nerve. She should be married, and she wasn't.

'That's where I disagree.' One corner of his mouth quirked into a smile. 'I find single people are usually more career-motivated. They have less distractions away from work. They're less likely to leave the office early, or skip work to look after the kids. I'm sure as head of HR you've come across such issues.'

Her first assumptions about Stephen Stokes had been correct. He was a dinosaur. Outdated and a misogynist.

He wasn't referring to 'people' in the workplace; he was airing his views about working women.

Despite huge improvements in equality laws, it was still women who were most likely to have their working day disrupted by childcare issues. Something she was trying to address by improving the hospital's policies concerning not just childcare commitments, but carers in general. She wanted to ensure that as employers they offered reasonable adjustments in the workplace to allow for anyone needing additional support.

'Do you have children?' His eyes dipped to her knee.

Uncrossing her legs, she tugged on the hem of her suit skirt. 'Perhaps I could draw your attention to the new recruitment policy the hospital introduced last year, which removed asking any unnecessary personal questions from the application process. Basing a recruitment decision using such information was deemed to be inappropriate and outdated.'

He grinned. 'Ah, a feminist.'

'I support equality in the workplace, if that's what you're implying. I also consider myself to be professional, non-judgemental and impartial. My aim is to assess an application purely on its merits.'

He laughed. 'I know that's the party line, but let's face it, there's more to a person that a few embellished career highlights on a CV.' He rested his weight on one hand, revealing an expensive gold watch beneath his shirtsleeve. As his body edged closer to hers, an unpleasant waft of strong aftershave filled her senses. 'I like to delve a little deeper and find out a person's true character. I want to discover the inner workings and what drives them to succeed. Like, for instance, are you in a relationship?'

Sarah felt an instant flush hit her cheeks. 'I don't see why that's relevant.'

'That's a no, then?' He smiled. 'In my experience, when given the opportunity, women love to tell you all about their romantic liaisons.'

Talk about sexist. Sarah pushed back against the chair, trying to create some distance. 'Not this woman.'

His grin widened. 'Why, is it scandalous?'

She adopted what she hoped was a stern expression. 'It's private.'

'I'm divorced,' he said, getting up from the desk, much to Sarah's relief. 'Two grown-up kids.' He handed her a photo frame. 'My son's training to be a doctor, like his old man. And my daughter's working as an architect.'

Sarah nodded politely at the photo of two smiling people with their father's confident posture, exuding self-belief, and with a slight smidgeon of arrogance.

He replaced the photo frame on the desk. 'I'm currently single. I love travelling, fine dining and buying expensive art. I spend my weekends on my boat, and most evenings I enjoy trips to the theatre, opera and dining with friends.' He tilted his head. 'There, you see? Not so hard to expand on the boring CV, is it? Now it's your turn. Give me a snapshot of Sarah Haynes. Who is she away from work?'

As much as she wanted to tell him where to stick his impertinent and intrusive questions, she knew her career would suffer if she did. That said, no one was going to bully her into revealing more about herself than she was comfortable with.

Drawing in a shaky breath, she forced herself to meet his gaze. 'As I've already explained, my life away from the hospital is private and I intend to keep it that way.' She stood up. 'Now if you'll excuse me, I have work to do. I'm extremely busy.'

Seemingly amused, he followed her over to the door. 'Most women find me easy to open up to. I'm a good listener.'

Ugh. She doubted that. She suspected his favourite pastime was talking about himself. 'Thank you for the meeting. I won't take up any more of your precious time.'

'Until next time,' he said, holding the door open for her.

What a miserable thought. The less she had to endure the new medical director, the better.

Sarah headed back to her office, glancing over her shoulder to ensure he wasn't following her, and trying to shake off the lingering scent of his aftershave that seemed to have permeated the fibres of her suit jacket.

As she reached the open-plan area where her colleagues were stationed, she heard Georgia's distinctive dirty laugh. 'We're talking seriously hot. Like, holy hell, yes, please, I'll-have-me-some-of-that hot.'

Aged thirty, Georgia could be mistaken for a recent uni graduate. Excessive partying, Tinder hook-ups and rolling into work with smudged eyeliner and matted hair was a common occurrence. Her maths skills and dedication to the role of finance assistant saved her from ever being reprimanded when her non-work activities interfered, but she walked a fine line some days.

Sarah reached their workstation in time to hear Jafrina's reply. 'Honestly, Georgia, that's hardly an appropriate way to speak about a work colleague.'

Georgia swung around in her chair. 'Calm down, Miss Prim-and-Proper. I'm just commenting on the quality of his aesthetic.'

Jafrina tutted. 'It's demeaning.'

Unlike Georgia, Jafrina was conservative, quietly spoken and her idea of a wild night was staying up past ten p.m. Something Sarah could definitely relate to. She was far more Team Jafrina than Team Georgia.

'Blokes love being objectified. Isn't that right, Tyler?' Georgia swivelled around to grin at the only male member of the team. 'Back me up here. Would you be offended or flattered if a woman called you hot?'

Tyler's deep throaty chuckle was a welcome sound in the office. 'I'm staying out of this.' But then he grinned. 'Honestly? Yeah, I'd quite like it.'

Georgia slapped her hand on the desk. 'You see?'

'To be fair, when you're in a wheelchair, it doesn't happen very often.' He pointed downwards. 'This thing isn't exactly a turn-on for most women.'

'Oh, please,' Georgia scoffed. 'Don't give me all that crap about the wheels hampering your game. I've seen your wife; she looks like Halle Berry.'

Tyler grinned. 'This is true.'

'And you have two equally stunning kids. So don't you go telling me she doesn't find you hot. The evidence says otherwise.'

Jafrina adjusted her headscarf. 'Georgia, really. This is hardly appropriate talk. Not everyone judges people based on their looks, or their—'

'Bedroom prowess?' Georgia nodded downwards. 'It's all right, Jafrina. You're allowed to say the words. You are married, after all.'

Sarah cleared her throat. 'Looks like I've returned just in time. Busy working, I see.' She tried to look stern, but her team knew her well enough to know it was a front.

'We were just discussing the hotness of the new doctor,' Georgia said, flicking her long brown hair over her shoulder. 'You seen him yet?'

Sarah tried to keep a neutral expression. It wouldn't be professional to voice her opinions about the new medical director. 'I've just had a meeting with him.'

'Ooh, lucky you. Is he single?' Georgia looked at her expectantly.

Sarah headed towards her office. 'Divorced, apparently.'

'Excellent! Decent bloke?'

Sarah paused by her office door. 'The jury's out on that one.'

'Oh, well, it might take a while to get to know him. Persevere, I say.'

Sarah had no intentions of doing anything of the sort. 'No, thank you. He's a work colleague, nothing more.' She headed inside her office and removed her jacket, which still reeked of aftershave.

Georgia appeared in the doorway. 'Yeah, but single, good-looking men do not come along every day. You need to suss him out, see if he's worth pursuing.'

Sarah sat down behind her desk. 'Not going to happen.'

'You don't have to marry the guy, just have some fun.' Georgia slumped onto one of the visitor chairs. 'When was the last time you hooked up with anyone?'

Sarah logged onto her computer. 'None of your business.'

'That long, huh? You need to get back out there and start dating. It's the only way to get over a shitty break-up.'

Sarah sighed. 'I'm fine being single, thanks.'

'But you're not fine, are you? You never go out at weekends, and you won't let me set you up with any of my friends. You won't even try internet dating.'

Sarah looked over at Georgia, who was sprawled across the chair, one court shoe dangling from her foot. 'I'm not interested in having a relationship, Georgia. Why is that so hard for you to understand?'

'Who said anything about a relationship? I'm talking about having some fun.'

'I have fun.' Sarah sounded defensive, but she was tired of being criticised all the time. She wasn't the one responsible for ruining her life. Josh Hamilton had done that. She was entitled to feel aggrieved.

'Yeah? Like what?'

Sarah let out an exasperated sigh. 'I watch movies… I visit antique shops. I have *fun*.'

Georgia raised an eyebrow. 'Blimey, even Jafrina has more fun than you do, and that's saying something. You know she had a dinner party on Saturday night? How many twenty-seven-year-olds host dinner parties, for crying out loud.'

Jafrina appeared in the doorway. 'Thank you, Georgia.' Her voice made Georgia startle and lose her shoe. 'Not all of us have the same level of immaturity as you do. I'm quite content with my family life, thank you. Maybe you should try it, instead of staggering home blind drunk every night.'

Georgia shuffled around to face her. 'Listen, I'm out there living my life. There's plenty of time to host dinner parties when I'm forty. For now, I'm sampling what life has to offer.'

'How adult of you.' Jafrina rolled her eyes, before turning to Sarah. 'Not that I agree with Georgia, but would it really be so terrible to meet someone? You have so much to offer. You're kind, smart—'

'Smoking hot.' Georgia incurred a glare from Jafrina.

'I was going to say *attractive*.' Jafrina turned back to Sarah.

Sarah tried to hide her agitation. 'I know you mean well, but seriously, guys, I'm not interested. I'm happy living alone. I have no desire to get involved with a man.'

'Not even the new hot doctor?'

'Not even him.' Sarah shuddered. Definitely not him.

Georgia tutted. 'No taste, some people.'

'Now, can we please get on with some work?' Sarah gave them a pointed look and waited for them to leave her office. It was exhausting to keep defending her decision to remain single, but life was easier that way. She liked her space. She liked having control of the remote, and going to bed at eight p.m. so she could flick through antique magazines.

Occasionally she missed company. She'd be lying if she said she didn't find the bed too cold in the winter, and often found herself talking to herself, or crying for no reason.

Sometimes she even allowed her mind to drift back to a happier time when Josh wasn't blowing hot and cold and messing her around. But that would only result in more tears and misery, so it was best left in the past.

Time passed quickly for the remainder of the day. She only became aware of the late hour when her colleagues shouted goodbye from the doorway and headed home for the night. She needed to pack up too. She might be off men, but she still had a certain male canine waiting for her at home. A situation she really needed to do something about.

Forty minutes later, she was pushing open the door to her dark and quiet flat, and feeling a sense of trepidation.

'Fred?' she called out, wondering where he was. It was her first time leaving him alone in the flat and she half excepted to find mauled cushions, or pee on her expensive oriental rug.

'Fred, where are you?' More silence. Had he escaped? If so, how? The flat was secure... unless someone had reported her and the landlord had called around and confiscated him. Panic coursed through her. She couldn't keep him long-term, but she wasn't quite ready to say goodbye to him just yet.

And then she heard scurrying coming from her bedroom. This was followed by a thump, which preceded her switching on the overhead light and seeing Fred's guilty expression gazing up at her. Coupled with the rumpled duvet, it was all the evidence she needed. 'Have you been on my bed?'

Fred looked at her, as if to say, *Who, me?*

'Yes, you. What did I say about climbing on the furniture, you naughty dog?'

He trotted over, head hanging low, and slumped by her feet. He then rolled onto his back, legs splayed, and made a pathetic whining noise.

'Don't think you can fool me with a doe-eyed expression, Fred Basset. I'm made of sterner stuff.' But then he blinked up at her and she couldn't stay mad with him any longer. 'Daft animal.'

His wounded demeanour changed the moment she crouched down. His tail began wagging and he knew telling-off time was over. Talk about manipulative.

As Sarah stripped off her work clothes and put on her jogging bottoms, Fred began barking and scurrying around in circles.

'Shush, will you!' She crouched down and tried to quieten him. 'You need to keep quiet, or you'll end up at Battersea Dogs Home. You'll probably end up there anyway, as I can't keep you, but that's life. It's unfair, I know.'

He was too buzzing to stay still. At least he'd stopped barking.

Now all she had to do was get him out of the building without being seen.

Sarah was not cut out for covert operations. As she bundled Fred down the stairs, her pulse was thumping so hard she could barely make her legs work. Waiting until she was sure the guy in Flat 2 wasn't about to make an unwanted appearance, she sprinted past his door and almost dragged Fred down the stairs.

It was only when she was at the end of the road and heading towards Wandsworth Park that she allowed herself to slow to a walking pace. Fred looked disgruntled. She guessed partly from being dragged down the stairs, but mostly at being forced outside in the cold.

For all Sarah's threats to take Fred to the rescue centre, she'd still gone out and bought a lead, a dog bowl and a bag of treats. She didn't need a psychologist to analyse her behaviour. She knew full well that delaying rehoming Fred was as much about filling a gap in her lonely life as it was about saving him from a stint in kennels.

Dwelling wouldn't solve her issues, so she broke into a jog, only to be pulled back when the lead reached full stretch. Stumbling to a halt, she turned to look at Fred, who had planted his feet firmly on the ground and was refusing to budge. 'Seriously? You're not going to run?'

He shook his head – or he appeared to, because dogs didn't shake their heads; that would be insane. Either way, Fred was not the athletic type, it seemed.

It took all of Sarah's efforts to get him to walk around the park. She ended up static jogging, trying to run without actually moving, which was challenging to say the least.

Thirty minutes later, having failed to break a sweat, Sarah and Fred were heading home. So much for a nice spot of exercise. Fred was less active than Mrs Kelsey.

When their building came into view, Fred sped up. 'Oh, now you speed up,' she said, pulling on his lead. 'Shame you couldn't have jogged like that in the park.'

As they reached the building, Mrs Kelsey was shuffling out of her flat with an armful of recycling.

Sarah dropped behind the low wall and pulled Fred closer. 'Keep your head down, Fred.'

His sudden yelp made the older woman stutter to a halt. 'Who's there?'

Sarah prayed Fred would stay silent.

'I have security cameras,' she shouted. 'Don't think I won't call the police if you're up to no good. Come on, you good for nothings, show yourselves.'

Sarah stayed hidden. She didn't think Mrs Kelsey did have security cameras, but she didn't want to risk finding out.

'Think it's clever to harass an old lady, do you?'

Oh, so she wasn't above using the 'old' card when it suited her. Sarah rolled her eyes, causing Fred to give her a strange look.

'I'll be watching, don't think I won't be.' There was a loud crash as the woman's recycling landed in the bin.

Sarah peered over the wall and watched Mrs Kelsey shuffle back inside her flat. The light in the living room switched off and Sarah could see the net curtains twitching as the silhouette of Mrs Kelsey hovered by the window.

Sarah became aware of a neighbour opposite looking over as he exited his car.

Her behaviour was attracting unwanted attention. 'Like it or not, Fred, we're going to have to make a run for it.'

His look of *No way* did little to settle her nerves as she shoved him forwards.

'On my count of three. One... two...'

Swiping Fred up in her arms, she ran towards the steps, praying that even laden down with Fred's weight, she was still faster on her feet than Mrs Kelsey.

By the time she'd raced up the steps, her legs were burning and Fred was sagging in her arms – which meant that when the door of Flat 2 opened and the occupant stepped into the hallway, she had no way of avoiding him and they smacked into each other.

She screamed.

He yelled, 'What the hell?'

And Fred made a run for the stairs.

Sarah watched his wobbly brown and white bottom disappear with far more speed than he'd managed on their walk. It was like he knew he couldn't be seen. That had to be a coincidence, right? No dog could be that smart.

'Hey, are you okay?'

Sarah realised she was lying on the hallway floor. How had that happened?

She blinked up at the man. Lucas, her new neighbour. It hadn't been her imagination then? He really was as good-looking as she'd remembered from their first meeting. Maybe she had concussion? She rubbed her forehead. 'I'm fine, I think.'

'Are you sure? Did you hit your head?' He was bending over her, his face so close she could see every feature in high definition. Dark blonde hair, startling blue eyes, and… seriously? Who had a jawline like that? Was he some kind of model sent to torment her?

He smelt good too. Not like Stephen Stokes with his overpowering aftershave, but a subtle scent of something woody. His shirt was open at the collar, revealing a smattering of blonde chest hair that matched the stubble on his chin. He was seriously… *hot*, as Georgia would say. And Sarah didn't like that one little bit.

She shuffled away from him and, using the banister rail, hauled herself upright. 'I'm not hurt. No damage. Apologies for running into you. I hope you're okay.'

'I'm fine, but you took quite a spill. D'you need me to check you over?' He moved towards her and rested his warm hand on her forehead. Swear to God, she felt the floor shift beneath her. Large, smooth hands, softer than a pillow, firm enough to feel his fingers caressing her skin.

The universe was not playing fair. Not fair at all. Not content with throwing Josh into her life and letting him stomp all over her, the fates were now shoving this man into her universe. A tall, wide, god-like creature who could double for Chris Hemsworth as Thor.

'Nope, not fair at all.'

He frowned. 'What's not fair?'

'Oh, er… nothing. Just… rambling. Excuse me. I need to go.'

'You need to check on your dog, right?'

'What dog?' She backed away so fast she hit the wall. 'I don't have a dog. No dog in my life. You're mistaken.'

He ran a hand through his hair. 'You were carrying a dog when you ran into me. I just saw it head upstairs.'

'Really? Well, I wonder who that belongs to? A stray, no doubt. Shame, really. Anyway, I need to go.' She made a dash for the stairs.

'Why the rush?'

'I need... the loo. Yes, that's it. The loo. I'm busting. Excuse me.' She bolted for the stairs, tripping up them, and leaving him with a wide-eyed, confused expression on his very handsome, chiselled face.

You see? This was why she avoided men. They made her say and do crazy things. Things she later regretted.

Fred was waiting for her at the top of the stairs. He looked relieved to see her.

Almost falling through her flat door, she slumped against it and slid to the floor. Fred trotted over and gave her a strange look, one bushy eyebrow raised.

'I know, Fred. You don't have to say it. I feel the same way. Something tells me we might be in a spot of trouble.'

Chapter Four

Thursday, 8th December

A lot had happened during Lucas's first week in the UK. He'd started his locum work at the hospital, he'd managed to incur a penalty charge notice for 'stopping in a box junction' while driving the Bentley, and he'd experienced two further bizarre encounters with his neighbours. Mrs Kelsey had accused him of stealing a parcel from her doorstep, and the woman above had smacked into him with her dog, and then denied having a dog. Mostly, his week had centred around looking after his sister.

'I don't know how it came to this.' Harper's voice was muffled through another batch of crying. 'Sure, we'd been arguing more, but isn't that what happens when kids come along?' She grabbed a handful of tissues from the box on the desk. 'Running a family is stressful. All I wanted was a little support. Is that so much to ask? I had a decent career. I gave it up to start a family. The next thing I know, I'm being replaced.' She sobbed harder, and Lucas reached across to rub her back.

Poor Harper, this was not something he wanted for her. She didn't deserve this. He'd spent the weekend trying to be a supportive brother and listening patiently while she relayed the difficulties in her marriage, but it was hard going. To see someone you loved so crushed was heartbreaking. He felt utterly useless.

Stocking up on groceries and running errands had seemed too inadequate, so he'd suggested seeking legal advice as a way of helping. Harper hadn't been keen at first; she worried it would incite further angst between her and Paul and prevent a reconciliation, but she needed to fight her corner. And so far, Paul had been calling the shots.

The solicitor waited for the crying to subside. 'There's a third party involved?'

Harper nodded and snatched more tissues. 'Not that he had the guts to tell me himself. I found out from a mutual friend. She thought I knew about Laura. Well, I didn't. He said he needed to go away for a few days to clear his head.' She paused to blow her nose. 'Things had become so toxic between us disagreeing all the time that I thought: *Sure, go away, it'll do us both good.* But he never came back. A few days turned into a week, then two, and the next thing I know, he's rented an apartment across town and is living with this Laura woman.'

Lucas wanted to brain Paul. What a spineless way to behave.

Harper shook her head, her unwashed hair tied back in a scruffy ponytail. 'And this was a woman who'd been all charming and sweet to me at the work's summer barbeque, even though she was screwing my husband behind my back. Talk about two-faced.'

The solicitor waited a beat. 'Have you asked your husband what his intentions are? An affair doesn't always signal the end of a marriage. Has he told you what he wants?'

Harper's body sagged. 'He wants a divorce.' She buried her face in her hands.

Lucas leant over and hugged her. 'He said that?'

'Last night on the phone. He wants to sell the house so we can divide the profits and he can buy a place with Laura.'

Lucas wasn't an angry person by nature, but he sure despised his brother-in-law right at that moment. Paul knew Harper was feeling vulnerable, and he was sticking the knife in, taking advantage of her weakened state. It was cowardly, and cruel, and Lucas would be telling him so the next time they met. For now, he needed to focus on Harper.

The solicitor made a few notes on her pad. 'Have you discussed childcare arrangements?'

Harper shook her head. 'Not really.'

The solicitor rested her arms on the desk. 'Let me ask you this: what do *you* want, Mrs Evans?'

'Doesn't seem to matter what I want. He doesn't love me any more. There's nothing I can do about that.'

Lucas flinched. 'He told you he doesn't love you?'

Harper's face contorted with pain. 'He said he'd always love me, but he's no longer *in love* with me. He sees me more like a sister than a wife.'

Lucas cradled his sister in his arms. No wonder she was hurting so bad. Someone telling you they no longer loved you was hard to hear. He'd experienced the same thing in his senior year of college. Difference was, he hadn't been married and with two kids. That took the pain to a whole new level.

The solicitor placed her pen on the desk. 'If the marriage can't be saved, then we need to look at your options moving forwards.'

Harper clawed at her hands. 'What options? Paul's the one who earns the money and pays the bills. I've no idea how I'm going to cope without him providing for us. If I can't look after the boys then I'm scared they'll be taken away from me and I'll be left with nothing.'

Lucas placed a hand over Harper's, stopping her from scratching at her skin. The back of her hand was red-raw.

The solicitor spoke softly. 'Firstly, let me reassure you that UK divorce laws are intended to ensure both parties leave the marriage on an equal footing. This means your husband is required by law to provide for you and your children while they're still in education. If your circumstances improve in the coming months and years, which hopefully they will, any agreement will be adjusted accordingly. Until that time, I'm confident we can secure you a decent level of child and spousal maintenance that will enable you to provide for your children.'

Harper didn't look overly convinced, but she nodded anyway. 'What about the house?'

'That depends on a number of factors. For the time being, he cannot enforce a sale. I'd advise you to stay put and defer any questions about finances to me. I'm assuming your husband has engaged the services of a solicitor?'

Harper nodded.

'Then let us hash out the details between us and see if we can come to a settlement you're both happy with. Please be assured that you are my priority, and I'll be doing my utmost to secure you the best possible deal.'

'Thank you. But I don't have the money to pay you.'

Lucas squeezed her shoulder. 'I'll take care of that. Don't worry.'

She looked at him through bloodshot eyes. 'You can't pay for my divorce, Lucas.'

'Sure I can. I'm not leaving you without legal representation. It's not up for debate. No arguments, okay? It's what brothers are for.' He turned to the solicitor. 'What happens now?'

'I'll make contact with Mr Evans and request the details of his solicitor. In the meantime, I'd like you to think about what you'd ideally like the outcome to be, Mrs Evans. For example, do you want to stay in the house, which would be co-owned with your husband? Or would you rather sell up and move somewhere you own outright? Would you prefer a lump sum settlement, or monthly alimony payments? What would be acceptable in terms of childcare arrangements? Weekend visits? Weeknight sleepovers? These are all things you need to think about carefully. Once I know what you want moving forwards, I can build a case and try to secure a deal for you. But it's key that I know what the priorities are, and what you're prepared to compromise on.'

Harper wiped her eyes. 'I'll have a think about it.'

The solicitor stood, an indicator that the meeting was drawing to a close. 'May I suggest we schedule another meeting for next week? I'll ask my assistant to contact you to fix a time.'

Lucas stood up and extended his hand. 'Thanks for your help.'

'My pleasure.' The solicitor moved to the door and opened it. 'I'm glad you have your brother here to support you, Mrs Evans. We all need an ally during these difficult times. Good day to you.'

Harper was quiet as they left. He guessed she had a lot on her mind.

They walked down the busy high street and past the quaint coffee shops and independent grocery stores. He'd expected to find diversity in London, but the extent blew him away. There was Indian, Chinese and Moroccan cuisine, Polish and Punjabi convenience stores, halal butchers and rows of Jewish jewellers. There was even an American store, selling everything from leather ranch hats to little models of the Statue of Liberty.

'What time do you have to be at the hospital?' Harper asked, as they reached the car.

'Half an hour. I can come over later, though. Maybe we could get takeout and watch a movie?'

Harper nodded. 'I'd like that. Thank you.' She hugged him hard. 'I don't know what I'd do without you.'

'I have your back,' he whispered, holding her tight and wishing he could make things better for her. 'We'll get through this together, okay?'

She kissed his cheek. 'Love you.'

'Love you too, sis. Always.'

He waited until she'd driven off and disappeared into the traffic before heading for the Underground. The novelty of driving a fancy Bentley had worn off pretty quickly. There was never anywhere to park, the roads were so busy it took forever to get anywhere, and the parking fees were crazy. When he'd realised moving around by Tube was quicker and easier, he'd handed the car keys back to his sister.

Besides, he'd wanted the London experience. There was nothing more British than travelling on the Jubilee Line, where people stared at the floor, and if you dared say hi, they scowled at you like you were a serial killer.

These were all things he'd encountered during his first week, and something he'd been assured by his new colleagues was perfectly normal. Friendliness was viewed with suspicion and caution. It was seen as a mask for an ulterior motive. He'd never understand such scepticism.

Another anomaly was the language barrier.

He'd have laughed if someone had told him he'd need an interpreter working in London, but he'd only lasted thirty minutes during his first shift at the hospital before having to track down his nursing assistant and ask what a 'dicky ticker' was.

It turned out to be slang for heart failure. He now knew that 'mince pies' was cockney rhyming slang for 'eyes'. 'Farmer Giles' was 'piles', and 'Mutton Jeff' meant 'deaf'. There was a whole new language out there he knew nothing about.

He made it to the hospital with a few minutes to spare and found his nursing assistant waiting for him in his consulting rooms. 'Hey there, Carla. How y'doing today?'

Carla's face broke into a smile. 'Good, thanks, Dr Moore. How are you?'

'Just peachy. And please, call me Lucas.'

She feigned shock. 'And defy hospital protocol? It's more than my job's worth. I'm required to address you as Dr Moore during clinic hours, and I'm never one for breaking the rules,' she said, sneaking a chocolate from her top drawer. 'Except when it comes to sweets. Then I revolt. You want one?'

'Hell yes.' He accepted the offer of a chocolate. 'Who made these dumb rules?'

She shrugged. 'The powers that be, I guess.'

Carla was late forties and the perfect nursing assistant, efficient, friendly and joyful. She attributed her happiness to getting divorced. The best decision she'd ever made, apparently. With her only son away at university, she spent her free time walking four dogs, volunteering at the local food bank and attending various events with her girlfriends. They played darts in a league, tasted wine at fancy vineyards and met every Saturday to go cold-water swimming. All of which she'd never been able to do while she'd been married.

Maybe he should introduce Carla to his sister? An example of what the future might hold.

'Who's my first patient?' he said, hanging up his jacket.

'You were due to see Mr Jones about his dodgy waterworks, but he's running late, so I've rebooked him for later this afternoon, which means you have a gap before your first appointment.'

Lucas raised an eyebrow. 'Dodgy waterworks? Is he having problems with his plumbing?'

Carla grinned. 'Kind of.' She pointed downwards. 'Trouble peeing.'

Lucas snapped his fingers. 'Ah, waterworks. Right, I get it. Does anybody in this country ever use the correct anatomical description?'

'Rarely. It's our repressed upbringing,' she said, checking the computer screen. 'You have fifteen minutes before Mr Summers is due.'

Lucas rolled up his shirtsleeves. 'How come I recognise that name?'

'He's the chap you saw on Monday and requested bloodwork for.'

'Ah, dicky ticker man.'

Carla laughed and handed him the file. 'That's him. I have his results here.'

'See? I'm picking up the lingo no problem.'

'You're like a native already.' She checked the watch on her blue nurse's tunic. 'Would you like me to fetch you a coffee before surgery starts?'

'That's okay, Carla. I can fetch my own.' He skimmed through the file. 'In fact, let me get you one. What would you like?'

Carla pretended to faint. 'You're going to get me coffee?'

'Sure, why not?'

Her hands settled on her hips. 'A doctor fetching a nurse coffee?'

'Am I breaking protocol again?'

'Of the highest order. There'll be an uprising. Don't let the consultants catch you; they break out in hives at any perceived threat to their hierarchy.'

'I'll be discreet,' he said, heading for the door. 'Plus, I like to live dangerously. What would you like? Latte? Cappuccino? Americano?'

Carla laughed like he was the funniest guy on the planet. 'What are you like?'

'Did I say something amusing?'

She came over and patted his shoulder. 'There's only one type of coffee available. Instant. But thanks for the laugh, I needed that.'

'Are you saying you brought me that awful stuff because that's all they had?'

'Yep. Although they do have a selection of teas. Earl Grey, English breakfast and camomile. We take our tea very seriously.'

He rolled his eyes. 'Well, you need to start taking your coffee seriously.'

He went in search of the food hall, which he'd now learnt was called a canteen. Tomorrow he'd be bringing in a flask.

As he joined the queue, his attention was drawn to the woman standing in front of him. It was her hair that sparked his interest. Long, dark and glossy, like the mirror glaze his mom used on her cakes. Added to the faint waft of camomile, and he was transported back to Monday evening when he'd got up close and personal with his new neighbour. Not in a romantic sense, more like his high school wrestling days.

'Hey, there,' he said, clearing his throat as the queue shuffled forwards. When she didn't respond, he tapped her on the shoulder. 'Remember me?'

Her shoulder twitched, as if she was shrugging him off, before she glanced back and her face switched from a frown to shock. 'You?'

He gave a little wave. 'Yep, it's me. Lucas. Your neighbour. Sarah, right?'

Her brown eyes grew wide, and he might have enjoyed the sudden flush of pink in her cheeks if she hadn't groaned like he was all her nightmares rolled into one. As she stepped away from him, she landed on the foot of the woman in front, making her yelp.

The woman spun around. 'Jesus, Sarah, mind what you're doing with those heels.' Her frown disappeared when she spotted Lucas. 'Well, hello there, Dr *Moore*!'

Lucas frowned. 'You know who I am?'

'I make a point of getting to know all the new doctors.' Her smile turned flirtatious. 'I mean, *staff*. It's not like I'm only interested in the doctors.' Her laugh was loud, and she made no attempt to hide the fact that she was checking him out. She stuck out her hand. 'Georgia Brown – I work in finance.'

Lucas shook her hand, struggling to withdraw it when she didn't immediately let go.

Georgia nudged Sarah in the ribs. 'This is Dr Moore, Sarah. Remember me telling you about the new doctor?'

If Georgia Brown was drooling like he was her next hot meal, then her colleague was looking at him like he was dog food. Apt, really, considering the other night.

'You… work here?' she said, panic in her eyes.

'Started this week, covering maternity leave for one of the general practitioners.'

'You're a doctor?' She didn't sound impressed.

'I'm not sure they'd let me loose on the patients if I wasn't.'

'Ooh, he does sarcasm.' Georgia nudged Sarah again. 'Unusual for an American. I like it. So, where are you from, cowboy?'

'Duluth, Minnesota.'

'Cool, not that I know where that is, but it sounds exotic.'

He raised an eyebrow. Her geography was worse than his. 'Not really.' He focused on Sarah, who was looking rather pale now the colour had drained from cheeks. She was wearing a smart navy suit, so he figured she wasn't medical staff. 'What do you do at the hospital, Sarah?'

'Oh, she's head of human resources,' Georgia said, answering for her. 'One of the top brass. Very important. Total badass.'

Lucas smiled at Sarah. 'I'll know who to come to if I have any issues.'

Georgia nudged Sarah again. 'You hear that? He's going to come to you if he has any issues. Lucky you.'

Sarah briefly closed her eyes.

Lucas knew how she felt. It was time to put her out of her misery. Him too. 'Anyway, nice seeing you again, Sarah. Small world, huh?'

She offered him a weak smile. 'Indeed.'

He nodded behind her. 'The queue's moving.'

It took a moment for her to catch on. 'Oh, right. Yes. The queue.' She turned away and scuttled forwards on her heels.

'See you around?' he called after her.

'You can count on it!' Georgia said, grabbing Sarah and whispering in her ear.

That was his third strike now. The woman was cute as hell, but clearly not interested in being friendly. He should take the hint and back off, but it didn't stop him wondering about her. *Some folks are dealing with a battle we know nothing about*, his mom would say. Maybe she was right. Perhaps Sarah had issues that had nothing to do with him. Or maybe she just didn't like him. It was a depressing thought.

'You know anything about a woman called Sarah?' he asked Carla, when he returned to the consulting room with their coffees. 'Head of human resources.'

Carla took her coffee from him. 'Sarah Haynes? Of course. Total sweetheart. Why?'

'You say "total sweetheart", but three times I've tried to talk to her, and three times she's shot me down in flames.'

Carla sipped her coffee. 'Don't take it personally. It's not you.'

'It sure feels personal. She looks at me like I'm the devil.'

Carla shrugged. 'It's a male thing.'

He paused, his coffee carton halfway to his mouth. 'Come again?'

Carla went over and shut the door. 'You didn't hear this from me, but Sarah was jilted five years ago on her wedding day.'

Lucas lowered his coffee. 'For real?'

'Sadly, yes. There she was, standing at the altar, all smiles and looking like a fairy princess in her white dress and sparkly tiara, and he never showed up.'

'You were there?'

She nodded. 'Quite a few of the staff were. It was awful. She was so humiliated, poor love. She didn't come into work for a month afterwards. She couldn't face anyone.'

He slumped into a chair. 'I'm surprised she's still working here.'

'I don't think she would be if she hadn't been promoted,' Carla said, with a sigh. 'But it was her dream job; she didn't want to turn it down. Besides, I think she needed the distraction. She threw herself into work afterwards. She's been brilliant too, completely changed this place for the better. Working conditions have really improved since she's been doing the job.'

He nodded slowly. 'Good for her.'

'Yes... except, well, the experience has left her a little bruised.'

He didn't doubt it.

'A lot, actually. I don't think there's been anyone since. You know, romantically.'

Lucas blinked. 'Seriously? No one?'

'Not that I know of. So, you see, you mustn't take it personally. It's not you. It's men in general.'

Lucas sat forwards in his chair. 'What, like all men?'

Carla nodded.

'Well, that's just plum crazy.'

'Try telling her that.'

Chapter Five

Sarah usually looked forward to her Friday evenings. They were spent curled up on the sofa with a takeaway, a glass of wine and watching an old movie. As she drew the curtains and dimmed the lights, it was like shutting out the world. She liked the peace and quiet, and a chance to unwind from the working week, so being coerced into joining her colleagues for 'welcome drinks' at a trendy wine bar was not her idea of fun.

'It's not like I'd even be missed,' she complained to Georgia, as she was virtually dragged down Fulham Road, shivering from the cold. 'They'll be so many people, no one's going to notice if I'm not there.'

'You read the email. All staff are required to attend,' Georgia replied, striding out despite her skin-tight dress and pin-thin heels. 'You don't want to piss off the new boss, do you? Think of your job.'

'My job doesn't require me to attend social events outside of working hours.'

Georgia gave her an exasperated look. 'I don't see what the big deal is. No one's asking you to strip naked and dance. It's just welcome drinks for the new medical director.' She tugged on Sarah's arm. 'Aren't you the one always banging on about the importance of being a team player?'

'At work, yes.'

They reached the venue and stopped to gaze through the tinted glass front, emblazoned with the words *Vagabond* in bold modern typeface. 'And this is work, of sorts.'

Sarah raised her eyebrows. 'You're not going to be drinking, then? Or dancing? Or flirting?'

Georgia laughed. 'Hell, yes.'

'Right, so it's not a work event. It's a social event, and one I don't want to attend.'

'Really?' Georgia feigned shock. 'I'd never have guessed. You hide it so well.' She pushed open the door. 'Look on the bright side: Doctor Moreish might be here.'

'His name is Doctor *Moore*,' Sarah replied, her words absorbed by the throb of bass music and loud chatter.

Georgia turned to her. 'Coat off, please.'

Knowing there was no point resisting, Sarah shrugged off her coat, and immediately felt out of place. This was not your average local pub. The walls were painted dark teal, with rows of industrial steel racking filled with fancy wine bottles. Strings of exposed bulbs were strung around the room, their warm glow providing a soft ambience, in contrast to the loud noise.

'And we don't need this.' Georgia removed Sarah's scarf. 'Try loosening up a bit.' She stuffed the scarf into Sarah's coat pocket. 'You're not at work now. And you want to look hot for Doctor Moreish, don't you?'

Sarah slapped Georgia's hand away when she started unbuttoning her shirt. 'That's quite enough. And I've no interest in Lucas Moore, or any other man, for that matter.'

Georgia smiled. 'Lucas? First name terms, eh? Interesting.'

'Not interesting at all.' Despite her objection, Sarah's cheeks grew warm.

Georgia grinned. 'Now, stop scowling. Slap on a smile and pretend like you're enjoying yourself. You want to impress the new boss, don't you? Seeing as how you're so focused on your career, and all that.'

It wouldn't be appropriate for Sarah to voice her opinions on Stephen Stokes. The more dealings she had with him, the more alarmed she became. Only yesterday he'd sent her a friend request on Facebook. Talk about unprofessional. But Georgia wouldn't see it that way. She'd probably tell Sarah she was being uptight and reading too much into it. So she bit her lip and kept quiet.

In truth, the new medical director was the real reason why she hadn't wanted to attend tonight's event. It was tricky enough avoiding Stephen during work hours; she didn't need the headache of having to dodge him after work too.

Taking Sarah's hand, Georgia dragged her towards the bar. 'Time for alcohol.'

The wine bar was as Sarah had expected, crammed full of people looking stylish in the latest fashions, as they laughed, knocked back the booze and checked each other out. It was an advert for the young and trendy – all the things she wasn't.

They battled their way to the bar and ordered drinks, before searching for somewhere to sit. Georgia wanted a central spot, with clear views of the room to ensure she was the centre of attention. 'I've not syphoned myself into this dress for nothing,' she shouted over the noise, exchanging flirtatious glances with a man at the bar. He gave her clingy black dress an approving look and offered to pay for her drink.

'It's too loud in here.' Sarah pointed away from the crowds. 'I'm going to find somewhere quieter. You stay here and enjoy yourself.'

Georgia fluffed up her mass of hair. 'I'll come and find you later.'

Sarah smiled. 'Have fun.'

'I intend to.' Georgia returned her attentions to the man at the bar.

Leaving Georgia to flirt, Sarah made her way across the room, aiming for an alcove tucked away at the back. Jafrina was already seated there, along with Tyler, whose wheelchair didn't quite fit under the designer table.

Relieved to be heading for safer ground, Sarah made a beeline for them. She always felt on edge in crowds – although, she hadn't always felt that way. Being humiliated in front of a hundred-plus people had been the catalyst for withdrawing from mass socialising. She didn't need a therapist to tell her why feeling conspicuous in a crowded room would act as a trigger. She was intuitive enough to work that one out for herself.

Faking a confidence she didn't feel, she waved at various colleagues as she squashed past them, pretending to feel more at ease than she did. Everyone else was dressed up for a night out. It hadn't occurred to her to bring a change of clothes. But then, she hadn't intended to be here. It was only constant pressure throughout the day from her team that had persuaded her to come. Her plan was to make small talk for twenty minutes, enjoy one drink and then escape as soon as possible. Besides, once the alcohol started flowing, no one would miss her.

'Sarah, you came.' A hand caught her arm before she could reach the safety of the alcove. 'I wasn't sure whether you'd be here. You didn't reply to my secretary's message?'

All the relief she'd felt moments earlier drained out of her. Using the momentum of twisting to face him, she dislodged Stephen's hand from her arm. 'Apologies, I meant to reply to Rosetta's message, but I got caught up with a work matter.'

She always made a point of using his PA's name in the hope he'd take the hint and stop referring to such an experienced employee as his 'secretary'. But he seemed oblivious to his condescending manner. Or maybe it was intentional.

There was a calculating air about Stephen Stokes that was extremely off-putting. He was wearing a black shirt with the top few buttons undone, no doubt intended to show off his tanned chest and gold chain.

Behind him, a group of doctors were gathered together, including Lucas Moore, her new neighbour. When Lucas glanced over, his face broke into a huge grin… which might have been quite comforting, if she hadn't been so rattled by Stephen's ambush. Lucas was also wearing a fitted black shirt, but on him it didn't look creepy. Quite the opposite, in fact.

'You mustn't focus so much on work,' Stephen was saying, using the excuse of a surge in the crowd to edge closer. 'Everyone needs social time away from the office to relax and unwind.'

Spoken like the entitled consultant he was. A man who had reached the point in his career where he now called the shots. Sarah didn't have that luxury; she was still proving herself as a senior manager. If she didn't give her job total focus, she'd be out on her ear.

Stephen's gaze dipped to her mouth. 'Can I get you another drink?'

She lifted her glass, trying to preserve the minimal gap between them. She wished the crowd would disperse so she could escape. 'No, thanks. I still have this.'

'That won't last long. We can't have you running out.' He snapped his fingers at one of the junior administrators nearby and sent her off to the bar for a bottle of champagne. 'I'm sure you won't say no to a glass of fizz.' It was delivered as a statement rather than a question, so she didn't bother replying. 'No work tomorrow, so let your hair down.' He lifted his hand as if he was about to touch her, forcing her to jerk backwards, resulting in her spilling wine down her front.

Her hand immediately came up to stop him approaching. 'It's fine. I can manage.'

'Someone's edgy tonight.' Stephen's eyes were now locked on her see-through wet shirt, and it took all her willpower not to chuck the contents of her drink in his face.

Feeling self-conscious, she buttoned up her suit jacket, trying to divert his stare elsewhere. The scent of malt whiskey, mingling with his strong aftershave, confirmed her theory that Stephen Stokes had been knocking back the shots.

'Excuse me. I need to wash this wine off before it stains,' she said, aiming for a gap in the crowd in the hope of escaping.

'Not so fast.' Again, he caught her arm. 'Why haven't you accepted my friend request on Facebook?'

'I'm not a fan of social media.' Which was entirely true. Since being jilted she'd deleted nearly all of her accounts. Most of the comments had been kind and consoling, but reading about how wretched everyone felt only added to her shame. Friends of friends had started messaging her. They were sorry to hear about her ordeal. How awful. Did she have any idea? Surely, she must have had a clue things weren't right? Like somehow it was her fault for being naive and she should have seen it coming.

And then the nasty remarks had appeared. How Josh must have had a good reason for dumping her. Had he found something out? Maybe she'd been unfaithful? This was followed by a host of responses, people falling into two categories: those defending her, and those supporting the rumours. It had been torture. So, she'd removed herself from public scrutiny.

'I couldn't find you on LinkedIn or Instagram,' Stephen continued, his face uncomfortably close. 'And when I googled you, nothing came up. Strange, for a young person to be off-grid. Anything I should know about?'

He'd googled her? She felt slightly sickened at the idea he'd been so intrusive, but equally relieved that his search hadn't thrown up anything about her disastrous non-wedding day. It was her biggest fear, that somehow her humiliation would reach a wider audience than it already had. 'There's nothing you should know. Like I said before, I prefer to keep my personal life private.'

'But you do have a Facebook account?'

'I limit it to close friends and family.'

'I'm a friend,' he said, opening his arms, no doubt aiming for sincerity, but making her skin crawl.

'I'm not friends with anyone from work.'

'I'm sure you can make an exception. How else am I supposed to get to know you? I've invited you to lunch three times this week and each time you've turned me down. I'm starting to think you're avoiding me.'

There was a challenge in his expression, as though he was daring her to reject him again.

It was then that she realised Lucas Moore was watching her, a questioning expression on his face. Her distress must have been visible, because his gaze switched between her and Stephen, and then he mouthed, 'Are you okay?'

Her instinct was to reassure him she was fine. Resisting assistance of any kind was her default setting these days. She'd vowed never to rely on another man again. But that was when she was fully in control of a situation, and not feeling increasingly unnerved by Stephen's unwanted attentions. Common sense told her she needed an ally.

So when Lucas tilted his head, waiting for her response, instead of batting away his offer of help like she'd normally do, she shook her head, indicating that she was not okay.

He nodded in understanding, although quite what he was going to do, she had no idea.

'I'll get my secretary to arrange something for next week,' Stephen said, oblivious to the distress he was causing her. 'Think of it as a working lunch, a networking opportunity, appeasing the boss to ensure your career stays on track.'

Was he threatening her? She tried to step away, but someone blocked her escape.

'And accept my friend request, okay? You don't want to offend the boss.' There was an edge to his voice.

Thankfully, Lucas appeared in that moment, almost shoving Stephen to one side so he could step between them. 'Ah, here you are!' He rested his warm hand on her arm. 'Sorry I was so long; I got caught chatting with some guy from paediatrics. You okay, honey?'

Honey? Sarah felt her eyes grow wide.

Lucas turned to Stephen. 'Hey there, Stephen. Good seeing you again. Great party. This is some venue.' His grin was big and open and totally beguiling. She could feel several sets of eyes turning in their direction. 'You'll have to excuse me if I steal my girl away, only I haven't seen her all day.'

When Lucas's large hand slid into hers, she was so alarmed she audibly whimpered.

'You have a good night, sir.' Lucas gently pulled Sarah with him as he moved away. 'Thanks again for the invite. It's real sociable of you.'

Sarah wasn't sure whose expression was more shocked, hers or Stephen's. Shock that switched to annoyance as Stephen watched her being whisked away by Lucas, his expression darkening by the second.

'I'd prefer to handle Stephen myself,' she hissed, allowing herself to be led through the crowded bar – even though she hadn't been handling the man at all. That was beside the point.

Lucas kept hold of her hand. 'I get that you're mad with me for pretending we're involved, but—'

'I'm not mad,' she admitted, causing him to abruptly stop.

He turned to her, one eyebrow raised. 'You're not?'

She screwed up her nose. 'Well, maybe a bit.'

He grinned. 'I figured as much. Sorry, but it was all I could think of to get you away from him.'

'I realise that. And honestly, I'm more grateful than mad,' she admitted, trying to hide her disgruntlement. He'd rescued her, after all. 'Despite my best efforts, Stephen wasn't taking no for an answer, so thank you for coming to my aid and getting me out of a very uncomfortable situation. I really appreciate it.'

Lucas's expression softened. 'No worries.' He eased her into a space near the exit. 'I'm guessing you've had enough for tonight?'

She nodded. 'More than enough.'

'Then let's get out of here.' He collected their jackets from the stand and angled her towards the door.

'Is he following us?' she asked, joining Lucas outside.

He glanced back. 'Not sure. A bunch of people are looking out the window. How convincing do you want this to look?'

She blinked up at him. 'How do you mean?'

'Being involved. Making Stephen believe we're an item. A hug might seal the deal.'

'A hug?'

'Only if you're comfortable with that?' He waited, not pressurising, letting her make the decision.

Her brain struggled to compute the array of conflicting thoughts whizzing around her head. She didn't know this man. He could be an abuser. Then again, he'd rescued her from Stephen. They were standing on a main road. How much danger was she really in?

'Just a friendly hug,' he said, as if reading her mind. 'Nothing more. Playing for the crowd.'

She kept her eyes away from the window. 'Are they still watching?'

He glanced over. 'Yep, still watching.'

She swallowed awkwardly. 'Okay, then.'

'Okay?' He waited until she'd nodded her consent before stepping closer and sliding his arms around her.

He smelt of beer and that same woody scent he was wearing the other night, which must contain some sort of illegal aphrodisiac, because the smell seemed to be doing strange things to her insides. She felt boneless and had temporarily lost the ability to speak. She had no idea whether she was shaking from shock, fear or the cold. A tiny voice in her head alerted her to another reason, but she quickly dismissed it: the idea that she fancied Lucas Moore was ludicrous.

His hands rested gently on her back. 'You've gone quiet on me. You okay?'

Was she okay? She had no idea. She was standing on a busy street being hugged by a man she hardly knew. It was surreal, to say the least. It was also impossible to focus when she could feel his firm chest, the tickle of his stubble and the power in his arms. She needed her barriers back in place. And quick. 'You can let go of me now.'

He stepped away, and a draught of cold air immediately hit her, coupled with a strange sense of disappointment. She reasoned it was nostalgia. It had been a long time since anyone had held her, even if the brief moment of pleasure had now evaporated, leaving her wistful and shivering.

He zipped up his jacket, and then held out her coat for her. He was a gentleman, she'd give him that.

Turning around so she could slide her arms into her coat meant she was facing the wine bar window and could see her work colleagues staring at her open-mouthed.

Oh, heavens. The gossips would love this.

When she turned to face Lucas again, he had his hand outstretched. 'One last piece of theatrics. I'll let go as soon as we're out of sight.'

Sighing, she slipped her hand into his, not because she didn't want to, but rather alarmingly, because she did. 'This is turning into a very strange evening.'

'Tell me about it.' He squeezed her hand. 'And maybe try smiling? You looked kind of freaked out. Like I'm trying to kidnap you.'

'Oh.' She pulled her lips into a tight line. 'Better?'

He laughed. 'Been a while, huh? Come on, showtime's over.'

Hand in hand, they walked off down the street, just like any other couple out on a date. Except this felt really weird. Although perhaps not as weird as it should do. A feeling exacerbated by the warmth of his hand, firm grip and the soft feel of his skin.

'How come you have such soft hands?' she asked, without thinking. Those few sips of wine had loosened her tongue. Fancy asking such a question. What was she thinking?

'I moisturise,' he said, his thumb trailing over her skin and making her forget her own name. 'I'm a modern man.'

Needing a distraction, before she did something crazy, like lift his hand to her lips so she could breathe in his scent, she glanced back at the wine bar, only to see Georgia's shocked expression pressed against the glass. Her friend grinned and then gave a double thumbs-up before snogging the window.

Boy, this was going to take some explaining on Monday.

The temperature had dropped another few degrees and ice was beginning to form on the shop windows. The Christmas lights sparkled away and it suddenly felt very intimate to be holding this man's hand while walking along the frosty pavements towards Putney Bridge. She needed to be careful. A lesser woman might be fooled into having romantic thoughts, and that needed to be avoided at all costs. Her heart couldn't take it.

'Was that the first time Stephen's made a play for you?' Lucas asked as they crossed the road.

'I wouldn't call it a play,' she said, sliding her hand from his. They were out of sight now; there was no need to continue holding his hand.

'Trust me, it was a play. That man likes getting his own way.'

She'd arrived at the same conclusion. Although clearly Stephen had been drinking, so maybe that was a factor. Alcohol often made people act inappropriately. After all, look at her. Hadn't she commented on Lucas's soft hands? 'Hopefully he'll stop now. You know, now he thinks we're an item.'

Lucas gave a shrug. 'Maybe.'

They reached Putney Bridge, the soft glow from the lanterns misting against the lowering fog. It was a beautifully eerie sight. 'I'll leave it a couple of days and then tell people we broke up.'

'Sure. Whatever you think's best.'

It was so quiet on the bridge she could hear her heels clicking on the pavement surface. She glanced across at Lucas, hoping she hadn't offended him. It wasn't his fault she was off men. He seemed like a perfectly decent man. She should make more of an effort. It wouldn't hurt to be civil for one evening. 'How are you finding life in the UK?'

He seemed surprised by the question. She couldn't really blame him; she hadn't exactly been overly friendly with him so far. 'Good, I guess, for the most part. I came over to visit my sister. She married an English guy, but they're going through a divorce, and she's finding it tough. I wanted to be here to support her. For a while, anyway. I start a new job back home in January.'

So it was a short-term visit? It wasn't like she was interested. 'In Duluth?'

He turned to her. 'You remembered where I'm from?'

It was no big deal. She had a good memory, that was all.

He smiled. 'The job's in Houston. Different state entirely.'

'Are you looking forward to it?'

'I guess. It's a teaching role at the hospital, so I'm excited about that.'

'At least it'll be warmer than the UK. You must be hating this cold weather.'

'Are you kidding me? This isn't cold. Last winter we had temperatures of minus thirty-five in Minnesota.'

'Minus thirty-five?' She'd stopped walking. 'Goodness. I thought minus one was cold. I don't think I could cope with those kinds of temperatures.'

'You get used to it. Most folks have snow ploughs and chains on their tyres, so life mostly keeps going. I love this fog, though. You don't get this back home.' He looked over the edge of the bridge. 'Look at that. It's beautiful.'

She joined him and looked down at the Thames, dark and foreboding. The fog hovered above the water, glistening and sinister, like a scene from a Sherlock Holmes movie. 'I think so, but most people prefer the warmer months. Not me – I like the winter.'

Lucas smiled. 'Big fan of Christmas, huh?'

She pushed away from the wall. 'Not Christmas, just winter. I avoid anything to do with the festive season.'

He looked puzzled. 'Why?'

She turned away, chastising herself for revealing such an intimate fact about herself. That glass of wine had a lot to answer for. 'What's Duluth like?' she said, walking off at pace. 'I've never been to the States.'

It was a few seconds before he caught up. 'It's a great place to visit. Lots of open space and country parks. We had a vacation cabin on the North Shore of Lake Superior.

It looked out across the water, not another building in sight, just the lighthouse in the distance.'

'Sounds idyllic. Was that with your family?'

'Yeah, although they don't live there now.' He fell into step beside her. 'My parents divorced a while back and moved away, so I have no ties there now. No ties any place, in fact. I'm looking to lay down roots somewhere. Houston seems like as good a place as any.'

She pushed her hands into her coat pockets. 'I hope it works out for you.'

'What about you? Where's home for you?'

'London. I've never lived anywhere else.' They reached the end of the bridge and turned towards Oxford Road. The lights from the busy Boathouse pub bled across the water, the inside packed full of Friday night revellers.

Lucas glanced at her. 'Do you want to live someplace else?'

'I'm not sure,' she said, with a shrug. 'My parents live in Devon now, so who knows, maybe I'll end up living near them at some point. My brother still lives in London, so it's not like I don't have family close by.'

As they reached their building, a familiar voice cut through the frosty night air. 'I want a word with you, young lady!'

Sarah flinched. 'Oh, gawd, what now,' she mumbled, wishing she could avoid another grilling from her neighbour.

'What's with all this noise I keep hearing on the stairs?' Mrs Kelsey yelled, straining her neck to see. 'Sounds like barking. You got a dog up there?'

Sarah crossed her fingers behind her back. 'A dog? Me?'

Lucas stepped into the lamplight. 'Sorry, Mrs Kelsey, that'll be me.'

'You?' She shook a fist at him. 'You got a dog?'

'No, but I work out. It involves a lot of shouting. It's probably that you can hear. Sorry.' He subjected her to a disarming smile – a smile that would melt the hardiest of souls, except that Sarah suspected Mrs Kelsey had no soul, so it was a lost cause.

'You telling me there's no dog up there?'

'I promise, I don't have a dog, Mrs Kelsey.' He gave Sarah a discreet wink. 'Why don't you head back inside; it's cold out here.' He nudged Sarah towards the steps. 'We're heading up now. See you tomorrow.'

'I can deal with the likes of Mrs Kelsey,' Sarah grumbled, frustrated that Lucas was coming to her rescue for a second time that evening.

When he reached the top step, he turned to her. 'You want to admit to having a dog up there?'

Sarah was two steps down, so at a distinct height disadvantage. He was tall enough as it was. 'What makes you think I have a dog? I don't have a dog.'

Both his eyebrows lifted. 'Sure you don't.' He turned and headed towards his flat. 'Night, Sarah… say hi to Fred for me,' he called back, before disappearing inside his flat, wearing a huge grin plastered across his annoyingly handsome face.

Sarah slumped against the wall.

So much for keeping Fred a secret. Her cover was blown.

Chapter Six

Saturday, 10th December

Lucas couldn't remember the last time he'd bought a woman flowers. Maybe his mom on Mother's Day. But here he was, walking back from the Putney Exchange carrying a huge bouquet of winter roses. The woman at The Flowersmith had referred to him as *darlin'* a lot, and wished him good luck when he'd confessed the flowers were for his attractive neighbour.

He'd need all the luck he could get, as buying Sarah Haynes flowers was not the action of a sane man. But what could he say? He'd never been able to resist the appeal of a wounded woman. And despite her tetchy exterior, Sarah wasn't as tough as she made out.

'*Oi!* You there. American fella.'

Lucas paused when he reached the building steps, figuring whoever was shouting across the street could only be referring to him. He turned to see Mrs Kelsey leaning on her walking frame by her front door.

'That's right, you. I need your help.'

Lucas glanced up longingly at Sarah's flat, before sighing in resignation and heading down the steps to the basement flat. 'What can I do for you, Mrs Kelsey?'

'Leaky tap in the bathroom. You handy with a wrench?'

'Not in the least, but I'm happy to take a look. What happened?'

'How the hell should I know.' She gave him an incredulous look; her skin was sallow and grey. She didn't look well. 'The blessed thing started leaking water.'

'Have you called a plumber?'

'And pay weekend rates?' she scoffed. 'Don't be daft. You'll do.'

It was hard to resist such charm.

He followed her inside, watching as she shuffled along, her worn slippers dragging against the equally worn matting. Her yellow hair had white roots showing, and her dressing gown was dirty at the bottom. There was a definite shake to her hands and she had large patches of purple bruising visible on her paper-thin skin.

He covered his mouth as he entered her flat, his senses struggling to process the array of aromas. Old cigarette smoke was the predominant odour, mixed with air freshener and stale wine. The lounge was small and crammed with large pieces of furniture. There were two bottle-green armchairs and a two-seater couch positioned in front of a walnut coffee table. Side cabinets were covered in magazines, and newspapers were thrown across the worn carpet, alongside dirty dinner plates and empty mugs. Discarded inhalers and opened packets of steroids explained the purple bruising.

'Through here,' she said, shuffling down the hallway.

Placing his flowers on the cabinet, Lucas followed her and eased himself into the tiny bathroom. The small window was cracked and covered in mould. Limescale tarnished the plugholes and there were urine stains around the toilet pan.

Mrs Kelsey was wheezing badly. 'Can you fix it?'

Lucas looked to where she was pointing. A sodden towel was wrapped around the base of the sink. 'Do you have any tools?'

'Whatever's in the cupboard.' She shuffled into the hallway and opened a cupboard door. Inside he could see a nebuliser machine and boxes of unopened salbutamol. 'This was my late husband's,' she said, handing him a worn leather toolbelt. 'Threw most of his stuff out, nowhere to store it. But I kept this. No idea why. Sentiment, probably.'

Lucas took the toolbelt and crouched down to inspect the sink. 'When did your husband die?'

'Ten years ago. Heart failure.'

He glanced up. 'I'm sorry for your loss.'

'Me too. It's no fun living like this,' she said, coughing and banging her chest. 'Pete had the right idea. Never got ill, was still working in the building trade at seventy, and then one day, gone. Just like that. No suffering, no lingering pain, just never woke up one day. I should be so lucky.'

Lucas used the wrench to loosen the bolts. 'Are you finding life difficult, Mrs Kelsey?'

She gave him an incredulous glare. 'No flies on you.'

He felt water dripping down his arm. 'Do you have any family close by to support you?'

'What's it to you?'

'I'm a doctor. I'm concerned about your welfare.' He reached over for some toilet paper and placed it under the drip.

'A doctor? Don't get me started on doctors, waste of space the lot of them. You can never get hold of one, and when you do, they refuse to come out.'

He wiped his hands on the towel, removing a smudge of grease. 'Have you tried arranging a home visit?'

'Course I have, but do they come? No, they don't. I'm not considered housebound. What do they think this here walking frame is for, eh? Drying me washing on? Daft buggers.'

Lucas cleaned the greasy pipes. 'When was the last time you saw a doctor?'

'No idea.'

'Do you mind me asking what ailments you suffer from?'

'I suffer from nosy-parkers like you sticking their nose into my business. Now, you able to fix that leak, or what?'

She was feisty, that was for sure. 'Maybe.'

'What do you mean, maybe? Either you can or you can't. Which is it?'

He turned to face her. 'If I help you, then you need to help me.'

'How can I help you?' She looked disgruntled.

'By letting me fix a date to come back and give you a health check.'

'Bugger off. I don't need some American hack getting personal with me. You even properly trained?'

He rolled his eyes. 'I assure you, I'm fully qualified.' He refitted the bolts. 'Funnily enough, they have COPD in the States too. I'm guessing that's what you have? Chronic obstructive pulmonary disease?'

'Smartarse. You been looking through my stuff?'

'No need, your symptoms are obvious. Do you have any electrical tape?'

'This ain't a hardware store.' But she rummaged through the cupboard and handed him a roll of surgical tape. 'This do?'

'Perfect.' His fingers brushed hers as he took the tape and he was shocked at how cold she was. 'Emphysema?'

'Something like that.' She sounded sulky, her lips forming a pout.

'I don't like the sound of your breathing.'

'Well, I don't like the sound of your voice, so neither of us are happy.'

He couldn't help laughing. 'Do you want this leak fixed, or not?'

'Fine. But no funny business.' She pointed a finger at him. 'You keep your hands to yourself.'

'I won't do anything you don't give consent for, okay?' He wound tape around the pipe.

She rubbed her chest, her wheezing pronounced. 'I suppose.'

'I've tightened the bolts and temporarily sealed the pipe with tape, but I think the washers need replacing. I'll check on the leak when I call around to give you a health check on Tuesday.'

'Tuesday? I can't do Tuesday.'

'You told me you don't go anywhere.'

'Doesn't mean I'm not busy.'

'All day?'

Her eyes narrowed. 'Pushy, ain't you?'

He stood up and brushed dust away from his jeans. 'I'll call around on my way home from the hospital. Don't even think about not answering the door.'

'What are you, a mind reader?'

'I'm worried about you, Mrs Kelsey.' He washed his hands in the sink.

'Yeah, well, don't even think of asking me to quit smoking.' She turned to leave. 'It's the one ruddy pleasure I have in this world.'

Having dried his hands, he followed her down the hallway into the lounge.

She stopped by the cabinet and inspected the bouquet of flowers. 'You bought these for the woman upstairs?'

'Yep.'

'You know she's likely to throw them in your face?'

'I do.'

'Yet you're still going to try?'

'That I am, ma'am… sorry, Mrs Kelsey.' He collected plates and mugs from the floor and carried them through to the kitchen, which was no better than the rest of the flat. Piles of washing-up filled the sink and there was a faint smell of outdated food. 'Why do you give her such a hard time?' he asked, returning to the lounge.

'Who?'

'Sarah, your neighbour.'

'I don't.' She sounded indignant. 'I treat her like anyone else. She's all right, as neighbours go. Better than most. Helps me out occasionally.'

'That's nice of her.' He took the rest of the crockery through to the kitchen. 'Can I wash these up for you?'

'No, you bloody can't.' She waited until he'd returned. 'And you would say that; you're smitten with her.'

He thought about it. 'Not smitten. Intrigued.'

'Either way, you're wasting your money buying her flowers. Now stop messing about with my stuff and be off with you. You're getting on me nerves.'

He pulled out his wallet. 'Do me a favour: if your breathing gets bad, call me, okay.' He handed her his card. 'Here's my number. Day or night, any time. You call me.'

She averted her eyes. 'Whatever.'

When she wouldn't take the card, he placed it by the phone on the side cabinet. 'Have a nice day, Mrs Kelsey.

See you on Tuesday.' As he left her apartment and stepped onto the porch, he turned back. 'Don't forget, call if you need me.'

The door slammed shut in his face.

Bending down, he called through the letterbox. 'A "thank you" might have been nice!'

'Sod off!'

Smiling, he headed up the steps, wondering if there was something about this building that attracted spiky women who weren't quite as tough as they made out.

Puffed from running up three flights of stairs, Lucas knocked on Sarah's door, smiling when he heard barking, followed by muffled attempts to quieten the dog. No dog, his arse.

The door opened a fraction and a pair of dark brown eyes fixed him with a glare. 'Yes? Oh, it's you.'

'Nice to see you too. Can I come in?'

Her eyes narrowed further. 'Why?'

'I'd like to meet Fred.'

Silence followed.

'What, no snarky comeback? Maybe Mrs Kelsey would like to meet him too; shall I go fetch her?' He turned to leave.

'Quit with the sarcasm.' She yanked open the door and he struggled not to laugh. Her hair was loose and she was wearing leggings with fluffy red socks. Her overlarge T-shirt was printed with the slogan, *I May Be Wrong, But It's Highly Unlikely*.

'Nice outfit.'

'I wasn't expecting visitors.'

He handed her the flowers. 'These are for you.'

She gave him a suspicious look. 'Why?'

'Because that's what boyfriends do: they gift their loved one's flowers.'

She blew her bangs from her eyes. 'You do know you're not my real boyfriend?'

'I do.'

'So why the flowers?'

'To keep up with the ruse. Can I come in?'

She stepped back to allow him into her apartment. 'But no one's here to see it, so what's the point?'

He gazed around her apartment, which was scarily similar to Mrs Kelsey's, only cleaner. Much cleaner. Ridiculously cleaner. Obsessively so. There was a strong smell of furniture polish.

'Ever heard of Instagram? You post a photo about how fabulous your boyfriend is, and what a sweetheart he is for buying you flowers, and everyone will coo and like the post, and you'll give the appearance of being coupled up and not open to the advances of people like Stephen Stokes.'

'I don't do Instagram,' she said, raising her eyebrows. 'And did you really just use the word "coo"?'

'That's a word, isn't it?'

'For the likes of Mrs Kelsey, yes. Not for anyone under the age of seventy.' She carried the flowers over to a large mahogany dresser. 'What are you, twenty-five?'

'After seven years of medical school? Hardly. I'm thirty-five.'

She unearthed a strange-looking vase from the dresser. 'You look younger.'

'Thank you. How old are you?'

'Same as you.' She plonked the flowers in the vase. 'And there you have it. Life's biggest cruelty. You're thirty-five and look twenty-five; I'm thirty-five and look forty-five.'

'You do not look forty-five.' He nodded to the vase. 'And what is that thing?'

'Art deco.' She headed for the kitchen. 'And I may not look forty-five, but I feel it.'

He followed her, leaning against the doorframe so he could watch her fill the vase. 'And why's that?'

'Men. They've aged me.'

'Men? Or man, singular?'

She shut off the tap. 'None of your business.'

'Fair enough.' He'd wondered if she'd tell him about her break-up, but she didn't offer anything further. 'Why are you so grumpy today?' He had to move quickly to get out of her way.

'I'm always grumpy.'

He followed her into the lounge. 'You weren't last night. You were almost friendly.'

'Yeah, well, it wore off.' She dumped the vase on the glass coffee table, making it rattle.

'Can I meet Fred?'

She closed her eyes briefly. 'I suppose there's no point denying his existence?'

'None whatsoever.'

'Fine. Stay here.'

He used the delay to check out her apartment. Wooden floorboards, bulky period furniture, heavy drapes at the window and a fancy chandelier. The walls were painted deep green, a contrast to the large red rug, and he felt like he was on the set of a murder mystery. The only glimpse of modern life was the flat-screen TV and an iPad lying on the coffee table. There were no photos anywhere, just a painting of a Twenties flapper hanging on the wall.

Sarah returned with a short dog trotting behind her. 'Fred, this is Lucas.'

'Hey there, fella.' Lucas dropped to his knees and the dog scurried over, his soft brown coat as clean as the furnishings. 'What's his story?'

Sarah perched on the arm of the couch. 'I found him on Putney Bridge shivering and hungry. He looked up at me with those pathetic brown eyes and I caved.' She gave a shrug. 'Mug, or what?'

He waited until she looked at him. 'Big brown eyes kind of make me go soppy too.'

She pinned him with a look. 'I can't be charmed.'

He laughed. 'You planning on keeping him?'

'Not allowed. No pets policy in the tenancy lease. He's had a check-up with the vet, and he seems healthy enough, but he doesn't have an identity microchip, so there's no way to locate his previous owner. I keep threatening to take him to Battersea Dogs Home, but it's like he knows and starts whimpering and I give in.' She picked up a cushion and hugged it to her chest. 'One more day, I say, but the next day it's the same. Who knows, maybe this week I'll finally take him.'

Fred rolled onto his back and started whimpering, his legs in the air like he'd been shot. Lucas laughed.

'See what I mean? He could win an Oscar for that performance.'

Fred righted himself and jumped onto Lucas's lap. 'The longer you keep him, the harder it'll be saying goodbye.'

'Tell me something I don't know.'

'It's a tough one.' He ruffled the dog's ears; he was an affectionate animal. 'You lived here long?'

'Five years.'

He looked around. 'I'm guessing the place came furnished?'

'No, this is my stuff.' She frowned. 'Why?'

'Nothing. It's just a bit… outdated.'

'It's not outdated. It's antique,' she said, looking outraged. 'These are collectors' pieces. Sought after, I'll have you know.'

'By who? Miss Marple?'

She threw the cushion at him. 'I like it.'

The cushion landed on Fred. 'Good for you.'

She folded her arms. 'Anyway, what's wrong with it?'

'It doesn't look very… you.' Fred began tugging on the cushion.

Sarah came over and tried to remove the cushion from Fred's teeth, but he wasn't letting go. 'What do you mean, it doesn't look like me? Why not?'

He shrugged. 'It's too serious.'

'Well, I am serious. I'm an extremely serious person,' she said, failing to see the irony as she rolled around the floor engaged in a tugging game with Fred.

'I bet you weren't always. What happened?'

'I told you. A man happened.' Fred landed on her chest, winding her and pinning her to the floor.

Lucas leant over and smiled down at her. She had really pretty eyes. The was a moment of stillness when their eyes met and he felt a little… what was the word Mrs Kelsey had used…? Smitten. He cleared his throat. 'What did he do?'

'He turned up at my flat with flowers and criticised my furniture.'

Lucas laughed. She was fun to spar with. 'Want to join me for a walk in the park with Fred? We could stop off somewhere for coffee?'

A beat passed, almost as if she was tempted, but thought better of it. 'No can do.' She rolled onto her front and got up.

'Tomorrow?'

She straightened her T-shirt. 'Nope.'

'Maybe some other time.' He got up from the floor. 'And before you say no again, remember I am your boyfriend.' He opened his arms. 'Is this any way to treat the man you love?'

Her hands went to her hips. 'We broke up, remember?'

He handed her the cushion from the floor. 'Enjoy your flowers. And don't forget to post about them on Instagram.'

'Yeah, not going to happen,' she called after him, as he walked off.

He waved a goodbye. 'See ya, Fred… don't let her take you to the pound.'

Fred began barking and sending Sarah into a panic as she tried to quieten him. 'Thanks for that!'

Lucas headed down to his apartment, grinning. Why he was grinning, he had no idea. A sane man would know when to quit.

But he'd never been one for quitting.

Chapter Seven

It was fair to say that in all her time working at the hospital, Sarah had never walked into her office on a Monday morning and been greeted with cheering and a round of applause. Talk about embarrassing.

Georgia was balancing precariously on an office chair and punching the air. Jafrina had her hands clasped and was looking all doe-eyed and wistful, and Tyler had a grin splitting his face that was almost as wide as his dreadlocks.

She knew exactly why her colleagues were looking so excited, and it filled her with dread.

'Go, Sarah!' Georgia yelled, followed by an ear-piercing whistle.

'We're so happy for you,' Jafrina said, exchanging an awkward high-five with Tyler, who laughed and said, 'You're a dark horse, Sarah Haynes. You kept that quiet.'

Sarah tried to shush them. 'For goodness' sake, calm down, will you. This is a hospital, not a children's play park. Get off the chair, Georgia. You'll break your neck.'

Georgia saluted and climbed down. 'Whatever you say, boss.' She shimmied over, her creased shirt untucked from her skirt. 'Someone's got a boyfriend,' she sang, thrusting her hips forwards. 'Someone's getting some action… someone's getting—'

'Stop that!' Sarah tried to look stern. This was why she kept quiet about her private life. She hated all this intrusion and attention. 'It's completely unprofessional.'

'We're just so pleased you've found someone,' Jafrina said, looking pristine in her uniform. 'And Doctor Moore seems so lovely.'

'He's smokin', all right.' Georgia fanned her face.

'He seems like a cool bloke,' Tyler agreed.

'I think you mean *hot*,' Georgia said, followed by more hip thrusting.

'Will you please stop!' Sarah raised her hand. 'Apart from the inappropriateness of discussing this at work, I'm sorry to disappoint you, but there's nothing going on between myself and Doctor Moore.'

'Bullshit.' Georgia shoved her shirt inside her skirt. 'We saw you Friday night, smooching. All that crap about not wanting to go to the bar? And then ten minutes later you're snogging Doctor Moreish and leaving the venue with him. That was fast work, by anyone's standards. Even mine.'

'I was doing nothing of the sort,' Sarah objected, checking no one had entered the office and could over-hear. 'There was a brief… hug, after which he walked me home, and then left. That's it.' She tried not to dwell on hugging Lucas Moore; the memory still had the ability to befuddle her thinking.

'That's it?' Georgia looked confused. 'But he stayed the night, right? Please tell me you didn't squander the opportunity to get your kit off?'

'Keep your voice down,' Sarah shushed, moving towards her office door in the hope of cutting short the conversation. 'I assure you, nothing happened. And nothing's going to happen. It was a momentary lapse on my part, and something that won't be repeated.'

Georgia slumped onto her desk. 'Why the hell not?'

'Yes, why not?' Jafrina repeated. 'He seems so lovely.'

Sarah looked at her colleagues' expectant faces, their previous delight rapidly fading. 'I'm sure he is; I'm just not looking for a relationship right now. We've agreed to go our separate ways.'

Georgia thumped the desk. 'Well, hell, Sarah! What's wrong with you?'

'Nothing's wrong with me; I'm content remaining single.'

Jafrina came towards her. 'I know getting back out there is scary, but would it really be so terrible to give love another go? Couldn't you go on a few dates? I'm sure once you get over the initial fear, you'll realise that being with someone can be really quite magical.'

Georgia padded over in her bare feet. 'A little Disney for my taste, but the woman's got a point. Listen to your fairy godmother; she knows her stuff.'

'He seems like a decent bloke,' Tyler interjected, keeping a safe distance. 'I was chatting to him at the bar on Friday and he's a straight arrow. No alarm bells.'

They didn't need to tell her Lucas was a decent bloke; she was painfully aware of that herself. Add in his handsome face, broad shoulders and confident bluster, and he was just the sort of man who could cause a woman serious damage. Tyler might not be hearing alarm bells, but she certainly was.

Jafrina took her hand. 'Everyone knows Tyler's an expert at reading people, so if he says Lucas is okay, then there's nothing to be afraid of.'

'That's as may be.' Sarah withdrew her hand, unwilling to hear any more comments about how wonderful Lucas Moore was. 'But I'm still not interested in getting romantically involved with him. Or anyone else, for that matter.'

Georgia stomped back to her desk. 'You're rejecting him before he can reject you,' she said, slumping into her chair. 'Classic masochistic behaviour.'

'I prefer to think of it as self-perseveration,' Sarah retaliated, feeling increasingly flustered. 'Besides, he's only in the UK for a month. Pursuing anything romantic would be foolish and utterly pointless.' Something she'd reminded herself when he'd turned up at her flat on Saturday and bamboozled her with flowers and charmed her dog. Of course, he'd also criticised her furniture, so the man wasn't perfect.

'Unless it's the real deal?' Jafrina suggested tentatively. 'You might fall in love?'

Heaven help her. Sarah could think of little worse.

'And if nothing else, at least you'd get a good seeing to.' Georgia squeezed her feet into her shoes. 'For a whole month, and with no strings. Sounds perfect to me.'

'Well, not to me.' Sarah had had enough. 'Now, can we please get to work. I appreciate your enthusiasm regarding my lack of a love life, but there's going to be no happy ever after on this occasion.'

'But—'

'Discussion over.' Sarah raised her hand. 'Work, please.'

Turning away, she stepped into her office, embarrassed at being the subject of gossip, but also feeling like a fraud for deceiving them. It wasn't like she could tell them the real reason why she'd gone off with Lucas Moore. Her issues with Stephen Stokes were a matter for her alone to deal with. And, however mortifying it was to be embroiled in a romantic interlude, she just had to hope the ruse would be enough to deter the medical director from harassing her further.

It took a moment for her to spot the huge bouquet of red roses sitting on her desk. When she did, she recoiled as though she'd stumbled across a dead body. Instinct made her spin around, only to see two grinning faces peering in through the office window, before Georgia and Jafrina scurried back to their desks like a couple of kids playing knock down ginger.

So that's what had fuelled their interest? Damned bloody Lucas had sent her flowers again.

Chucking her bag and coat onto a chair, she picked up the bouquet and marched from her office. 'Don't say a word,' she barked as she strode across the open-plan space, barely able to see above the mass of deep red stems.

Their scent was so overwhelming that she was quite giddy by the time she reached Lucas's consulting rooms.

'Is he here?' she asked Carla, his nursing assistant.

Carla looked up from behind her computer, her eyes growing wide as she took in the sight of Sarah obscured behind the array of flowers. 'Lucas! You're needed.'

Lucas appeared from a treatment room. 'Someone looking for me?'

He looked like a character from an American hospital drama, with his pale-blue shirtsleeves rolled up and his stethoscope hanging around his neck, like he was ready to save a small child's life. Why did he have to look so good?

He grinned when he saw her. 'Nice flowers.'

'No, not nice flowers,' she said, plonking them onto Carla's desk, making the water in the bottom splosh. 'Totally inappropriate flowers.'

Lucas looked puzzled. 'Come again?'

She rested her hands on her hips, trying to appear assertive, rather than glad to see him, which made no sense whatsoever. 'What did I say about giving me flowers?'

Carla's mouth dropped open. 'You gave her flowers?'

Lucas shrugged. 'I did, but—'

'It was bad enough you showing up at my flat with a bouquet,' Sarah said, wishing he had a stain down his shirt or something, anything to dull the impact of his blue eyes. 'But at work?'

Carla was now openly gawping. 'You went to her home?'

Lucas glanced at Carla. 'I did, but—'

'When we explicitly agreed that we weren't going to… you know… see each other.' Sarah was starting to regret her outburst. She should have waited until there wasn't an audience.

Carla stopped even pretending not to listen. 'Ooh, this is getting interesting.' She sat back in her chair. 'Don't mind me. Please, continue.'

Sarah cleared her throat. 'It's hardly appropriate when we've… "broken up",' she said, using air quotes.

'You've broken up already.' Carla looked dismayed. 'I didn't even know you'd started dating!'

Lucas rubbed his forehead. 'It was a brief affair.'

'Very brief.' Sarah folded her arms across her chest.

Carla looked between them. 'And now it's over? So soon?'

Lucas sighed. 'Apparently so.'

'Definitely so.' Sarah pointed to the flowers. 'So, what's with the flowers?'

Lucas looked uncomfortable. 'They're not from me.'

Sarah opened her mouth, but then her brain caught up with her ears. 'They're not?'

'Nope.' He lowered his voice. 'Although I can guess who did send them. In which case, you might want to rethink our "*break-up*",' he said, mirroring her use of air quotes.

Carla leant forwards in her chair. 'Does that mean you're getting back together?'

'No,' Sarah said, even though her bluster was rapidly waning. The flowers weren't from Lucas? She'd just made a right fool of herself.

Lucas's gaze softened. 'Sure about that?'

'Quite sure. I'll deal with this myself.' Mortified at her mistake, and wanting to escape as quickly as possible, she almost ran across the room. She stopped by the door and turned back. 'Sorry, for you know… bursting in here and having a go. I just assumed they were from you.'

Lucas lifted his hands. 'Easy assumption. They were last time.' His smile was warm and kind and she hated the way it made her feel, all wobbly and foolish. 'I'm here if you need me. Or, you know, you change your mind about… us?'

'Thanks, but I'll be fine.' Head down, she made to leave.

'Don't forget your flowers!' Carla gestured to the bouquet.

'You keep them, or better still, give them to a patient.'

'Of course, love.' Carla's smile was sympathetic, which only made Sarah feel worse. 'Shame to see them go to waste.'

As she scuttled down the corridor, her skin burning from humiliation, she overheard Carla say, 'Well, someone's been busy. Care to elaborate?', which only made her run faster.

It hadn't occurred to her the flowers might be from Stephen. What a fool she was.

As she rounded the bend, she screeched to a halt. Further down the corridor she could see Stephen Stokes heading her way with one of the nursing staff. Dealing with Stephen in the state she was in was the last thing she needed, so she reversed her steps and raced back down the corridor away from him.

As Stephen's voice grew louder, she knew time was running out. The moment he rounded the corner, he'd see her. Panicking, she yanked open the door next to Lucas's consulting rooms and almost threw herself inside.

As she slammed the door behind her with force, a broom slipped from its hook and smacked her on the shoulder. Great, she was hiding in a cleaning cupboard. Could today get any worse?

Pressing her ear against the door, she tried to hear what was happening on the other side.

Stephen's voice grew louder. She held her breath, willing him to keep walking and not discover her hiding in a cleaning cupboard. What possible excuse could she provide for being in here? She would just look unhinged. Her job would be at risk.

Annoyingly, far from continuing down the corridor, he seemed to stop right outside where she was hiding. Her panic levels increased another level.

She looked around the room, hoping for another way out, but there was only a small window at the back, no other exits. She didn't even have her phone with her, so she couldn't call Georgia and ask her to distract Stephen so she could escape.

Then she remembered she was on the ground floor; the window opened onto the flowerbeds at the side of the hospital by the car park. Could she climb out?

Stepping over the metal wheely-buckets, she carefully made her way towards the window. It lifted upwards, leaving a medium-sized gap at the bottom. Bending down, she pushed her torso through the gap, checking to see if she had enough room to climb out. The drop below was a good few feet, but the landing would be soft. Except for the rose bushes. They might scratch a bit. Could she make it?

'I hope you're not thinking of jumping?'

The woman's voice made Sarah startle so hard that if the window had been bigger she might have fallen out. She turned to see Carla leaning out of the adjacent window, smoking a cigarette. 'Goodness, you scared the life out of me.'

'I would say "Please don't grass me up," seeing as smoking on the premises is strictly against hospital protocols,' she said, drawing on her cigarette. 'But seeing as you're attempting to climb out of a cleaning cupboard window, I'm guessing my secret is safe.'

'I can explain,' Sarah said, hoping she wouldn't have to.

'No need. I've heard the rumours. Stephen's a piece of work.' She stubbed out her cigarette on the wall. 'I'll fetch the cavalry.' She disappeared inside before Sarah could stop her.

Cursing, Sarah tried to wriggle through the gap before realising if she continued she'd land headfirst in the flowerbed. Reversing, she turned around and eased one leg out of the window. Holding on to the wall racking, she lifted her other leg, only just managing to push it through the gap before the inevitable happened.

'I thought Carla must've been smoking weed,' Lucas said, from below. 'There's no way you would seriously attempt to climb out of a window. But here you are, doing just that. Do you need a hand?'

'No.' She was aware that her bum was now hanging out of the window, her skirt stretched so tight that she feared it might split. 'On seconds thought, yes.'

'You realise I'll have to touch you?'

She bit her lip. What had she ever done to deserve this? 'Fine. But no funny business.'

'My game does not involve manhandling women incapacitated by hanging out of a window. And why are you climbing out of a window?' he said, sliding his arms around her legs.

'I'm trying to avoid Stephen.'

'A little drastic, don't you think?' His grip tightened as he tried to balance her on his shoulder.

'Probably.' Especially as the end result was having Lucas's face squashed into her backside.

'Are things really that bad?'

'All I know is that he makes my skin crawl.' She eased her body fully out of the window, gripping hold of the ledge so she didn't fall. 'He's constantly wanting me to attend unnecessary meetings, have lunch with him, and he won't take no for an answer. I have no idea whether he's being genuine and it's his way of bonding over work, or whether he's pushing for more. Maybe I'm being paranoid.'

'I doubt it. Don't let go of the window ledge.'

'I've no intentions of letting go.' She was past the point of no return now, her torso hanging out of the window, and hoping and praying no one was watching. 'I was convinced the roses were from you.'

'I wish they had been.'

'Why do you say that?' Her knees scraped painfully against the wall.

'You had no worries about putting me in my place. Not so easy to do when it's the guy paying your wages.'

'Exactly.'

'Right, I think I've got you. You can let go.'

'You only *think* you've got me? Could I have a little more assurance than that, please?'

'I'm standing on soft soil. Your entire body weight is resting on my shoulder. If I drop you it'll cause me as much pain as you. Trust me, this is the best assurance I can give.'

'Fair enough.' She took a deep breath. 'Here goes.'

She released her hold and immediately dropped a few inches, before a pair of strong arms caught her and held her aloft.

She was now lying in Lucas's arms, in a flowerbed, in full view of the car park. And she'd thought her day couldn't get any worse.

Lucas smiled down at her. 'We made it.'

He was ridiculously close. Inevitable, really, seeing as how she was lying in his arms. But still, did he have to smell so good? Was it necessary for him to work out so much? And why did one hand have to be quite so close to her breast? 'Can you put me down, please?'

'Sure.' He carefully lifted her out of the flowerbed and onto firmer ground. 'You okay?'

'I'm fine.' When she glanced up from straightening her skirt, she was met with a pair of raised eyebrows. 'What?'

'No gratitude for rescuing you?'

She let out an exasperated sigh. 'Thanks, I guess.'

'Heartfelt.' Grinning, he wiped his feet on the grass to remove the loose mud. 'You know what this means?'

'Enlighten me?'

'We need to get back together.'

She closed her eyes. 'Oh, God.'

'Do you have to look so horrified?'

She opened her eyes. 'Sorry, it's just that I've spent the morning trying to convince my team there's nothing going on between us. A rumour that isn't going away if anyone saw you lifting me out of a window.'

'I appreciate it's not nice being gossiped about, but which is easier to deal with, Stephen coming on to you… or your team teasing you about me?'

'The latter,' she admitted, feeling disgruntled.

'Then it's official.' He hit her with a big smile. 'We're dating.'

'*Fake* dating,' she corrected.

'Not much difference, just less of the good stuff.'

'None of the good stuff.' She stepped away; there was only so much Lucas Moore she could take. He was interfering with her equilibrium. 'This is not a real relationship.'

'You want to be convincing, don't you?'

'Fine, but there are boundaries.' She brushed grit away from her sore knees. 'Especially at work.'

'Is hand-holding okay?'

'No.'

'The occasional touching?' He gently brushed her fringe away from her eyes.

She batted his hand away. 'Far too intimate.'

'So, that's a no to hair-touching.' His smile told her that far from being offended, he was enjoying toying with her. 'How about lingering glances?' His eyes locked on hers, and for a moment it was liked she'd been stunned into stillness. There was a weight to his gaze that made her a little dizzy. This man was highly dangerous.

It was also extremely hard to look away. It had been a very long time since a man had looked at her with such wanting. Ever, in fact. But then she remembered he was play-acting. She blinked to break the spell. 'I'm head of HR, remember?'

'Kissing?' He was definitely teasing her now.

'Definitely not kissing.' She placed her hands on his chest to keep him at arm's length. 'Just stick to the basics. That's more than enough.'

He laughed. 'Fair enough. What about meeting up for coffee? That's safe?'

'Let me check my diary and I'll get back to you.'

He rested his hands over hers. 'Your hands are freezing… and we need to go for coffee now.'

'I can't go now. I'm supposed to be working,' she said, letting his warm hands alleviate the chill. She'd remove them soon. When they were warmer. There was no rush. 'I've barely been here half an hour; I need to get back to my team.'

'Stephen will only track you down and demand to know how you liked the flowers. He needs to see you with me so that he gets the message you're not available.'

'Available? I'm not a taxicab.'

'Interested, then. Either way, it'll be easier to reject his advances if he thinks you're with me. The more visible we are, the harder it'll be for him to make a play during work hours.' He nodded to where the takeaway van was parked up. 'How about a compromise? We get coffee from the van.'

She could certainly do with a hot drink; she was starting to feel the cold. Apart from her hands, which were nice and toasty. She'd move them soon. Really soon.

'It's up to you,' he said, with a shrug. 'I'm only trying to help.'

'I know you are, although I have to question why?'

His eyes lifted to the sky. 'I'm asking myself the same thing.'

'What's in it for you?'

'Absolutely nothing.' He smiled down at her. 'Other than doing a fellow human being a favour.'

His smile made her want to wrap her arms around him and warm the rest of her body. Instead, she did the sensible thing and slid her hands out from underneath his. 'Fine. Takeaway it is.' They headed over to the van. 'And I know what you're thinking,' she said, sensing him watching her with an amused smile.

'What am I thinking?'

'That you don't normally have to work this hard with a woman. I imagine you have a harem full of hotties all clamouring for your attention back home.'

He laughed. 'Why would you think that?'

'Oh, please. You own a mirror. Look in it.'

He stopped walking. 'Is that your way of saying you think I'm handsome?'

She gave him an exasperated glare. 'You're passable.'

He resumed walking. 'Flattered, I'm sure.'

'So how many women do you have on the go?'

'None.'

'I find that hard to believe. There must be at least one?' They joined the end of the queue and she rubbed her chilly arms.

'Nope, no one. I'd like there to be, but I've been single for a while.' He rested his hand on her shoulder.

She shrugged him off. 'Stop that. People will see.'

'I thought that was the idea.' He turned to her, one eyebrow raised. 'So it's okay for you to ask questions about my love life, but I can't do the same?'

'Somehow I doubt your romantic history is as traumatic as mine.'

'That's quite an assumption. I've had my heart broken. Several times, in fact.'

That was a surprise. She imagined him impervious to heartbreak; he seemed too... robust to be floored by love. 'Then why keep putting yourself out there?'

'Because if I don't, I'm never gonna meet her, am I?'

The queue shuffled forwards.

Sarah waited a beat before asking, 'Her?'

'The woman of my dreams. My one and only. My true love.'

'I can't work out whether you're being romantic or sarcastic.'

'Both.' His grin widened. 'Americano for me,' he said, reaching the front of the queue, before turning to Sarah. 'What can I get you, honey?'

'Tea, please. One sugar. And quit calling me *honey*,' she said, elbowing him in the ribs.

'Coming right up, sweetheart.' The serving guy placed two cartons on the counter.

Lucas looked indignant. 'So it's okay for him to call you sweetheart, but I can't call you honey? And I'm your boyfriend. Talk about hurtful.'

The serving guy poured their drinks. 'Aw, let him call you honey, sweetheart. The lad's in love. Anyone can see that.'

Lucas burst out laughing. 'You see? He gets it.'

Sarah glared at the serving guy. 'Please don't encourage him.' She took her tea. 'Thank you.'

Lucas collected his coffee and took a sip as they wandered off. He immediately grimaced. 'You people really can't do coffee in this country. How's your tea?'

'Fine.' She was still mulling over his previous comment. 'So, you're a believer in the whole *happy ever after*?'

'Now who's being sarcastic.' He took another sip of coffee. 'I think most people are. Isn't that what keeps us going? Optimism and hope. Whatever's happened in the past, we need to believe the future will be brighter.'

'You really are annoyingly optimistic.'

He grinned. 'Besides, I like being in love. It's fun.'

She sipped her tea. 'Not always.'

'But when it is, it's great. Isn't that worth fighting for?' His expression was open and honest, and for a moment she almost believed him… until reality kicked back in.

'Depends what you have to lose.'

'I figure it's more about what you have to gain.'

'That's because you're American. You have a more positive outlook on life than us Brits. We're experts at doom and gloom.'

'So I'm learning.' His expression softened. 'You must have been happy once?'

'If I was, then it's been obliterated.'

Lucas took another sip of coffee. 'Then he wins.'

'Who?'

'The man who hurt you. Do you really want to give him that much power over you? I can't drink any more of this.' He threw the remaining coffee into the flowerbed and binned the carton.

Sarah averted her eyes. 'He ruined my life.'

'But your life isn't over, not by a long way. Don't let him ruin your future too. Just like you don't want Stephen Stokes to ruin your career. Talking of which.' He nodded behind her.

She glanced over to see Stephen walking towards his flashy silver Mercedes. 'You're right, I don't.' She turned back to Lucas, her heart racing with a panic. She couldn't allow him to make her feel that way. She was tougher than that.

'So, what are you going do about it?'

She swallowed, trying to control her breathing. 'Has he seen us?'

Lucas discreetly glanced over. 'Yup. He doesn't look happy.'

'Good.' She placed her tea carton on the ground. 'Then I'm going to do this.' Mustering her inner bravery, she reached up on tiptoes and kissed Lucas Moore.

It was brief, fleeting, a mere glancing of her lips brushing his, so that anyone watching would think it perfectly innocuous. Nothing really. Blink and you'd miss it. And yet it set off a tingle in her blood so fierce that she felt like she'd touched an exposed electrical socket.

She stepped back, slightly stunned, and wondering what she'd just done.

Lucas looked equally stunned. 'Well, that'll work.' He closed the gap between them. 'Maybe do it again, just to be certain he saw.'

'Oh, he saw,' she said, patting him on the chest. 'And don't push your luck, matey.'

Lucas laughed. 'Can't blame a guy for trying.'

She walked away with her head held high, even if there was a definite shake in her hands.

It felt good to have shocked both men. To act out of character. To have the upper hand. A little niggle also told her she'd lit a fuse, and there were bound to be repercussions, but for now, she was okay. Better than okay. Empowered. Even if she had resorted to climbing out of a window to escape Stephen.

She just hoped she knew what she was doing.

Chapter Eight

Lucas had to ring the doorbell twice and repeatedly knock before he finally heard Mrs Kelsey shuffling along the hallway to answer the door. He knew she was home; he'd seen her curtains twitching when he'd arrived. If she thought ignoring him would make him give up and leave, she was mistaken. He could be stubborn too.

'All right, all right… keep your hair on,' she grumbled as she slowly opened her front door. 'Where's the bleedin' fire?'

'Hi there, Mrs Kelsey.' He tried to charm her with a smile, but she wasn't that easily won over and gave him a dirty look. 'Are you going to let me in?'

Her bloodshot eyes narrowed. 'Why would I do that?'

'It's Tuesday. We arranged for me to come over and give you a health check, remember?'

'I don't remember nothing of the sort. Go away.' She tried to shut the door, but he wedged his foot in the gap.

'That's not very neighbourly. Can I at least come in for a cup of coffee? I've just finished a hectic shift at the hospital.'

'Not my problem.' But she shuffled away on her walking frame, leaving the door open, which he took as permission for him to follow.

The apartment was just as stale and messy as it had been at the weekend. A few mugs had reappeared in the lounge, along with two inhalers, but when he glanced in the kitchen, he spotted the same pile of washing-up by the sink. 'Do you cook for yourself, Mrs Kelsey?'

'What's it to you?'

'I'm concerned you might not be taking care of yourself. Why don't you take a seat and I'll make us a drink?'

'Don't you go calling the social on me,' she said, shuffling over to an armchair and almost dropping into it, clearly lacking the strength to lower herself down. 'I don't want no busybodies coming over here and taking me off to one of them psychiatric places. I've still got all me marbles.' She tapped the side of her head. 'I don't need no fellas in white coats turning up and putting me in a straightjacket.'

Lucas ran a bowl of hot water and searched for washing-up liquid in the cupboard beneath the sink. 'That's not going to happen, Mrs Kelsey. I assure you, I won't be contacting anyone without your permission.' He found some Fairy liquid and added a large squirt to the water. 'But I think you have a slightly outdated view on what help is available these days. There are all sorts of organisations that can provide support to ensure you stay living independently.'

'Like what?'

He began washing up. 'Someone to help around the home and run chores for you. Or perhaps a befriending service to provide company for you. It must get lonely living here by yourself.'

'I don't need the likes of you feeling sorry for me. And what are you doing in there?'

'Just making myself useful, Mrs Kelsey. You didn't have any clean mugs.'

She tutted. 'Bloody busybody.'

'You're not the first person to accuse me of sticking my nose into other people's business. I appreciate it can be annoying.'

'Too bloody right it is.'

He smiled. 'It's not about feeling sorry for you – it's about letting you know what services are out there that might improve your quality of life.' He rinsed the dishes. 'How's that a bad thing?'

'I don't like strangers in my home.'

'They'd only be a stranger the first time they visit. After that, you'd get used to them being here.' He drained the sink and used a tea towel to dry the crockery. 'Wouldn't you like someone to take you out occasionally? Maybe to the shops, or for a coffee, or lunch? Or someone to chat to and do a puzzle with? I notice you like wordsearches.'

'Nosy bugger, aren't you?'

'I prefer to think of it as observant,' he said, tidying away the crockery 'I saw the puzzle books on the table.' He stuck his head around the door. 'Have a think about it. I promise I won't make any enquiries if you don't want me to.'

'Big of you.'

He filled the kettle and searched for coffee. Her cupboards were bare, as was her fridge, just a few cans of soup and a packet of rice, but he did find a jar of instant coffee and some long-life milk. It was evident that Mrs Kelsey was struggling to care for herself, but he needed to tread carefully. She was a proud woman who clearly wasn't open to the idea of getting help.

'Here we are,' he said, carrying two mugs of coffee into the lounge and placing them on the table. 'I have biscuits in my bag. Let me fetch them.'

She frowned as he reached for his holdall. 'That's an odd thing to carry in your medical bag.'

'You'd be amazed what's in here. Mary Poppins has nothing on me.' He removed a squeaky toy, which almost made her laugh... almost. 'Distraction tactics for children, or dogs, or both. The biscuits come in handy for patients with diabetes. Sometimes a quick burst of sugar is needed. Here we are.' He opened the packet of chocolate bourbons and left them open on the table. 'Help yourself.'

She didn't hold back and swiped two, confirming his theory that she hadn't eaten for a while. She was all skin and bones underneath her maroon kaftan.

Taking a sip of coffee, which wasn't the worst he'd experienced in the UK, he nodded to a framed photo on the sideboard. 'Nice picture – is it family?'

'That's my son, Nigel,' she said, not looking at the photo. 'He lives in Australia with his wife and two daughters. That photo's about five years old. My granddaughters are teenagers now. Not that I see them. I don't see neither of my kids.'

Lucas was mildly shocked at how much information she'd revealed, having expected one of her snarky remarks telling him to 'butt out'.

He sipped his coffee, waiting to see if she'd say any more.

'My daughter, Keeley, lives in Los Angeles,' she said, licking chocolate from her fingers. 'No idea what she does out there. Something to do with technology.'

'Does she have a family too?'

'No idea. I don't think so. According to her brother, she's gay, but she's never said nothing to me about it, and I don't like to ask. I guess she'll tell me when she's ready. Or maybe not. It's not like it matters either way. They don't make no effort to come see me.'

'That's sad. I imagine you must miss them.'

She reached for a tissue and blew her nose. 'I can't blame them. Parenting never came natural to me. They complained I was too hard on them. They were closer to their dad, my Pete. Since he's been gone they've drifted away.'

Lucas placed his mug on the table. 'Do they know you're having health issues?' He picked up his medical bag. 'May I?'

She gave a short shrug, which he took as confirmation. 'They wouldn't be interested.'

He removed his stethoscope from his bag so he could examine her chest. 'Do you speak to them on the phone?'

'Occasionally. But what's there to talk about? I don't know nothing about their lives and they don't wanna hear about me ailments. Can't blame them for staying away.' She began coughing and he heard a definite rattle in her chest.

He switched his stethoscope to her back. 'Breathe in for me.'

She took a deep breath and held it, before coughing again. 'Last thing I want is to turn out like me parents,' she said, banging her chest. 'All they did was moan, even though I did everything for them and looked after them until they died. What thanks did I get? Bugger all. And now I'm in the same situation. Tough luck, huh?'

'It's hard to keep a relationship going when you live so far apart. I'm in the same situation.' He searched for his thermometer. 'My parents are divorced and live in different states, and my sister's here in the UK. We're definitely not as close as we used to be… I'm going to check your temperature, okay?'

'Do what you like. It's not like I care.'

Her temperature was higher than he'd like. 'You don't care about your wellbeing?'

'What's the point? I'm just sitting around waiting to snuff it. The quicker it comes, the better for everyone.'

'That's a sad outlook.' He checked her oxygen levels and took her blood pressure. 'Do you have any friends who live locally?'

'What do you think?'

'Would you like more company?'

She gave him a stern look. 'Who'd want my company? I'm better off keeping out of everyone's way.'

He held the spirometer to her mouth. 'I need you to take a deep breath and exhale as much air as possible into this reader for me. Can you do that?'

'Course I can; I ain't stupid.' She blew into the gadget. They repeated the test three times; each time her lung capacity dropped. 'I'm tired now.'

'Don't worry, I'm done.' He packed up his bag. 'I'm pretty certain you have a chest infection, Mrs Kelsey. That's probably why you're feeling run-down and your mood is so low. I'm going to prescribe you antibiotics and a course of steroids to help boost their effectiveness. Have you taken prednisolone before?'

'Can't remember.'

'I'll collect the medication tomorrow and bring it over and explain how to take it. In the meantime, continue using your inhalers, both the reliever and the preventer, and you might benefit from using your nebuliser tonight. Plenty of fluids, and I want you to call me if your breathing deteriorates further. Okay?'

'Okay.'

He stilled. 'What, no resistance?'

She gave a small shrug. 'I guess you're only trying to help.'

'I am.' He stood up. 'You'd also benefit from eating something. I noticed a few cans of soup in the cupboard. I'd like you to have one of those this evening. Would you like me to heat it up for you?'

'I can do that myself. I'm not incapable.'

'No, but you are unwell, Mrs Kelsey. And like it or not, I'm worried about you. So expect to see me again tomorrow, and the next day, and no doubt the day after that.'

She rolled her eyes. 'Jesus, I'll be sick of the sight of you.'

'I guarantee it.'

And then something amazing happened, Mrs Kelsey smiled. 'Cheeky blighter. Now get out of here. I've had enough of you prodding and poking me for one night. You can see yourself out. And hand me that remote before you leave.'

He did as asked, checking his card was still by the phone before he left. 'Night, Mrs Kelsey. Call if you need me.'

'*Oi*, laddie...?'

He stopped by the lounge door. 'What do you need, Mrs Kelsey?'

'I need for you to stop calling me Mrs Kelsey. My name's Diana.'

He tried to hide his shock, although he wasn't able to hide his grin. 'Good night, Diana. See you tomorrow.'

Leaving her apartment, he headed up the steps to his place, still smiling. All the medical stuff aside, he loved his work because of moments like that. It might seem like a tiny breakthrough, but he notched it up to a win nonetheless. The formidable Diana Kelsey was finally thawing.

The cold hit him the moment he opened the door to his apartment. A chill was blowing through the place, making it feel like an ice box. Had the heating system packed up?

Flicking on the hall light, he followed the draught, which lead him to the big sash window in the lounge area. He'd left the window open? Damn it.

And then he remembered using the fire escape this morning to empty the trash. The large recycling bins were stored in the service yard at the back of the building, so it was easier to use the spiral metal staircase leading down to the service area than exiting the front of the building and having to walk around the block.

Walking over, he shoved the window closed with a thud, but as he turned around he saw something move on his couch. What the hell? There it was again: the cushions moved. It was too small for a person. Had an animal climbed in through the window? What animals did they have roaming loose in London? A fox? Cat? Rat? Had a panther escaped from London Zoo?

He switched on the side lamp, ready to pounce, only to be met by a pair of huge brown eyes. 'Fred…? Is that you?'

The dog rolled onto his back, begging for a tummy rub.

'Make yourself at home, why don't you.' He walked over and crouched down. 'Does your mom know you're here?'

Loud banging on his front door made them both startle.

'I'm guessing not.' He got up and headed for the door. 'Coming!'

'Have you seen Fred?' Sarah said, the moment he opened the door.

'Hi to you too… and yes, he's here.' He stood back to let her in.

'You have my dog?' She brushed past him, looking annoyed, and smelling a damned sight sweeter than she sounded. 'Why do you have my dog? How did he get in here? How long has he been here? You didn't think to let me know? Is he okay?' She swung around, searching for her companion. 'Where is he?'

'Jesus, that's a hell of a load of questions. You're making my head hurt. And he's on my couch.'

He followed her through to the lounge, where she launched herself at Fred. 'There you are!'

'I think he came in through the fire escape. I've only just got home, so I've no idea how long he's been here.'

Sarah cupped the dog's face in her hands. 'You had me worried, Fred. I've been looking all over for you. I thought you'd been run over. Or dognapped. But no, here you are, acting like Lord Muck.'

Lucas perched against the armchair. 'Who's Lord Muck?'

'A haughty person with ideas above their station. Like Fred here.' She tried to look stern. 'And don't try the whimpering act on me; it won't work.' She gave him a cuddle, not seeming to care if it crumpled her work uniform. 'Maybe your punishment will be a trip to Battersea Dogs Home tomorrow. I should, you know.'

Fred's whimpering increased.

Sarah glanced up at Lucas and blew her bangs away from her eyes. 'What are you grinning at?'

'I'm getting an insight into you as a mom. Tough love, huh? You know darned well you ain't taking him to the pound tomorrow.'

Sarah raised an eyebrow. 'Ain't?'

'Sorry, I've been spending too much time with Mrs Kelsey. Her accent is rubbing off on me. What is she, like a cockney, or something?'

'Closer to Essex I suspect, but she's definitely got that *EastEnders* twang.' She pulled Fred onto her lap. 'And why are you spending so much time with Mrs Kelsey? Are you a glutton for punishment?'

'I've no idea what that means, but I've been visiting her because she's poorly and refuses to see her own doctor.'

'Oh.' Sarah frowned. 'I hope she's okay. Anything I can help with?'

'Does anyone do food shopping for her?'

'Apart from me, I've no idea. When I ask her if she needs anything, she usually tells me to bugger off and stop interfering and to mind my own business. Recently I've started leaving a few bits on her doorstep and running away before she sees me.' Sarah shivered and rubbed her hands together. 'Why's it so cold in here? Is your heating broken?'

'I left the window open by mistake.'

'Oh, right.' When she looked up, she gave him a questioning look. 'What? Why are you looking at me like that? What have I done?'

'You haven't done anything. It just occurred to me that you're a really nice person.'

She gave him a loaded look. 'And this is a shock?'

'You normally hide it so well.'

She poked her tongue out. 'I can be nice.'

'I know you can. I'm teasing.' Smiling, he slumped into the armchair. 'How was work today? Any issues with Stephen?'

'Call me chicken, but I arranged back-to-back staff appraisals so I was never alone, even for a minute.' She unclipped her hair and let it tumble onto her shoulders. 'Three times I saw him hovering outside my office looking annoyed because I was forever in a meeting.'

'Doesn't sound like he's getting the message.'

'I know.' She grimaced. 'He sent me a curt email asking for an urgent meeting. Can't say I'm looking forward to it.' She looked around the room. 'Your flat is very different to mine. It's very modern.'

He had a flashback to her holding the art deco vase. 'You don't like modern, right?'

'Not when it comes to furniture, but this is quite nice.' She seemed genuine enough. She certainly looked comfy on his couch. She fitted right in. Fred too.

He looked around at the cream walls, wooden furniture and black leather couch. White kitchen and bath, blinds at the windows, wooden flooring. No rugs. No fuss. No clutter. Just a few cushions and a large cheese plant. 'It suits my needs.'

She crinkled her nose. 'What's that smell? It's divine.'

'Vegetable tagine. I've discovered the wonders of a crockpot. I'd never used one before. It's great. I threw a bunch of stuff in the pan this morning and twelve hours later I have dinner.'

Sarah stopped rubbing Fred's ears. 'Twelve hours?'

'Too long?'

'Did you have it on the low setting?'

'No idea.' He got up and headed for the kitchen. 'Are you an expert cook?'

'Not in the slightest. Although I am a fan of eating. I like my food.'

'Glad to hear it.' He lifted the lid. It looked fine. It smelt even better. 'Want to join me for supper? I have plenty.'

'I should say no.'

'Why should you?' He switched off the heat and stuck his head around the kitchen door. 'Oh, I get it. You think it's a *date*, or that I'll assume you like me. Or it might start rumours that you don't really hate men.' He snapped his fingers. 'You know, you might have a point. I mean, two people eating tagine together is pretty racy. Scandalous, in fact. You'd best leave now.' He gave her a pointed stare. 'Or you could stop fretting and just eat the damned food.'

'Fine, I'll eat the damned food,' she said, throwing a cushion at him. 'There's no need to be sarcastic.'

Fred jumped off the couch and grabbed the cushion, thinking it was playtime.

Lucas dropped to his knees and tried to rescue the suede accessory before it was decorated with bite marks. 'I'll make a deal with you. I'll stop being sarcastic, if you stop being so defensive and reacting as though everything I do is an attack on you.'

'I don't do that,' she said, sounding offended. 'Fred, stop that. Let go!' She removed the cushion from his grip and stood up. 'Is that really what I do?'

She looked so wounded that he felt bad for ribbing her. 'You're bruised, I get it. But I am not the enemy here. I have no agenda, no ulterior motive. I'm a guy visiting London for a few weeks to see the sights and spend time with his sister. That's it. I am not on a mission to persuade you to marry me.'

She stepped back, feigning hurt. 'You don't want to marry me? Why not? What's wrong with me?'

He lifted an eyebrow. 'Now who's being sarcastic. And it was you who kissed me, remember?'

'Well, I don't want to marry you, either,' she said, shoving him playfully in the chest. 'And you know why I kissed you. It was a necessary evil.'

'Well, I'm glad we've got that sorted. So, we can skip the part where you suspect me of trying to seduce you and just hang out. Fake dating. Real mates.' He held out his hand. 'Deal?'

She shook his hand. 'Do you have any couscous?'

'I'll take that as a yes.' Rolling his eyes, he returned to the kitchen. 'And yes, I have couscous.'

Ten minutes later, they had lap trays and were on the couch eating tagine, with Fred sitting between them staring longingly at their food. The place had warmed up, and Sarah had removed her suit jacket and kicked off her shoes. With her hair loose and colour in her cheeks, she looked less uptight, bordering on relaxed. An old Fred Astaire and Ginger Rogers movie played quietly on Film4, and he had to admit it was nice to have some company.

'How's your sister doing?' she asked, accepting the offer of more wine.

'Not great,' he admitted, filling his own glass. 'I had dinner with her last night. My nephews are staying with their dad this week, so I took Harper to The Ivy, a fancy restaurant near Leicester Square. You know it?'

'Everybody knows The Ivy. Very few of us mere mortals get the luxury of eating there. It's quite well-to-do.'

He tilted his head. 'Well-to-do?'

'Posh. Elite. Where all the celebs dine.'

'Oh, right. Well, that's where I took her.'

He thought back to how a few years before, Harper would have loved being taken to a fancy restaurant. She'd have dressed up and ordered something exotic from the menu. But last night she'd looked sullen and pale. She was distracted, and hadn't eaten much; she'd just pushed her food around the plate.

Sarah was watching him. 'I'm guessing it wasn't great?'

'The food was fine, but my sister wasn't.' He pushed his empty plate away. 'She's so angry. I try changing the subject, but the conversation keeps coming back to Paul and how she wants him... how can I put this?'

'Dead?' Sarah took a sip of wine.

He blinked at her nonchalance. 'How did you know?'

'It's a common phase,' she said, tucking her hair behind her ears. 'Step five, or something, in the break-up process. Rage. Anger. The desire to dismember the person with a blunt shovel. Been there, got the T-shirt.'

'You're telling me this is normal?'

'Absolutely.' She took a slug of wine. 'Haven't you ever felt that way?'

'Never.'

'Then lucky you. I can tell you from experience it's not pleasant. Especially if you're not normally a violent person. Having murderous thoughts can be quite unsettling.'

He rubbed his forehead, wondering about his own romantic history. He'd never felt that crushed. That enraged. Hurt, sure. Sad and heartbroken, but never so mad that he'd want to commit homicide. If that's what love did to you, had he ever really been in love? He would have said so, but now he wasn't so sure. 'So how do I get her over it?'

'You don't. She needs to work through it in her own time. She won't always feel this angry. Has she been through self-loathing yet? Endless crying? Denial? Destruction of property? That was my least favourite. I cut up an entire wardrobe of clothes in less than an hour. It only occurred to me afterwards that all I was left with were the pyjamas I was standing up in.' She lifted her glass and took another mouthful. 'This is fabulous wine, by the way.'

'I'm glad you like it. Want some more?'

'Better not, work tomorrow. I'm already feeling a bit squiffy.' She got up and carried her tray through to the kitchen. 'Thanks for dinner. Want a hand washing up?'

'I have a dishwasher.'

'Ooh, fancy you, Mr Mod-Cons. I only have a sink.'

He placed his tray next to hers on the countertop. 'Is Harper safe to be left alone, do you think?'

Sarah turned to him. 'Better to let her rage. The quicker it's done with the better. Did you enjoy your tagine?'

'I did, until I discovered my sister's murderous intentions are perfectly normal. I may have indigestion now.'

Sarah hesitated, as if she was uncertain about voicing something. 'Would you like me to talk to her? I've been where she is. Maybe I can help. Or at least empathise.'

'Seriously?' Lucas barked a laugh. 'You've hardly come through it unscathed. You're the most messed-up person I've ever met.'

Her face fell. 'Well, that told me.'

He instantly felt bad. 'Aw, shit. Sorry, Sarah. I didn't mean that.'

'Yes, you did. And it was a fair comment.' She tried to smile, but he could see it was an effort. 'Who am I to give advice when I can't even accept the kindness of a nice American man without suspecting him of trying to seduce me? I should sort my own life out first, right? Better go,' she said, heading for the door. 'Come on, Fred. Time to go home.'

'Sarah… wait.' He followed her into the hallway. 'I didn't mean it like it sounded.'

'It's fine, really. No harm done.' She gave a quick wave without turning back. 'Night, Lucas. Dinner was lovely. Thanks so much.'

She disappeared up the stairs with Fred trotting behind her.

Lucas slumped against the doorframe, feeling like a complete shit. So much for making gains with Mrs Kelsey; he'd blown it with Sarah. And she was the last person he'd ever want to hurt.

He was such a fool.

Chapter Nine

Thursday, 15th December

After a trying couple of weeks at work, not helped by the incompetent builders who had taken over two weeks to fix the wheelchair ramp, Sarah was finally able to sign off the work and confirm with the local authority that the Queen Adelaide Hospital was compliant with Disability Discrimination Act regulations.

It was a weight off her mind, but any relief she felt was short-lived when she returned to her office, and Georgia said, 'You have a visitor waiting for you in your office.'

Sarah glanced over, wondering if it was Lucas, but knowing it was more likely to be Stephen. She hadn't seen Lucas since Tuesday – not since he'd told her she was the most 'messed-up person he knew'. The truth had stung. His apology note slid under her door later that night was heartfelt, but not enough to ease her embarrassment. Avoiding him was safest.

'It's the boss,' Georgia said, making a slicing motion across her neck. 'He's been waiting for ages. It must be important. Are you in the shit?'

'Not as far as I know.' Sarah's stomach flipped at the idea of dealing with Stephen. Could she sneak out before he spotted her? It was tempting, but she didn't want her colleagues witnessing such a blatant affront to the hierarchy.

'Best go and see what he wants,' Georgia said, her desk covered in glitter from the tinsel wrapped around her computer screen. 'Maybe it's a pay rise?'

Sarah doubted that. She'd been actively avoiding Stephen all week. He'd clearly got tired of waiting for her to respond to his messages and had hunted her down.

Steeling herself, she headed for her office. It was the only space devoid of festive decorations. Her team had gone full out this year with a real tree, ceiling garlands and an inflatable Santa perched on one of the chairs, looking like he worked there. Thankfully, her team knew better than to decorate her office and had left the space festive-free.

Stephen was flicking through the papers on her desk when she entered, which immediately put her back up. He might be head honcho around here, but HR records were confidential. The staff had a right to their privacy.

'Busy day?' he said as she hung up her coat.

'No different to any other day,' she said, rebuttoning her suit jacket in an effort to look business-like. 'There's always something that needs my attention. This afternoon it was inspecting the new wheelchair ramp at the rear of the building.'

'A woman of many talents.'

She didn't return his smile. 'Can I help you with something?'

'You've been avoiding me.' He walked over to the door and closed it. Her office suddenly felt very confined, even with the glass front.

'I've been busy.'

He looked around the room, probably looking for clues about her and failing to find any. She'd deliberately kept her workspace neutral. Mainly because she had nothing to add: no photos of a partner or children, nothing to indicate anything about her personal life. Instead, the studded walls were filled with posters promoting equality and dignity in the workplace – something she hoped Stephen might take note of.

'I've requested several meetings,' he said, his eyes landing on her.

'I'm aware of that.' She headed over to her desk. 'And I've replied to your messages requesting an agenda. I'm not sure what's so urgent we need to meet up. Your predecessor was content with monthly management meetings and email updates.'

He leant against the door. 'I prefer a more hands-on approach.'

'Unfortunately, I don't have enough space in my diary to accommodate that.' Sarah busied herself tidying papers on her desk.

'You're refusing to meet with me?'

She pulled open a filing cabinet drawer, trying to stem the shake in her hands. 'I'm simply asking for more consideration of my time. A collective meeting with the other department heads where a number of topics can be discussed would be more time-efficient.'

'You're making it hard for me to get to know you, Sarah.' He moved away from the door. 'I want us to be more than colleagues. I care about you. I'd like for us to pursue a relationship outside of work.'

Sarah stilled. Had she heard right? If she'd been unsure about his intentions before, she was left in no doubt now.

'Are you free this evening? There's a new Greek restaurant down the road from where you live. Shall a book a table for seven? I can pick you up.'

Several things whizzed around her head. He knew where she lived? He wanted more than a work relationship? She focused on the immediate issue. 'I have plans tonight.'

He watched her fumbling with the filing cabinet. 'Tomorrow evening, then?'

'I'm busy tomorrow.'

'I'm sure you can rearrange your plans.' His hand rested close to hers on the desk. 'Tomorrow night it is.'

She pulled away. 'I'm sorry, but no.'

'Why not?'

She straightened and hoped her voice wouldn't betray her. This was a power play and she needed to stay strong. 'I'm not interested in pursuing a relationship with you, Stephen.' There she'd said it. Clear. Concise. Forceful. Job done.

'I don't see why not.' He seemed unperturbed. 'I'm a successful man. I have a lot to offer. I'm single and I've admitted I like you. Why wouldn't you be interested?'

Was he for real?

'I think we'd work well together.' He fixed her with a supposed seductive look. 'You need to stop being so stubborn. Live a little. Explore this great opportunity being presented to you.' His grin was wide and confident, and in that moment, she realised how deluded Stephen Stokes actually was. He was like the baddie in a superhero movie, seduced by his own power and success, impervious to rejection or insult.

'As I've said before, I don't like mixing work with my private life,' she said, glancing at the door and praying someone would interrupt. Anyone. Even Knob the Builder would be a welcome distraction at this moment in time.

Stephen's smile faded. 'We both know that's a lie. You left my drinks evening last Friday with Doctor Moore, and I saw you kissing him in the car park on Monday. If it's okay for you to cavort with him, there's no reason why you can't extend the same courtesy to me.'

Sarah was so shocked she almost swore. And she never swore.

'I disagree,' she said, choosing her words carefully. 'Even though my relationship with Doctor Moore is none of anyone else's concern, it's my decision who I become friendly with. I don't have to justify that, or explain myself.'

Stephen's smile was back. 'Dinner tomorrow evening, then?' He stood and headed for the door. 'I'll pick you up at seven.'

'I am not going to dinner with you,' she blurted loudly, inviting curious glances from Georgia and Jafrina, visible through the glass.

Stephen frowned. 'Why not?'

'Because I don't want to,' she said, opting for the brutal truth. Subtlety wasn't getting her anywhere.

He sighed. 'You just need to get to know me, Sarah.'

'I don't want to get to know you.' She was barely holding on to her composure.

He folded his arms across his chest, his feet shoulder-width apart. It was an assertive pose. Masculine. Imposing. Meant to intimidate. 'You've yet to explain why. What's stopping you from accepting a dinner invitation?'

He really wasn't backing down, was he? Being honest and admitting she didn't want to go out with him wasn't penetrating his thick skin. Which left her with only one option. The 'fake dating' card.

'Because, as you've already alluded to, I'm in a relationship with Doctor Moore.' Her words sounded strained, even to her own ears. 'Lucas… Lucas Moore.' She hoped her lie wasn't too obvious and the heat in her cheeks wasn't undermining her efforts to appear convincing. 'We've started dating. It wouldn't be appropriate for me to accept a dinner invitation with another man.'

'You can't have been dating that long,' he said, frowning. 'Hardly enough time to get attached. I fail to see why you can't see me as well. Isn't that the way things are done these days? Multiple dates with multiple men, sampling the pool before making any commitments?'

What an arrogant man. She straightened her shoulders. 'I've no idea, but as far as I'm concerned, dating one man is enough… and that man is Lucas Moore.'

Stephen's expression darkened. 'You have feelings for him?'

'That's really none of your business… but yes… yes, I do.' Years of working on her self-esteem and independence flew out of the window. She'd vowed never to rely on any man ever again. And here she was, acting like a lovestruck teenager, declaring her feelings for a man… albeit fictional. 'And I really am very busy, so please respect my decision and leave me to get on with my work.' She strode over to door and yanked it open before he could stop her.

Stephen clenched his jaw. 'You know he's only here for another couple of weeks?'

'Please leave.'

'You'll change your mind,' he whispered. 'And when you do, I'll make that dinner reservation.'

It took all her effort not to slam the door on his retreating back. Maybe she would have if her hands weren't shaking so much, but all her strength had drained out of her. Arrogant, awful man. The worst kind of bully. Full of self-importance and an inflated ego the size of Mars.

Feeling dizzy, she slumped onto a chair and rested her head in her hands. She wasn't sure whether she wanted to scream, cry or throw furniture. All three, probably. This was why she avoided men. They never listened. It was all about what *they* wanted, and how *they* felt, never about what was right for her. She was sick of it.

'You all right, boss?' The sound of Georgia's voice made her look up.

'Actually, I'm not.' She rubbed her temples. 'A sudden migraine. I need to go home.'

'Crikey, I've never known you off sick before. You want me to call an Uber?'

'I'll be okay. The walk will do me good.' She collected her coat and bag. 'See you tomorrow.'

Georgia followed her into the main office. 'Seems daft to come in for one day before the weekend. Why don't you take tomorrow off. Hopefully you'll feel better by Monday.'

'I might just do that.' She offered a weak smile. 'Thanks, Georgia. Night, everyone.'

Jafrina and Tyler muttered their goodbyes, unused to the boss leaving work mid-afternoon.

'Call if you need anything,' Georgia shouted, before turning to her work mates. 'Right... while the cat's away... it's time for some Christmas music!'

Leaving them to cause chaos in her absence, Sarah headed outside, praying no one would stop and speak to her. She wasn't up for conversation; her head was all over the place.

The last thing she'd wanted was to prolong any involvement with Lucas, and now she'd told the head of the hospital they were dating and that she had *feelings* for him. Avoiding Lucas until he returned home to the US had been her plan. It might not be mature, or even what she truly wanted, but it was necessary for her sanity. Because however she viewed it, she was annoyed with him.

Pushing open the exit door, she was hit by the cold winter air and drizzle gently falling from the darkening December sky. The weather matched her mood, gloomy and damp.

Flipping up her hood, she marched across the forecourt.

She wasn't annoyed with Lucas because he'd called her 'messed up' – that she could deal with. It was the truth, after all. She was annoyed because she liked him, and she really didn't want to. She enjoyed his company, which wasn't what she wanted. And worst of all, he'd reminded her what it was like to have a man in her life, to chat with someone and laugh with them. Until Lucas had crashed into her life, she hadn't realised how lonely she was, and that's why she was so annoyed. She'd been fine until he'd shown up.

Sarah might have walked straight past the woman huddled under the awning, if she hadn't made a sobbing noise. The sound of crying couldn't be ignored, so she stopped to check on her. 'Are you okay?' It wasn't unusual to find someone crying outside of a hospital. Patients were often given bad news. No one visited a medic if they were fit and healthy.

The woman wiped her eyes. 'Sorry, I didn't mean for you to hear. I'm waiting on my brother. He'll be here soon.'

Sarah knew the US was a big place, but this couldn't be a coincidence. 'Are you Harper?'

The woman looked surprised. 'Well, hey, how did you know?'

'Your accent is the same as your brother's. I'm Sarah; I live in the same building as Lucas.'

'You're Sarah?' The woman smiled. 'Jeez, he wasn't lying. You sure are pretty.'

Sarah jolted with surprise. 'He's mentioned me?'

'A little. He said you were nice. I think he's sweet on you.'

Compliment aside, Sarah still planned to avoid him.

She glanced at the woman's wet clothing. 'Does he know you're waiting? You're allowed to go inside, you know. You don't have to stay out here.'

'I'm not fit to be in company,' she said, wiping her wet hair away from her face. 'I'm kind of a mess; I don't want to embarrass him.'

'Would you like me to find him?' It seemed rude not to offer.

'That's okay. I'll wait till he's done.'

Sarah was torn. It was mid-afternoon. The woman would freeze to death if she stayed outside much longer. She was already shivering. 'It could be a while yet. How about you come home with me? It's not far. I live in the flat above him. At least wait in the dry for him.'

Harper's teeth were chattering. 'Sure you don't mind?'

'Of course not. Come on, this way.' They crossed the road and headed for Putney Bridge. 'Bad day?'

'Bad year, more like. Today was the worst. No one told me rock bottom had a basement.' Her laugh was self-deprecating. 'Lucas might've mentioned I'm going through a divorce. A messy one. This morning I showed up at my ex-husband's workplace and confronted the woman he left me for. Genius, huh?'

Sarah winced. 'A bold move.'

'I figured they owed me some answers.'

A silver Mercedes swept by so fast that Sarah had to pull Harper away from the road. She glared at the driver, hidden behind tinted glass. Was that…? Surely not?

'I'm the injured party,' Harper continued, seemingly oblivious to their near miss with the car. 'Me and my kids. Right? But do they get that? Hell, no. They stood there all superior and made it seem like I was the one acting unreasonable.'

Sarah moved to the outside of Harper, shielding her from the splash coming up from the traffic. 'That must have been hard.'

'It was humiliating. She looked at me like I was a piece of shit. And then she said if I didn't leave she'd call security. Man, I wanted to smack her pretty face. I didn't, of course. Sense told me I'd be the one arrested, so I left. I feel so damned angry… and cheated. I never asked for any of this.' She opened her arms, letting the rain drizzle down her face. 'How come my life gets upended and I don't get a say in it? It's like, he calls all the shots. He does what he likes and I'm expected to accept it without a fuss. Well, you know, I don't feel much like playing nice.'

Sarah managed to grab Harper before she fell into the path of a double-decker. 'I know that feeling.'

'You divorced?'

'Jilted. Come on, let's keep moving; the rain's coming down harder.'

Harper hooked her arm through Sarah's. 'Jilted? You mean, on your wedding day?'

Sarah wondered how much to divulge, especially following her conversation with Lucas, where she'd offered to help Harper, only to be told she was 'too messed up' to be of any use. But what he didn't realise was that only someone who had been through hell could truly understand the level of despair, rage and torment a person experienced when tossed aside like that. Harper needed an ally.

'Yep, in front of all my friends and family,' Sarah said, as the bridge lanterns flickered a few times before coming on. 'If he'd wanted to back out, why couldn't he have done it a week before? Or even the day before? Why wait until everyone was congregated at the church before deciding he didn't want to marry me?' She felt Harper squeeze her arm. 'He'd made this whole speech about how weddings were outdated, and as an independent woman I shouldn't be given away by my father. We should walk independently into the church and meet at the altar. Whoever arrived first would get the ball rolling.' Sarah sighed. 'Part of me wonders if he did that deliberately to maximise my humiliation.'

'Men are arseholes.'

Sarah sighed. 'I agree.'

'Except Lucas. He's one of the good ones.'

Sarah wasn't about to be drawn into that conversation.

They reached Oxford Road and crossed by the busy Boathouse pub. It was getting close to Christmas; the office parties were in full swing.

'Did you ever confront him?' Harper asked as they walked up the road, arm in arm.

'Not immediately – he disappeared off the grid. Even his family had no idea where he was. Having sent a lame WhatsApp message the day after apologising for running off and saying he needed space, he vanished.' Sarah noticed a set of headlights switch off as they approached her building. The silver Mercedes again. Stephen wouldn't go that far... would he?

'What did you do?'

Sarah had momentarily lost her place in the conversation. 'Oh... er... I didn't do anything, not for a couple of weeks. I was too stunned. I think I kept expecting him to come back. When he didn't, I moved in with my parents for a while.' Sarah pointed ahead. 'This is us. Mind the steps – they're slippery.'

When they reached the main door, Sarah let Harper go ahead. She glanced back. The silver Mercedes was still in darkness, the engine idling.

'That's Lucas's place on the left,' Sarah said, locking the main door behind her. 'I'm the next floor up.'

Harper wiped her feet on the mat. 'Have you heard from your ex since?'

Sarah climbed the stairs. 'About a month after I'd moved into this place, he showed up at my parents' house saying he wanted to talk. They refused to tell him where I was, but I agreed to meet him. I was curious to hear what he had to say.'

'What did he say?'

Sarah unlocked her door and headed inside. 'He was sorry and that he'd panicked, but he still loved me, and he wanted us to get back together. *Fred!* I'm home!'

Frantic noises came from the bedroom, followed by the scurrying of feet on her wooden floorboards. He'd been on her bed again, the little blighter.

Harper nudged Sarah's arm. 'Don't leave me hanging; what did you say to your ex?'

'I told him to piss off,' she said, dropping down and enveloping Fred in a hug.

'You did?'

'It wasn't the first time, you see.' She pushed Fred away when he tried to lick her face. 'You'll find towels in the bathroom. I'll fetch you some dry clothes to put on.'

'Thanks.' Harper went into the bathroom. 'Carry on, I'm listening! I want to know what happened.'

'Well, during the whole time we were together he constantly blew hot and cold,' Sarah said, heading for her wardrobe, Fred trotting behind. 'Things would be great for a while and we'd get close again, and then he'd pull away, saying he wasn't sure it was what he wanted.' She searched through her clothes, pulling out jogging bottoms, a T-shirt and a hoodie. 'The moment I gave up trying to persuade him to come back, he'd reappear and we'd start over again. It was only after the non-wedding that I had the headspace to analyse things properly. I realised he was drawn to what he couldn't have. When he had me, he didn't want me. When he thought he couldn't have me, he was interested again.'

Harper appeared in the bedroom. 'So, you kicked his sorry arse into touch?'

'I did. I'd had enough by then.' Sarah took Harper's wet clothes and placed them in a bag. 'Deep down I knew the same thing would keep happening, so I needed to resist his efforts to win me back.' She unearthed a pair of slipper-socks from the chest of drawers and handed them to Harper. 'Strangely, the more he tried, the more determined I became. I could finally see who he was. He didn't want me, not really. He just wanted what he couldn't have. I'd suddenly become unattainable.'

Harper pulled up the jogging bottoms. 'I admire you. I'm not so tough. I'm ashamed to admit, but I've begged and pleaded with Paul to change his mind. Shameful, huh? Not very women's lib.' She shoved her head inside the hoodie.

'Don't be hard on yourself. I'm sure if Josh had come back straight away I'd have done the same thing. It was only because I'd had time to focus on myself that I was able to tell him to take a hike.' She removed her suit jacket and kicked off her shoes. 'Wine or a hot drink? I have chocolate?'

'Chocolate sounds perfect. I've had enough wine; my liver's complaining.' Harper followed Sarah into the lounge. 'I messaged Lucas to tell him I was here. He's coming over. Hope that's okay?'

Sarah silently cursed. 'Sure. No problem.' So much for doing a good deed, she was being punished for it. 'Make yourself at home.' She flicked on the side lamps and glanced out of the window. The silver Mercedes had disappeared. Relief flooded her. She closed the curtains anyway. 'Fred, keep Harper company while I make drinks.'

The moment Harper sat on the sofa, Fred landed on her lap. 'You're a nice dog,' she said, stroking his ears. 'You think I'll ever stop wanting Paul back?'

'Maybe.' Sarah took the milk from the fridge and searched for a pan. 'At the moment you can't imagine a life without him. You're scared about the future. How you'll cope, how you'll pay the bills, how you'll look after your kids.' She scooped up two large helpings of chocolate. 'You're fighting to keep hold of your marriage. Most people would do the same.' Lighting the hob, she stuck her head around the door. 'All I know is, time can change things. One day, you can't get out of bed for crying, the next you find yourself having a good time and going out with girlfriends, or choosing a piece of furniture you know they'd hate. Suddenly you realise life without them isn't so bad, and you can cope just fine.'

Harper cuddled Fred close. 'Didn't you feel lonely?'

Sarah leant against the doorframe. 'There are different types of loneliness. Nothing's more soul-destroying than living with someone who no longer wants you. That's the worst type of loneliness. I'd rather be on my own any day.'

'Living with Paul this last year hasn't been great. I could feel us drifting apart, but the more I tried to fix things, the worse it got.'

Sarah felt for the woman. 'All you can do now is let things play out, one way or the other. In the meantime, my advice is to stop focusing on your ex and his new woman, and start focusing on yourself instead.'

Harper frowned. 'How do I do that?'

'Every time you find yourself dwelling, or thinking about what he's doing, or how he feels, stop and take a breath. Shake those thoughts from your mind and refocus on what *you're* doing. How do *you* feel? What do *you* want? What plans can you make to improve things? It doesn't have to be big things. Light some candles and take a bath. Book a babysitter and take yourself off to a spa resort. Go out for drinks with your girlfriends.'

'I bought a vibrator yesterday – does that count?'

Sarah spluttered a laugh. 'In terms of self-care, I'd say that definitely counts.' She returned to the kitchen and stirred the milk. 'Once he's stopped being the centre of your thoughts, you'll be surprised how you feel. If nothing else, you get to have some fun.'

'You're a good example of someone who's turned things around. Look at you, all fancy in your suit, with a good job, and a great apartment. A real role model.'

Sarah thought back to the way Lucas had described her the other day. He definitely hadn't used the words 'role model'. Maybe she was both. A messed-up role model. No one was perfect, after all.

'I do have a great job,' she said, carrying the mugs into the lounge. 'I'm in control of my life, and I like the choices I make. Whether it's buying soft furnishings, or what hobbies I do. My self-care comes first.'

'So, you have a vibrator too?'

Sarah nearly spilt the drinks. 'Well… I…'

'Good for you, girl. It's great to hear you're doing so well.' Harper sipped her drink. 'Ooh, this is nice.'

Slightly flustered, Sarah seated herself in the armchair. 'I'm doing okay, but if I'm honest, I'm struggling to clear one final hurdle. I've yet to start dating again.'

'You haven't dated anyone since? How long's it been?'

'Five years.'

'Five years? No wonder you need a vibrator.'

A knock on the door startled them both.

A situation made worse when Lucas called out, 'Hello!'

Sarah felt her face grow hot. She just hoped he hadn't heard their conversation about vibrators. Heading into the hall, she checked her appearance in the mirror and opened the door. 'Harper's through here,' she said, walking off before he could reply.

He caught her arm. 'Still mad at me, huh?'

'Why would you think that?' She turned to glare at him.

Before he could answer, Harper came into the hallway and threw her arms around him. 'Lucas! Am I glad to see you. Can I stay at your place tonight? The boys are with Paul.'

'Sure,' he said, meeting Sarah's gaze over the top of his sister's head.

'Thanks so much for the chocolate.' Harper turned to hug Sarah. 'And for the advice. It really helped.'

'Oh, well, you know… us girls have to stick together. Seeing as how we're so *messed up*, and all that.' She gave Lucas a pointed look.

Lucas flinched. 'You're not going to let me forget that, are you?'

Sarah's hands went to her hips. 'What do you think?'

A long beat passed where they both stared at each other.

Harper looked between them. 'Am I missing something?'

'No,' they said in unison.

'Don't forget your clothes,' Sarah said, handing Harper her bag. 'I hope things work out for you. Take care of yourself.'

'You too, girlfriend. I'll get these clothes back to you as soon as possible. And you take care of yourself, too.' Harper made a buzzing sound. 'Know what I mean?'

Sarah blushed.

Lucas raised an eyebrow. 'Anything I should know about?'

'Definitely not,' Sarah said, shutting the door firmly behind them.

That was one conversation she most certainly wasn't having with Lucas Moore.

Chapter Ten

Lucas wasn't needed at the hospital – they had enough locum cover – so he'd spent a relaxing day with his sister, if you could call drafting a response to Paul's solicitor's letter relaxing. But it was done now, all the points were covered and Harper had appreciated the support. She seemed less fragile today, still broken, but talking about the future rather than dwelling on the past. He figured that had to be a good thing. Whatever Sarah had said to her yesterday had helped, which just made him feel even worse about questioning her ability to act as his sister's counsellor.

His nephews finished school today for the holidays, so they'd taken them for pancakes at a joint in town. Both boys had eaten so much chocolate sauce they'd ended up feeling sick and were now on the couch watching one of the Marvel movies.

Harper seemed less morose after their trip out, so he'd left them to their evening on the couch, no longer concerned about leaving sharp knives in the house. Harper's rage seemed to have subsided, thankfully.

Ironic that instead of heading into town to see a show, or hanging out at a fancy bar in Soho like most guys his age, his Friday evening involved running errands for Diana Kelsey. She hadn't asked him, he knew she never would, but she was definitely less volatile now and a fraction more receptive to being helped.

He carried the shopping bags down the steps leading to the basement flat. It wasn't an ideal setting for someone with mobility issues. Navigating the steep drop, uneven paving and slippery surface in the dark was a challenge for him, let alone someone who used a walking frame.

He'd barely knocked when he heard her shuffling towards the door. She no longer resisted him visiting, which had to be a positive.

'You're late,' she said, opening the door.

'Nice to see you too.' He grinned at her. 'Missed me?'

'You should be so lucky. Get in here.' She headed off down the hallway, allowing him to follow. 'And close the door behind you.'

'Sorry I'm late; I took my nephews out for pancakes and then I had to stop off to buy provisions.'

She raised an eyebrow at the bulging carrier bags. 'You planning some kind of dinner party up there?'

'Provisions for you, not me.' He carried the bags through to the kitchen.

He noticed red polish on Diana's nails and took that as a good sign. She was taking better care of herself.

She waved a hand when he started unloading bags. 'I can't afford all that! You think I'm made of money?'

'Call it an early Christmas present,' he said, showing her the items. 'Ready meals for the freezer. Tinned soup and fruit. Yoghurts, milk and bread. I also got you chocolates and some cheesy biscuits as a treat. All easy stuff that doesn't need any preparation. Even you can manage to prepare a meal out of this lot.' He handed her a box of Celebrations.

'Cheeky blighter. I'm not incapable.' She carried the chocolates over to the coffee table. Her breathing was definitely less wheezy.

'You're looking better,' he said, switching on the oven and unwrapping one of the ready meals. 'Are you feeling any better?'

'Hard to tell. Me knees are aching, I can tell you that.'

'Do you have any medication for your arthritis?'

'Just the cream the pharmacist gave me.'

He picked up the tube lying on the side and read the label. 'This contains an anti-inflammatory. I wouldn't recommend using that with your COPD issues. I'll prescribe you an acetaminophen instead. It's still an analgesic, but it won't interfere with your breathing.'

'You could be talking Spanish for all I know. I just know me knees hurt.'

He popped the meal in the oven and found homes for the other items. 'Apart from your knees, are you okay?'

'No different to when you asked me yesterday. Or the day before that. It's not like anything happens in my life. I watched a rerun of *Heartbeat* this afternoon. Is that exciting enough for you?'

He came into the lounge and searched for his stethoscope in his medical bag. 'I've no idea what that is, but if you enjoyed it, then great.' He listened to her chest. 'Take a deep breath for me.'

'It was edge-of-the-seat stuff,' she said, with an eyeroll.

'I'm sensing sarcasm.'

'Clever boy.'

'Your chest is sounding better. Less crackle.' He took her temperature. 'I picked you up a couple of puzzle books and a jigsaw, and I got you this leaflet on social prescribing.'

'What's that when it's at home?'

'They provide complementary support to GPs for people like yourself who might need extra help. I mentioned it before, remember?'

'No.' She frowned at the leaflet.

'Someone from the organisation would visit and carry out an assessment. Then they'd match you with local services that could help. Whether it's a befriending service, physical activities, education or home help, they offer all sorts of things. I wish we had a scheme like this back home.' He checked the thermometer. 'Your temperature's normal. That's a good sign.'

'I don't like the idea of people interfering,' she said, rolling up the sleeve of her green kaftan so he could take her blood pressure.

'I get that, but why don't you let me refer you and then you can find out more. Seems crazy to say no to something before you've heard what they've got to say.' He made a note of her blood pressure reading. 'If you decide against it, no harm done. It might be good to hear what's out there. Did you know they run a games afternoon at the local church hall on Wednesday afternoons?'

'Games? In my state,' she scoffed. 'You're having a laugh.'

'Board games, not sports. Puzzles, quizzes, bingo, that kind of thing.' He packed away his bag. 'Sound good?'

She pouted like a small child. 'How would I get there?'

'A volunteer driver would take you and bring you home afterwards.'

'Got it all sorted, haven't you?' She shuffled over to the armchair and lowered herself onto it. 'You think you're so smart.'

'Only trying to help.' He stood up. 'So, can I refer you?'

'Do whatever you like. I doubt I'll do anything, though.' She reached for the chocolates.

'We'll see. Need anything before I go?'

'No, you can bugger off now.'

'Your dinner's in the oven.' He handed her the remote. 'The timer's on. Fish pie.'

She scowled at him and shoved a mini Milky Way in her mouth.

He tilted his head, waiting for her objection. 'Sound okay?'

'Thank you,' she said, although it clearly pained her to say so.

He grinned. 'You're entirely welcome, Diana. See you tomorrow.'

Leaving her to enjoy her chocolate, he headed upstairs to his apartment, glad to find it warm inside and he hadn't left the window open again.

Having ordered a curry online and opened a bottle of red, he chose a blues playlist on Spotify and flopped onto the couch, one arm under his head, letting his eyes drift shut.

As he lay there, wallowing in some downtime and drifting off to sleep, he was jolted awake by a loud crash outside. Blinking away sleep, he sat up and rubbed his face. Unsure whether he'd actually heard a faint scream, or whether it was his imagination, he headed over to the window to see what had caused the noise.

Lifting the sash window, he stuck his head out.

Jeez, it was cold. It was also pitch dark. There wasn't a single light shining onto the service area below; he couldn't see a damned thing. Then he heard a faint moaning sound, followed by barking.

Straining his eyes, he tried to see where the noise was coming from. 'Sarah…? Honey, is that you?'

'I'm not your honey,' came her disgruntled reply.

'Sarah? You okay?' When she didn't reply, he climbed onto the fire escape and climbed down the spiral metal steps leading to the service yard. 'Hey there, fella,' he said, encountering Fred along the way. 'Where's your mom?'

'I'm here… *Ouch.*'

He squinted, unable to see her at first, and then he spotted her. She was lying in a heap on the ground. Jesus. He jumped down the last few steps. 'What happened?'

'I fell,' she said, pushing herself into a sitting position. 'Stupid slippery steps.'

He crouched beside her. 'How far did you fall?'

She rubbed her elbow. 'Far enough for it to hurt.'

When she tried to get up, he stopped her. 'Hang fire a moment. Where does it hurt?'

She let out a shaky breath. 'Where doesn't it hurt. I just need to stand up.'

'Not until I've checked you over.' His eyes had adjusted to the dim lighting, allowing him to see better. 'Are you wearing pyjamas?'

'And what of it? I was planning an early night. I'd just got out the bath.' She was shivering. 'I'm cold. I want to move.'

'I know, but I'm the doctor and I want you to stay put.' He scanned her as he spoke, his eyes travelling from head to toe as he tried to assess the damage.

'I haven't broken anything. It's just bruising. Stop fussing.'

'Then stop moving.' His gaze landed on her feet. 'And I'm not surprised you're cold. You haven't got shoes on. What are those flimsy things?'

'They're called slippers. And seriously, Lucas, I'm fine.' She pushed his hand away. 'Just let me stand up.'

Reluctantly, he gave her space to stand up. She was clearly in pain; there was a lot of flinching and grimacing, and she had to use the metal railings to pull herself up. When she was finally upright, she gave him a triumphant look. 'See? Perfectly fine.' And then she crumpled forwards.

As he caught her, he could feel her ribs through the thin fabric of her nightwear. He could feel a lot more too: she was minus a bra. 'This is your idea of fine?'

She clung hold of him. 'Okay, I might be a little dizzy.'

The smell of camomile in her damp hair tickled his nose. 'Did you hit your head?'

'Among other things.'

He was torn between insisting she stay put until he'd assessed whether paramedics were required, or getting her into the warm so he could asses her himself. It was freezing out. She was barely weight-bearing, but lucid enough to be arguing with him, so logic dictated she wasn't critically injured. Moving her seemed like the better option, even if his medical training advised against it.

'Hook your arm around my neck,' he instructed, sliding one arm around her waist and the other under her legs so he could lift her. 'Let me take your weight... that's it. Slowly does it.'

Fred trotted up the steps ahead, glancing back as if to say, *Hurry up, humans.*

Easier said than done. Fred wasn't the one carrying one of the said humans. 'What were you doing out here, anyway?'

'Fred needed a wee.'

'You didn't think to put a coat on?'

She tutted. 'No, *dad*, I didn't. Crikey, you do make a fuss. And I wasn't planning on coming out here. I saw torchlight flashing about by the bins and I was worried about Fred's safety.' Her face winced in pain. 'I think Stephen might have followed me home yesterday.'

Lucas almost missed a step. 'He did what?'

'I'm not certain. Maybe it wasn't him, but a silver Merc was parked outside when I arrived back here with Harper.'

Lucas paused for breath; his thighs were burning from the climb. 'Did you ask him about it at work today?'

'I didn't go to work today. I couldn't face going in after yesterday's encounter, so I booked lieu time and stayed home.'

'Yesterday's encounter?' He steeled himself to hike the last few steps.

'Long story. The short version is that Stephen asked me to dinner; I said no. He pushed the issue, so I lied, and told him I was dating you. He didn't like that.'

Finally, they reached his window. 'I need to put you down.'

'I'm up another floor,' she said, pointing upwards.

'I don't have the strength to carry you up another floor. Besides, my medical bag's in here. I need to check you over.'

She looked disgruntled. 'I can do that myself.'

'You could, but you're not going to.' He leant her against the wall so he could climb inside. Fred followed him into his apartment.

She rubbed her side. 'You're being stubborn.'

'So are you.' He held his arms out. 'Take my hands.' He gently helped her inside, getting the first glimpse of the blood on her face and her grubby pyjama bottoms. 'I get that you're mad at me, but that's no reason for you to refuse medical help when you're clearly injured. And before you argue back, you have blood dripping down your face.'

She touched her head and winced.

'You can go back to being mad at me once I've patched you up.' He picked her up and carried her through to his bedroom. Fred trotted behind.

It was a moment before she spoke. 'I'm not really mad at you. I'm mad with myself.'

He kicked open the bedroom door. 'Why's that?'

'Because you were right. I *am* messed up. And despite having good reason for being messed up, I shouldn't be *this* messed up after this length of time. I knew that; I just didn't appreciate you pointing it out.'

He stopped by the bed and looked down at her. It had taken a lot of guts for her to admit that. 'I shouldn't have said what I did; it was uncalled for and mean. I'm truly sorry.'

Her eyes drifted away from his. 'That's okay.'

He lowered her onto the duvet and fetched his medical bag. 'Is the pain getting worse or better?'

Fred had jumped onto an armchair and was curled up in a ball.

'Better,' she said, looking into the glow of the slit lamp so he could check for concussion.

'Any dizziness?'

'It's better now I'm lying down. You have a comfy bed.'

He lifted her hair and saw the cause of the blood, a nasty graze on her forehead. 'Relax your head against the pillow so I can check for damage.' He felt his way around her skull, relieved that her head seemed to be intact. 'Tell me if it hurts.'

'The truth often hurts,' she said. 'But sometimes it's necessary.'

'I meant your head.'

'Oh, right… my head's fine, thanks.' She gave a little shrug. 'I'm just saying. Sometimes it's easier to see what's wrong in someone else's life than your own.'

He tried to focus on the job at hand, something that wasn't easy when she was looking at him with dilated pupils. He cleared his throat. 'I'm going to check the rest of you… is that okay?'

She nodded. 'I mean, I spend my days solving other people's problems. It's my job. The staff come to me with all kinds of issues and I provide them with solutions. Debt problems? Go to Citizens Advice. Relationship problems? Go to Relate. Tax issues? Contact HMRC. Whatever the problem, I research it and find a solution.' She recoiled when he touched her wrist. '*Ouch.*'

'Can you wiggle your fingers?' She did as he asked. It probably wasn't broken.

'But you can only do that if you know you have a problem, and I didn't. Well, maybe I did, but I didn't want to admit that I had a problem.' She shuffled onto one elbow. 'Do you think I have a concussion?'

He moved down to check her knees. 'Yes, but you're talking – that's a good sign. Lie down, please.'

'I might not be making sense,' she said, flopping down. 'Please ignore anything I say. I'm being weird.'

He smiled. 'You're being cute.'

'Please, I am not cute. I am spiky and defensive and sad.'

'You're also cute.' He pressed her tummy, hoping she didn't have any internal bleeding. 'And funny, and kind.'

This was a new experience for him, flattering a woman while medically treating her. 'Any pain when I press here?'

'No... And you don't like my furniture.'

He laughed. 'I like *you*. Isn't that more important?' He took her blood pressure, checked her oxygen levels and temperature. All normal. 'Want the verdict?'

'Give it to me straight, Doctor. I can take it.'

'Mild concussion, sprained wrist and extensive bruising.' He lifted her arm so he could prop a pillow under her wrist. 'And a nasty graze on your forehead, which needs cleaning and dressing. I can do it here, or I can take you to the nearest A&E.'

'Can you do it, please. I'm very comfy; I don't want to move.'

'Not a problem. Back soon.' He took a petri dish into the bathroom and filled it with warm water. This was not how he'd expected his night to go. Who would have thought Sarah would be lying on his bed, albeit battered from a fall. At least she'd forgiven him; that was something.

When he came back into the bedroom, her eyes were drifting shut. 'I guess buying the furniture was an act of rebellion,' she said, hugging one of his pillows to her chest. 'I'd always liked antiques, and Josh hated them, so when I got my own place I wanted to make it all about me.'

He pushed her hair away from her face and soaked a piece of gauze. 'Understandable.'

'I deliberately chose stuff I knew he'd hate. I think maybe I did that so he wouldn't want me back. *Ouch!*'

'Sorry, but I need to clean the wound.' He wiped dirt away from her forehead. 'You were saying?'

She closed her eyes. 'I didn't want another relapse. I'd taken him back so many times, I was sick of it. He could be very persuasive and charming, and it was hard to resist him. Jilting me was the final straw. I knew it was over and I needed to move on, but I was worried I might give in once he was standing in front of me.'

He tore open an alcoholic wipe. 'But you didn't.'

'No, I didn't.'

'This is going to sting.' He wiped the remaining blood away, ensuring the wound was clean. He could feel her tense beneath his fingers. 'You can relax now; the worst is over.'

She let out a breath. 'You didn't react when I said I'd been jilted, so I'm guessing someone already told you... Was it Harper?'

'Carla. I told her I liked you and she warned me off trying to get too close.'

She rolled her head to look at him. 'It didn't stop you.'

'No, it didn't.' He grinned and placed a gauze over the cut. 'I like a challenge.'

'I'm not a challenge; I'm insurmountable, like Everest. Or visiting Venus. I am the Invisible Triangle of women.'

'You really did hit your head,' he said, securing the gauze with tape. 'By the way, thanks for talking to Harper yesterday. Shows you how clueless I am when it comes to knowing what's best for her. Whatever you said really helped; she was all about focusing on self-care today.'

Sarah's eyes grew wide. 'She didn't mention... gadgets, did she?'

'Gadgets?' He grew curious. 'What kind of gadgets? Why are you blushing?'

'Nothing. Forget I said anything.' She buried her face in the pillow and made an odd squeaking noise.

Intrigued, he fetched a throw from the wardrobe and covered her with it. He'd quiz Harper tomorrow; she could never keep a secret. 'Warming up yet?'

Her face lifted from the pillow. 'Yes, thank you… And you know, talking to Harper helped me too.'

He took the pillow from her and eased it under her head. 'How come?'

'Giving her advice about moving forwards with her life reminded me I need to do the same.' She fixed him with those big brown eyes. 'I'm stuck.'

It took all his willpower not to kiss her. She was lying on his bed, looking up at him all doe-eyed and cute in her pyjamas, and his heart sped up a little. In other circumstances this would be a very romantic moment. 'I'm no expert, but I'm guessing admitting that has to be a positive step.'

'It's just knowing where to start.'

'How about starting with Christmas.' He kicked off his trainers and climbed onto the bed next to her.

'Excuse me?'

'You don't celebrate Christmas. I get it. It reminds you of a shitty time in your life. So, make some new memories. Let Christmas back into your life.' He arranged a couple of pillows behind him so he was propped up against the headboard. 'Wouldn't that be the ultimate payback for all the hurt your ex caused? To reclaim something he took from you?'

She seemed to consider this. 'Maybe.'

He reached for his laptop on the bedside table. 'What about a Christmas movie?' he said, loading Netflix. 'Here we go… *White Christmas*.' He angled his laptop so she could see.

She raised an eyebrow. 'Starting with the big guns, huh?'

'I hate to break it to you, but you're not going anywhere for several hours. I need to be certain that concussion doesn't get any worse. So we either lie here counting sheep, or we kill time watching a film. Which is it to be?'

'If it means you stop lecturing me, then the film it is.'

'Good choice. Snuggle up.' He lifted his arm so she could move closer. 'And I think you'll like it. Rosemary Clooney's character is all tetchy and suspicious. She thinks Bing Crosby is a cad, a man who's untrustworthy and running a scam, when really he's a genuine chap who's misunderstood and secretly has the hots for her.' He looked down at her, her face so close to his he could smell her hair. 'You know, she kinda reminds me of someone.'

'You're no Bing Crosby.'

'No?' He started singing, '*I'm… dreaming of a… white… Christmas…*'

Fred started barking and Sarah started laughing. 'Are you going to let me watch this film, or not?'

He grinned. 'I am.'

She rested her head against his shoulder and he felt her body relax. He'd missed this, getting cosy with a woman. It was nice. He brushed her hair away from her eyes and left his hand resting on her head, gently stroking her hair. She didn't object.

Fred jumped off the chair and joined them on the bed, curling up next to Sarah. They were just like a little family.

The film began playing and he switched off the side lamp. This was turning into a much better Friday evening than he'd imagined.

He'd just settled in next to her, smiling as her arm slid across his chest, when the doorbell rang.

His curry had arrived. And just when things were getting cosy.

Chapter Eleven

Sarah woke with a jolt after a restless night's sleep. At least she was in her own bed – unlike yesterday when she'd woken up in Lucas's. The thought made her groan. She hadn't intended to stay the night, but her battered state, coupled with strong painkillers and watching a soppy film, had lured her into sleep. The next thing she'd known, it was morning.

She'd rapidly escaped, needing space to gather her thoughts and prevent Lucas from getting the wrong idea, because however grateful she was for his caring attentions after her fall, cuddling up next to him and allowing him to stroke her arm and gently brush her hair wasn't behaviour she should be encouraging.

Once safely away from his hypnotic voice and muscular warm arms, she'd been able to think straight. Of sorts, anyway. It had taken a cold shower and a stern talking-to, but her defences were back in place. He was a nice guy. A *really* nice guy, and she welcomed his friendship. It was good for her: a way of regaining her trust and allowing her barriers to lower slightly. Ever so slightly.

As for anything else, she wasn't ready to venture back into the world of *real* dating. And besides, Lucas was leaving for the US soon, so there was no point getting too attached.

A day on the sofa watching TV had improved her spirits. She was still sore from her fall, but the strapping Lucas had applied to her wrist was helping to limit the pain, and her forehead had stopped bleeding. Feeling more mobile, she'd taken Fred for a walk and was now pondering how to spend the rest of her Sunday without dwelling on the issue of Stephen Stokes. The idea of facing him at work tomorrow made her feel sick. She still couldn't shake the idea that it had been him lurking in the service area Friday night.

A knock on the door sent Fred into a frenzy of excitement.

Shushing him, she headed over to answer it. So far no one had grassed her up to the landlord for having a dog staying with her, but she didn't want to push her luck.

'Morning!' Lucas sang as she opened the door, his beaming smile the only bright element on an otherwise murky December day. 'How are you feeling?'

'Better, thanks.' She stepped back to let him in, no longer averse to his visits. 'Did you have a good day yesterday?'

'I did, thanks.' He placed a large delivery box on the floor, crouching down to make a fuss of Fred. 'Harper took your advice and booked herself a spa day, so I took the boys swimming. We went to the theatre afterwards to see *Elf*, the musical.'

She couldn't help smiling at his enthusiasm. 'Sounds like a fun day.'

'It was.' He stood up and focused on her face. 'Any dizzy spells? Headaches? Nausea?'

The intensity of his stare was too much on a Sunday morning. She was in danger of coming over dizzy again, and not from the concussion. 'Nope, all good.'

He lifted her hand. 'How's the swelling?'

'Reducing. It's turning an attractive purple colour now.' She let him inspect her wrist, knowing there was little point making a fuss. He'd only switch on the charm and coerce her into letting him check her over, so why bother fighting it? Besides, he had soft hands. 'See, all good.'

He adjusted the strapping. 'In which case, do you fancy a trip out?'

She frowned. 'A trip out where, exactly?'

'It's a surprise. We'll only be gone a couple of hours. It's indoors so you won't get wet, and I've borrowed my sister's car, so no Underground to contend with.'

'You're going to drive?' She lifted her eyebrows. 'Is that wise?'

'Sometimes you have to live dangerously,' he said, making her laugh. 'Is that a yes?'

Her instinct was to refuse, but that's because she'd got into the habit of saying no to everything. Denying herself any opportunity to have fun was her default setting these days. But as Lucas had pointed out, punishing herself only allowed Josh to continue wielding power over her. It was time for that to stop. 'I'll fetch my coat.'

'Wow, that was easy. I expected a fight.' He pulled out an envelope from his pocket. 'By the way, this was sticking out of your mailbox downstairs.' She caught a waft of fabric softener as he handed her the gold envelope. He was wearing a soft green hoodie and relaxed jeans, the epitome of sports casual. 'It's an invite to the hospital's fundraising ball. I had one too. Sounds fun.'

Sarah tore open the envelope and read the card. True enough, it was an invitation to the ball, scripted in fancy glitter lettering and no doubt costing a fortune to produce. The sales team's motto was that you had to spend big to win big. The more an event cost, the more prestigious it appeared, attracting a more affluent crowd. Auctions at these events historically generated thousands.

It wasn't an event she'd been looking forward to. Everyone in couples, dancing the night away to a festive theme. No, thanks. It was a trigger on several levels. But as head of HR, she was expected to attend.

Sighing, she turned over the card, recoiling when she saw the hand-written message on the back.

Pick you up at 7 p.m. Hope the dress fits. Stephen x

Oblivious to her shock, Lucas picked up the box. 'I almost forgot, this parcel came for you. It was left by the front door. Someone must have dropped it off; there's no courier stamp. Just your name and apartment number.'

Sarah stared at the box. Stephen had sent her a dress? What was he thinking? This was a whole new level of impropriety.

Her silence must have alerted Lucas to her distress. 'What's wrong? Why have you paled?'

Wordlessly, she handed him the invite.

He read the message. 'Jeez, that guy really can't take a hint.'

'What am I going to do?' She stumbled towards the sofa, needing to sit down, before she fell down.

He followed her into the lounge. 'Report him for harassment.'

She blinked furiously, trying to clear her head. 'I know that's what I should do, but he's the boss. I'd have to report him to the board of directors, most of whom are men. It'll be my word against his, and they're bound to take his side over mine.' She rubbed her face. 'I'll just have to miss the ball.'

'And let him bully you?' Lucas knelt in front of her and took hold of her uninjured hand. 'Avoiding the situation will only prolong it.'

She shook her head. 'I can't face him.'

'Not on your own, you can't. But you won't be on your own, will you? You'll have me there. He won't try anything if I'm with you.'

'The ball isn't until Friday. I can't avoid him all week.'

'Then don't go to work. You've had a fall, you've got concussion. As your doctor, I'm recommending a week's rest.'

She slumped against the sofa. 'I certainly don't feel like going to work at the moment.'

'Then don't. Stay home. I've only got a couple of locum shifts this week. We can hang out and you can show me the sights of London I've missed.' He tried for a smile, but she could also see concern in his eyes.

'I'd feel guilty taking time off work.'

He tilted his head. 'When was the last time you took time off?'

She thought about it. 'I haven't taken any time off this year. Not even annual leave. I'm owed so much time I never get a chance to take it; I'm too busy.'

'Then a week is well overdue.' He moved to sit next to her on the sofa. 'Take the time off, Sarah. Remember what you said to Harper about self-care? It's time to put yourself first.'

She rolled her head to look at him. 'What about the dress?'

'Leave that to me.' He slid his arm around her. 'I'll hand it back to him personally tomorrow. I'll make it clear I don't appreciate him sending gifts to my girl.'

It was rather alarming to have him looking at her with such a serious expression. Especially when the moment extended into a very long, very intense stare. 'You can't do that,' she whispered, finding it hard to swallow.

'Why not? He's the one acting inappropriate. And it's not like I've anything to lose; I'm only here another couple weeks, then I'm gone.'

She looked away, trying not to feel disappointed. 'This is my battle, not yours.'

'And you've tried dealing with it, but he isn't getting the message. Maybe me confronting him will get through that dense skull of his.'

Accepting Lucas's help didn't feel very empowering. She should be able to handle the likes of Stephen herself, but she was at a loss as to what else to try. Maybe she did need his help.

'How about this?' He shifted position. 'Take the week off. Spend the time relaxing and having some fun, and then we'll go to the ball together. We'll act like, you know, all loved up, and make it clear to Stephen and anyone else watching that you're not interested in him.'

'And if he still doesn't get the message?'

'Then you've no option but to report him.' His expression softened. 'He came to your home, Sarah. You have physical evidence to back up your complaint. Written evidence too, with the invite, his emails, the dress. It's enough to support your claim.'

The idea filled her with dread, but she knew he was right. 'I don't want it to come to that. I love my job; I don't want to ruffle feathers.'

'I know, but this is getting serious. Sending you a dress? That's plain creepy.'

She closed her eyes. 'You're right, I know.'

'For now, try not to think about it.' He gently lifted her hand and kissed it. 'Let's go on our trip and forget about Stephen Stokes. He's a problem for another day. Okay?'

'Okay.' Opening her eyes, she slid away from him, alarmed by the buzz being kissed had set off in her blood. 'I'll fetch my coat.'

Leaving Fred tucked up on the sofa with treats, they headed out of the building and into the damp December air.

It was hard to shake off the impending sense of doom she felt at the Stephen situation. She had a feeling that avoidance was only going to get her so far. But what was the solution? Why was it so hard for him to accept she wasn't interested?

Despite her gloomy mood, she couldn't help smiling when she saw Harper's car parked at the roadside, one wheel bumped onto the kerb. 'Seriously? You're intending to drive that beast? What is it, anyhow?'

'It's a Bentley, and I'm getting the hang of it,' he said, bleeping the key-fob to unlock the doors with a loud *thunk*. 'If only there wasn't so much traffic in London. It would help if the roads were wider. And why are the parking spaces so small? How does anyone manage to park over here?'

She pointed to the faded brick sign at the top of the three-storey Victorian dwelling, depicting the build date. 'You do realise these houses were built long before cars were invented? Putney can be traced back to the Domesday Book of 1086 when there were only dirt tracks for horses and carriages.'

He feigned shock. 'London is that old? You don't say?' He opened the door for her.

'I might've known you'd respond with sarcasm,' she said, easing herself into the car. 'But Putney has a fascinating past, I'll have you know. It was the headquarters for Oliver Cromwell's New Model Army.'

Lucas extended the seatbelt for her and held it slack while she plugged it in. 'Bit of a history buff, huh?'

'Not really, I just think it's important to know about where you live… and why the roads aren't wider,' she said, failing to supress a laugh.

'Point taken. I'll refrain from commenting on road widths in future.' He climbed into the driver's side and started the engine. As he pulled away, a passing car honked their horn. 'Left-hand side, Lucas. Pay attention.'

'I thought it was just me who talked to themselves. Is it catching?'

'Yes. You're a bad influence.' The car jolted as he edged into the traffic, constantly looking around. It was amusing to watch him floundering; he was normally so assured.

She waited until they'd headed away from Putney and joined the A3 before glancing over. 'What about where you're from? Minnesota must have its own history. What's it like?'

'Where do I begin?' He turned up the heater. 'It's a big state for a start, the Land of Ten Thousand Lakes. Most people know it because of the Mall of America, the largest shopping mall in the US.'

'You mean, bigger than the Putney Exchange?'

He grinned. 'A hundred times the size. Further away from the cities, the terrain varies depending where you are. My previous job was working at the Mayo Clinic in Rochester.' He visibly ducked when a lorry sped by, making the car shudder. 'It's a rural area, with a Western theme. There's a bunch of farmer's markets and hobby farms too. It's big on agriculture. Plenty of rodeos. You like horseback riding?'

'Never been.'

He glanced over. 'Nothing like heading out on horseback to experience nature.'

'I can't imagine you in a cowboy hat. You're more male model than rustic rancher.'

'You making fun of me?' He gripped the steering wheel when a car cut them up.

'Not in the least. I'm just trying to imagine you on horseback. You don't seem like the rodeo type. More jock than cowboy.'

'You're right there.' He swerved the car onto a slip road. 'I played a bunch of sports in school.'

She glanced at the passing road signs, curious as to where they were headed. 'Where did you go to school?'

'Kiel High School. And then Columbia University, before completing my medical residency at the Mayo Clinic.'

She could imagine him as a kid. Sporty, handsome, straight As. 'I bet you were one of the popular kids at school. Teacher's pet.'

He lifted an eyebrow. 'Why'd you say that?'

'You're very likeable. And positive. I can imagine people being drawn to you.'

He laughed. 'You say it like it's a bad thing. Doesn't everyone want to be liked and fit in?'

'Not everyone has your attributes,' she said, watching the landscape become more rural. That was the thing about London: twenty minutes down the road and you were in the countryside. 'You make Ted Lasso look like Ebenezer Scrooge.'

'I've no idea whether that's a compliment or an insult,' he said, glancing over. He had such a warm smile. 'How did you end up working in HR?'

'There's nothing exciting about my journey. I took a degree in business psychology, and human resources seemed like a good fit. It paid well and there were plenty of opportunities for women to move up the ladder. You can't say that about many industries.' She unzipped her coat; the heater was making her warm. 'I worked in various positions within the NHS, before landing a payroll job at the Queen Adelaide. From there, I worked my way up. It's taken me a long time to get where I am.'

'Which is why you don't want Stephen ruining it for you.'

'Exactly. My career's everything to me. It's all I have.'

'Correction, it's all you *had*. Past tense. You're planning to move on, right? Expand your world.'

'Right.'

'Say it like you mean it,' he said, checking the satnav. 'Give it more conviction. *Believe*, as Ted Lasso would say. You're moving onwards and upwards, right?'

'Right.' She made a feeble attempt at punching the air. 'Go me.'

'Pathetic.' He tutted. 'You know, maybe it's time to branch out and expand your horizons. Ever thought about moving to the States?' They turned off onto a B-road.

'Lucas, the thought of moving borough fills me with anxiety, let alone another country.'

He laughed at that. 'Another example of being stuck, huh?'

'I'm a loser – you don't need to say it. A proper cliché.'

'Hardly. You have more gumption than any girl I've met. There's nothing you couldn't do, you just need to—'

'*Believe*. Yes, I hear you. And did you really just say I had gumption?'

'I watched *Mary Poppins* the other night with my nephews. I'm practising the language.'

'From the early 1900s.' She smiled. 'Next you'll be calling people "guv" and "ducky".'

A moment later, they pulled into a long driveway that was shrouded by enormous cedar trees. The cars ahead disappeared around a bend, and when they followed, a beautiful stately home came into view. It had a wide front, with grey stone walls and leaded windows.

'Here we are.' He pointed to a large sign situated on the immaculate front lawn.

The Spirit of Christmas.

Winter Art & Antiques Fair.

Her eyes grew wide. 'Christmas?'

'Mixed with antiques.'

'Clever.'

He did a double take. 'You mean, it worked?'

'I'll admit, I'm intrigued.'

They parked up in the neighbouring field and Lucas jumped out of the car and came around to help her out. Fumbling over trying to fasten her coat one-handed, she allowed him to zip up her coat and fix her scarf. She drew the line at letting him hold her hand.

'Selfie time,' he said, positioning her in front of the building. 'Instagram post.'

She stepped away. 'I told you, I don't do social media.'

'But I do,' he said, easing her back into position. 'Stephen has started following me. I'm keen for him to see this.' He snapped the shot just as Sarah turned to him.

'He's following you? Why don't you block him?'

'Then he won't get to see how happy and in love we are. Smile for the camera, honey.' He rested his cheek against hers and lifted his phone.

She tried to smile, but she suspected it looked more like shellshock.

'This is the best way of deterring him. Trust me... Hold still.' And then before she could escape, he kissed her cheek, snapping another shot.

'What the hell?' She rubbed her cheek.

Unperturbed, he showed her the photo.

Her eyes were wide, her cheeks were pink, and Lucas was kissing her. It was the perfect 'couple' shot. 'Will anyone else at work see this?'

'That's the plan. You need it to be convincing, and this is how we do it.' He pocketed his phone. 'Shall we head inside?'

Sarah was still reeling from being kissed. 'Might as well, now we're here.'

They headed for the queue at the entrance. She felt strangely at odds, partly perturbed by the events in her life, and yet somehow enjoying herself. Spending time with Lucas was a great distraction. She'd spent too long existing inside her own head; there'd been no one to challenge her reasoning, or offer an alternative perspective. Her fault, entirely. She'd cut people off, withdrawn from socialising and retreated into her safe, insular world. How dumb she'd been.

Shaking off her thoughts, she looked at the gorgeous architecture on display, grand ornate pillars, and a stone archway framing the oak door. Inside the building was just as impressive: oil paintings hung on the walls next to woven tapestries and coat-of-arms insignias.

They were directed into the first room, where a selection of period furniture had been staged to form a festive display by the fireplace. A mahogany desk took centre stage, with wingback chairs either side. The fireplace roared behind, the flames spitting embers onto the concrete flooring. The mantel was adorned with brass candelabras holding advent candles, and surrounded by a woodland garland. Small figurines on the desk formed a nativity scene.

Lucas cleared his throat. 'Interesting that you mentioned Oliver Cromwell earlier. Did you know he banned Christmas in the UK for twelve years? It was also banned in the US too, and in some areas it was only lifted in 1907. Can you believe that? Christmas was banned for over two hundred and sixty years.' He turned to her and smiled. 'And you thought *you* had an aversion to Christmas.'

Sarah folded her arms. 'Are you comparing me to Oliver Cromwell?'

'You're much prettier,' he said, nodding towards the next room. 'Shall we?' He led her through to the banqueting hall, where a number of vendors had set up stalls. Choral music played softly in the background and mulled spices filled the air. Above them, giant shimmering baubles secured with red ribbons hung down from the ceiling.

'Classy enough for you?' He was clearly pleased with himself.

'Consider me impressed.'

The first set of stalls sold a range of antique tree decorations. They had everything from Nordic soldiers to figurines of suffragettes holding up placards with 'Votes for Women' chalked onto them. There was even a French musketeer, complete with feather hat and musket-gun. Sarah had never seen such exquisite ornaments.

'Christmas decorations can be traced back to ancient Rome,' Lucas said, picking up a glass bauble wrapped in antique ribbon. 'They celebrated the pagan festival of Saturnalia. Homes were decorated in flowers and wreaths, and they'd host this giant feast where gifts were offered to the gods.'

Her hand went to her hip. 'For someone who doesn't like antiques, you seem to know a lot about their history.'

His smile was playful. 'Did you know, the first recorded Christmas trees were decorated with apples and candy canes? Pastries were added to the trees in the shape of hearts and stars.' He sounded like a really hot tour guide, which was oddly distracting. 'Traditional glass baubles didn't come into manufacture until the fifteen hundreds.'

'Blimey,' the woman running the stall said. 'He knows his stuff. You want to buy anything, love?'

Lucas charmed the woman with one of his smiles. 'We'd love to,' he said, touching Sarah's arm. 'What about these, honey?' He held up two small robins, their red breasts adorned with sequins. 'These would look cute on the tree.'

She frowned at him. 'What tree? We don't have a tree.'

He leant close and whispered, 'Pretend we do. It's what most regular human beings do at Christmas.' He straightened, leaving a chill where his warm breath had been. 'We'll take them. They look kind of art deco... right, honey?'

The woman laughed. 'He's a wonder, isn't he?'

Sarah rolled her eyes. 'Oh, he's certainly something all right.'

Lucas paid for the items and moved her on to the next stall. 'Another interesting fact. Did you know they played "Jingle Bells" during NASA's Gemini 6A space flight? It was part of a prank by the astronauts. They sent a message over the radio claiming they'd encountered a strange low-flying object travelling south from the North Pole. Mission Control only realised it was a wind-up when the music started playing.'

'Goodness, you're a mine of information.'

They reached a stall selling Christmas cards and he pointed to a vintage design. 'Queen Victoria was the first official person to send a Christmas card, but commercial cards didn't come into fashion until 1843. One of the original designs recently sold at auction for thirty thousand pounds. Imagine that?'

Sarah blinked up at him. 'How on earth did you know that?'

'I'm living in London now,' he said, with a shrug. 'I've been visiting museums.' He moved to the next stall. 'Hey, look at this.' Lucas handed her a brass lantern.

It took her a moment to focus her attention on the ornament. She had no idea Lucas knew so much about... well, stuff. The lantern was filled with a snow scene depicting four small golden birds singing in front of a brightly lit cottage. Everything was hand-painted and expertly crafted. 'It's beautiful.'

'It matches the robins we bought. Shall we get it?'

She viewed him cautiously. 'How come you know so much about Christmas?'

He looked sheepish. 'I didn't. I researched ahead of today.'

'Why on earth would you do that?'

'To remind you how magical Christmas can be. Letting a little festive spirit back into your life might be what you need to stop feeling so…' He shrugged. 'Stuck.'

Sarah could barely speak. 'You did that for me?'

'Of course.' He pinned her with one of his smiles. 'Now, are we buying this lantern?'

Sarah nodded.

Something odd was happening… she just didn't quite know what.

Chapter Twelve

When Lucas arrived at his sister's house ready to childmind while his sister and brother-in-law attended a mediation session, he hadn't expected to find Harper and Paul embroiled in another argument. Their raised voices could be heard even before Max had opened the front door.

Foolishly, he'd assumed they were making progress and had moved past the point of wanting to dismember each other. Apparently not. Today's argument was about the house sale. Or rather, Harper's refusal to put the house on the market. Her solicitor was pushing for an interim agreement, whereby Harper and the kids stayed in the house until the boys were in secondary school and allowed Harper time to restart her career and improve her financial situation. Paul's solicitor was pushing for a quick sale, a division of the assets and the divorce settlement to be finalised promptly. The end result was Harper and Paul yelling at each other and making an already testy situation even more toxic.

Having answered the door, Max ran back into the living room and joined his brother behind the couch. Lucas headed into the kitchen, arriving in time to witness Harper calling her husband a 'self-centred son of a bitch' and Paul accusing Harper of 'sabotaging his efforts to move on with his life'.

So much for mediation. It was full-on war in the Evans household.

It was therefore gone eleven a.m. by the time Lucas had calmed them down and Paul and Harper had left in separate cars to attend their appointment. *Good luck to the counsellor*, Lucas thought.

He'd given them a stern talking-to before they'd left, feeling like a parent berating his wayward teenagers. Constantly arguing was not going to resolve anything, he'd told them. They needed to stop lashing out, and find a way of reaching an agreement that worked for both of them.

When had he turned into the sensible one?

Having meekly apologised to their sons, kissed them and headed out the door, tails between their legs, the house descended into an uncomfortable silence.

Lucas had planned to stay in the house and entertain the boys, but both kids looked so traumatised he decided action was required.

'Right, come on, buddies,' he said, getting them kitted out in winter clothing. 'It's time for an adventure.'

With hats and scarves added to puffa jackets, they left the house hand in hand and headed for the Tube station.

'Where are we going?' Max asked as they crossed the road.

'To visit a friend of mine.' Lucas squeezed Max's hand. 'I thought you might like to meet her; she has a dog.'

'A dog?' Elliot's face broke into a smile. 'What kind of dog?'

'A basset hound, I think.' Lucas held their hands as they crossed the road. 'He's called Fred, and he has floppy ears and enjoys cuddles. I think you'll like him.'

Max nodded. 'I know I will.'

'Me too,' Elliot chipped in, the pair looking slightly less morose than half an hour earlier.

Forty minutes later, having played I spy on the train and eaten sticky jam doughnuts, they arrived at his apartment building and headed up the steps.

'Wave to Mrs Kelsey,' he said, spotting the woman peeking out from behind her net curtains. He half expected Diana to shout something grumpy, but she surprised him by waving and almost smiling before letting go of the curtain and disappearing from view.

He'd popped around to see her last night after his hospital shift and ended up staying for dinner. This had been followed by a game of Scrabble – a game in which she'd cheated, her words either being invented or extremely rude. He could only imagine how they'd react at the local church hall if she used that kind of language at their games afternoons. Maybe he should warn the liaison worker before she visited later this week. That was assuming Mrs Kelsey didn't change her mind and cancel the appointment. He hoped not. They were finally making progress.

'Here we are,' he said to the boys, as they reached the top floor. 'This is where my friend Sarah lives.' He tapped on her door.

Sarah's face was a picture when she opened the door and saw the three of them standing there. 'And who do we have here?' she said, beckoning them inside. 'The three musketeers?'

The boys laughed.

'This is Max,' Lucas said, removing his older nephew's hat to reveal his wavy blonde hair.

'And I'm Elliot.' His younger nephew held out his hand. 'I'm seven. I'm pleased to meet you.'

Sarah laughed and shook his hand. 'It's very nice to meet you, Elliot. What a polite young gentleman you are. My name's Sarah. And this is Fred.' She gestured to the dog, who had appeared from the lounge, looking excited at the idea of more playmates.

The boys immediately dropped to the floor and started petting Fred. It was instant love on both sides. There was lots of laughter and cuddling, and appreciative noises – especially from Fred. Max was rewarded with a lick, which removed a smudge of strawberry jam from his cheek. It was a relief to see the boys smiling.

Lucas touched Sarah's arm. 'I ran out of time to check on you yesterday – you doing okay?'

'I'm fine,' she said, lifting her bangs to show her healing forehead. 'My wrist is still painful, but the rest of me is okay. I had a quiet day; Fred and I watched the whole series of *Wednesday* on Netflix. He didn't like the were-wolves; he kept barking at the TV. How was your day? Did you manage to speak to Stephen?'

'He wasn't in work. I left the box on his desk with a note saying, *Return to Sender. Address unknown.*' He shrugged. 'I figured it worked for Elvis. Besides, I didn't want to write anything inflammatory in case he used it against us. I'm not at the hospital again until Thursday, and I didn't want him thinking you'd accepted the dress. Last thing we want is him turning up Friday night to pick you up.'

'Heaven forbid.' Sarah shivered. 'You did the right thing. Thanks for doing that; I appreciate it.' She turned to his nephews. 'Do you want to take your coats off, boys?'

'I thought we could head down to Wandsworth Park first,' Lucas said, joining in with petting Fred. 'I hear Santa Claus is visiting today.'

Elliot's eyes grew wide. 'The real one?'

'Of course not the real one.' Max was lying on the floor, stroking Fred's belly. 'He's too busy making presents for Christmas Eve.'

Sarah smiled. 'Ah, but Father Christmas is also a time traveller. He can be in several places at once, so I say we head down to the park and see for ourselves. What do you think?'

Max nodded. 'Can Fred come too?'

'Of course. I'll get his lead. The bathroom's just there if anyone needs the loo before we go.'

Elliot scrabbled to his feet and ran for the bathroom.

Lucas followed Sarah, hesitating by her bedroom door, out of earshot of the boys. 'I hope it's okay bringing them over. Things were a bit heated with Harper and Paul this morning. I thought they could do with a distraction.'

Sarah tied her hair into a ponytail. 'It's fine. They seem like lovely children.'

'They are.' He watched her pull on a fluffy blue hat. 'But I'm biased.'

She wrapped a scarf around her neck. 'They're lucky to have you in their corner.'

'It's going to be hard leaving them after Christmas.'

'I can imagine.' She slipped on her coat. 'Will they come and visit you in Houston?'

'I hope so. Although probably not very often.' It was a depressing thought. He'd enjoyed hanging out with them; he was going to miss them when he left.

She picked up Fred's lead. 'Ready when you are.'

They all bundled out of the apartment and headed downstairs.

Max looked puzzled when Sarah lifted Fred and hid him beneath her coat. 'Why are you doing that?' He looked up at her wide-eyed. 'Can't he manage the steps?'

'I have to keep him hidden, because I'm not supposed to have him here,' she whispered.

'Why not?' he whispered back.

'No pets allowed in the building, so until I can find him another home, I need to keep him hidden. Quick, before anyone sees.' She skipped down the steps, followed by Max, who was furtively looking around like a mini secret service agent.

'No one saw us,' he said, helping Sarah lower Fred to the ground. 'Where will he go?'

'Hopefully somewhere where he'll get lots of treats.' She ruffled Fred's ears.

Max patted Fred's head. 'Good boy. I hope you find a nice home.'

Lucas caught them up. 'Come on, let's go meet Santa Claus.'

As they headed down the road towards the park, the boys skipped along and chatted nonstop. Their conversations switched from one topic to another and overlapped as they vied for Sarah's attention. It was exhausting listening to them, yet amusing to watch. When Sarah asked them about their favourite hobbies, Max told her he liked drawing and football, and Elliot said he liked Lego and ring-tailed lemurs.

'I also like dressing up,' Elliot said, grabbing Sarah's hand and making her flinch.

Lucas intervened and took Fred's lead from her, relieving her of one exuberant mini male. 'Sarah has an injured wrist, Elliot, so be gentle.'

Elliot looked mortified. 'Sorry.'

'It's okay,' Sarah said, reassuring him. 'No harm done. How about you hook your arm through mine.' She positioned his arm inside hers to protect her wrist. 'That's better. So... who do you like dressing up as?'

As Elliot's little legs struggled to keep up, he told her about his favourite costumes, playing a fireman, and being Spider-Man. In return, Sarah relayed the story of when she was ten and she'd been given two pounds to spend at the local jumble sale, but instead of buying several items as she'd been instructed to do by her mum, she'd returned home with a huge sparkly ballgown that was far too big for her, but she loved and refused to take off for a whole week.

Elliot seemed to find this hilarious. 'Did you wear it to school?'

'I tried,' Sarah said, leading them across the road. 'But the school wouldn't allow it, so we had to find a compromise. In the end, my granny cut up the dress and made a throw for my bed and cushion covers out of the material. It was the only way they could stop me wearing the dress.'

Max laughed. 'That's funny.'

Lucas was amused too; it was a fascinating insight into Sarah's childhood. 'You mean, you used to be stubborn?' he said, feigning shock. 'Wow, I mean, no one would ever have guessed.'

Sarah glanced over her shoulder. 'Still sarcastic, I see.'

He grinned. 'You like it really.'

She rolled her eyes. 'It's my favourite trait.'

'Now who's being sarcastic.' He nodded ahead. 'Mind the step.'

Wandsworth Park came into view and a huge inflatable archway filled the entrance. Through the middle, Lucas could see a pen filled with reindeer and a marquee with *Santa's Grotto* written above. There was a stall selling candyfloss and toffee apples. Beyond was a bunch of people dressed as elves dancing about to 'Jingle Bell Rock'.

'Shall we say hello to the reindeer?' Sarah led them towards the animal pen.

'Which one's Rudolph?' Lucas asked the boys, who were almost running, they were so eager to meet the herd.

Elliot pointed to a reindeer with its head stuck in a bucket. 'That one!'

The boys climbed onto the wooden fence and peered closer, pointing to the animals. A wooden sleigh had been positioned inside the pen, adding to the illusion of it being Santa's base camp.

Lucas leant next to Sarah. 'Fred's not a fan of the reindeer,' he said, trying to hold on to the lead. 'Not that I blame him; they're three times his size.'

'There's nothing to be worried about, Fred,' she said, crouching down to fuss over him. 'Come to Mummy. That's it. Good boy.' Scooping him up, she cuddled him close. 'Daft animal.'

Lucas smiled at another little insight into Sarah's character. There was definitely a softer side beneath the prickly exterior. And then he saw her wince. 'Here, let me take him.'

She handed him over and rubbed her wrist. 'He's put on weight. Entirely my fault – I've been overfeeding him. But he'd been neglected; a bit of pampering was necessary.'

'And he milks it for all he can.'

'He's an impressive manipulator, that's for sure.'

Lucas watched her for a moment. 'Did you have pets as a kid?'

'We always had a dog,' she said, stroking Fred's ears. 'My first memory was of Tang-Lee the Pekinese; he liked to chew furniture and refused to leave the house when it rained. We had him for years. And then we had a corgi called Rusty, who sadly ran away a few weeks after we got him and was never seen again. And then there was Shandy, a Heinz 57 variety, who might've looked like a scruffy mongrel, but who was definitely lord of the manor. He had us all running around after him. Lovely dog. Bonkers, but lovely.'

Lucas's arms were aching under Fred's weight. 'You haven't had a dog since?'

'It's not been possible,' she said, with a shrug. 'Not living in shared accommodation at uni, and then moving into a rental place. Hopefully one day I can get one.' She kissed Fred's nose. 'One I can actually keep.'

'He's eating from that man's hand!' Max said, jolting them from their conversation. 'Can I feed him too?'

Sarah reverted her attentions to the boys. 'Absolutely.'

Lucas watched Sarah grab a handful of feed from a bucket and demonstrated how to feed the reindeer, encouraging his nephews to do the same. Max followed her lead, but Elliot was nervous and clutched her coat. Their confidence eventually grew, and it wasn't long before all three were stroking the reindeer and trying to guess which one was Prancer and which one was Vixen.

To anyone watching, they looked like a little family, and it gave him a pang of longing. He'd hoped to be in this situation for real by now. He'd spent so much effort concentrating on his career, and ensuring he had a stable future and was ready to support a family, that he'd kind of assumed the rest would fall into place. It hadn't, and he wasn't sure why.

Sarah moved away from the reindeer enclosure. 'Right, who's up for the bouncy castle?'

She sprinted off, followed by Max and Elliot, who laughed in that uncontrollable way only kids can, as they stumbled on the grass and nearly smacked into Sarah when they couldn't stop at the other end. Sarah was tickling them, which caused Fred to start barking.

'You have a very loud bark,' Lucas said, lowering the dog to the ground, his left ear ringing. 'You nearly deafened me.'

By the time he'd joined them, they'd removed their trainers and were climbing onto the inflatable castle.

Sarah bounced up and down in her socked feet. 'Are you joining us?'

'I'd better stay with Fred; he doesn't look keen.'

Sarah jumped off and came over. 'I'll stay with Fred; you have fun with your nephews. He's my dog, after all. Or, at least, his temporary custodian.'

'I'm fine watching.' Lucas smiled at her. 'Besides, it's fun seeing you enjoy yourself. I never knew you were such a child at heart.'

'I've no idea what you mean,' she said, poking her tongue out. 'I'll have you know, I'm very mature. The epitome of sophistication and poise.' She ran off and launched herself onto the bouncy castle, landing with such force she shot into the air, squealing.

He shook his head. 'Sure, real mature!'

For the next five minutes, he watched the three of them bouncing around, hitting the inflatable sides, and crashing into people. They fell over more times than they stayed upright. Max and Elliot could barely stand for laughing. Their cheeks were bright red, and their efforts to overcome gravity were hilarious. Sarah chased them, making them scream. When they fell over, she pulled them up. When they tried to catch her, she ran away. It was mayhem.

Lucas laughed when she looked over and pulled a face. She was running out of steam.

After taking an age to get up from her latest fall, she crawled over to the side and climbed off.

'I'm so unfit,' she said, panting heavily as she came over to where Lucas was standing.

'You lasted longer than most adults.' He caught her when she slumped against him. 'How's your wrist?'

'Sore,' she said, with a nonchalant shrug. 'It was totally worth it.'

He lifted her hand and checked for swelling. 'I had no idea you were hiding such a playful side.'

'Underneath all the bitterness, you mean?' She winced when he pressed her wrist. '*Ouch.*'

'Sorry. We'll need to ice that when we get back. No more activities for you today.' He removed her glove and gently massaged her forearm, trying to ease the pain.

She rolled her eyes. 'Okay, Doctor. I'll be a good girl.'

He lifted an eyebrow. 'You do realise the irony in making fun of me for being parental, when you've just been bouncing around like a five-year-old?'

'What can I say? There's something about being with kids that allows you to regress. No one bats an eyelid.

Of course, if I behaved like that in Lidl it'd be a different matter. I'd be escorted off the premises.'

He rubbed her cold fingers. 'Better?'

'Much.' She rested her forehead against his chest. 'You have very soothing hands. Must be all that moisturiser.'

He laughed. 'Would you prefer I had callouses?'

'Heavens no, you have the loveliest hands of anyone I know.' And then she lifted her head. 'For a man, I mean.'

He grinned. 'Men can't have nice hands?'

'Of course they can.' She stepped away, flustered. 'Ignore me. I'm exhausted from bouncing; I'm talking nonsense.'

He smiled at her flushed face. 'Did you ever want kids of your own?'

She didn't immediately answer.

When she did, her expression was sad. 'I guess,' she said, dropping down to pet Fred. 'It's something I try not to think about these days.' She stroked Fred's fur, a faraway look on her face. 'I did consider having a child a while back. You know, on my own.' She glanced up at him. 'But I know from my friends who are single parents it's not always easy. It can be hard work and utterly exhausting, so I decided against it. I was worried something would suffer, either my career, or the kid, so it seemed best not to pursue that route.' She stood up, accepting her glove and putting it back on. 'And as I'm not looking for a relationship, I've resigned myself to being childless.'

She feigned acceptance, but he could tell it was another mask, covering her sadness. 'It's not what you'd choose, though?'

She shrugged. 'It's not what I'd choose. Can't always have what we want, though, can we?'

'Shame, you're a natural. You'd make a great mom.' When she looked uncomfortable, he pointed to the dog. 'As Fred here can testify. Thoroughly spoilt.'

They were interrupted by his nephews bundling into them, exhausted and laughing, panting more than Fred after a run. Sarah put their trainers on for them, allowing them to catch their breath.

For some unfathomable reason, even though they hadn't known each other that long, Sarah was someone Lucas could visualise spending his life with. Which was totally illogical. But their brief interactions had given him a snapshot of what life with her might be like. Teasing. Laughing. Arguing. Pressing each other's buttons. She was fun to be around. Stimulating.

Ironic that when he'd finally met someone he could see himself settling down with, she lived in a different country. She also wasn't interested in dating. He'd managed to fall for a woman he couldn't have.

Sarah jumped up and clapped her hands. 'Who's ready to meet Father Christmas?'

The boys scrambled to their feet.

'Let's get over there; there's hardly any queue.'

The boys ran off, and once again he was struck by what a natural she was with them. It seemed crazy that she purposely denied herself the opportunity of meeting someone and having her own kids, but it wasn't like he was going to point that out. He couldn't imagine she'd appreciate his opinion. And he was having too much fun to ruin their day out.

They headed over to the marquee and joined the queue, which quickly shifted forwards. It was soon their turn to meet Santa.

Sarah led Elliot over to the big guy dressed in his characteristic red suit. She perched on a chair and pulled Elliot onto her lap. 'Can you believe it's really him?' she said, in an excited whisper. For someone with an aversion to Christmas, she was doing a good job of playing along.

'Hello, young man. And what's your name?' Santa Claus asked, in his deep rumbling voice.

'I'm Elliot Evans. I'm seven years old. And I'd like a ring-tailed lemur for Christmas.'

Santa Claus let out one of his *ho-ho-ho* chuckles. 'I hope not a real one? They can be tricky creatures. Maybe a toy lemur would be safer.' He leant closer. 'Have you been a good boy this year?'

Elliot nodded, his face full of awe.

'Then I hope you get what you wish for. Merry Christmas, young man.' He let out another *ho-ho-ho* and handed Elliot a bag of Haribo.

They swapped seats and Lucas took Max over to visit Santa next.

Max asked for drawing pencils and an England football kit. He told Santa he'd mostly been a good boy, except for the time he'd broken his dad's phone by hitting it with a football, and he didn't eat as many vegetables as he was supposed to, but apart from that he'd been a good boy.

Santa belted out another *ho-ho-ho* and whispered in Max's ear that he didn't like vegetables either, but he always ate his carrots, although he'd save a few for his reindeer.

Exiting the tent with bags of sweets and smiles on their faces, it was evident the boys' energy levels were flagging. So, after watching the elves 'Rockin' Around the Christmas Tree', Sarah suggested they head to the Smugglers Cafe in town for lunch.

Lucas wondered whether it was such a good idea spending so much time with someone he wanted, but who was never going to want him back. Was he being masochistic by torturing himself? But the idea of not seeing her was far worse. He'd be back home in the States soon; he wouldn't be able to see her at all then, and Jesus, wasn't that depressing.

After lunch, they ambled home, looking at the festive shop displays and enjoying the smell of roasting chestnuts.

As they passed an antique shop, Sarah paused to glance at the crafts set up in the window.

'Isn't that unusual?' she said, shielding her eyes from the low winter sun. 'I've never seen anything like that before.' She pointed to the collection of vintage-style silver and gold candles displayed on a gold frame. The frame was wider at the bottom, shrinking to a point at the top, making it look like a Christmas tree. 'It's so clever.'

'That would look great in your apartment,' he said, an idea forming in his mind. 'A nod to Christmas, but without being too full-on.'

Sarah seemed curious. 'They are pretty.'

Lucas needed allies to nudge her over the line. 'What about it, boys? Shall we get this display for Sarah as a thank you for a fun day out?'

'Yes!' Elliot jumped up and down, making Fred bark.

Max giggled. 'Fred likes it too.'

Ignoring Sarah's protests, Lucas headed inside and purchased the set.

It was a bit bulky to carry home, especially up two flights of steps, but it was worth the effort. The boys threw off their coats, hats and scarves, and began unwrapping the candles from their tissue paper. Sarah moved her furniture to make room in front of the fireplace, and together they set up the supporting frame and added the candles.

When they were done, Sarah stood back and admired the display. 'One final addition,' she said, placing the lantern Lucas had bought her at the antiques fair on top of the mantel. She positioned the robins either side. 'How does that look?'

'Perfect.' Lucas enjoyed seeing her smile. 'Do you have matches?'

Sarah fetched them from the kitchen and lit the candles. 'Doesn't that look festive.'

Lucas studied her, hoping she wasn't pretending for his sake. 'Is that okay?'

'Surprisingly so, yes.' She turned to him and smiled. 'Thank you for my gift. I love it.' She addressed the boys. 'I recorded a film earlier. Who wants to watch *Get Santa*?'

Elliot and Max raced for the couch, followed by Fred, who snuggled in between them.

Setting up the film and drawing the curtains, Sarah covered them with a throw. Within a few minutes of the film starting, their eyelids began drooping.

'You can sit here.' Max lifted the throw so Sarah could snuggle next to him.

Lucas sat on the floor in front of Elliot. He was rewarded with a foot pressed into his spine. He didn't care. With the light fading outside, and the candles flickering inside, he was content to sit back and watch an amusing film about a kid persuading his dad to help him break Santa Claus out of jail.

Lucas glanced behind at the scene on the couch. A lump formed in his throat as he watched Sarah, Fred and the boys cuddling on the sofa. This was the life he wanted. Family. Love. Laughter.

It was just a shame it wasn't something he could have. Not with Sarah, anyhow.

Chapter Thirteen

Wednesday, 21ˢᵗ December

Sarah couldn't remember the last time she'd fallen asleep during the day. It felt quite decadent to be laid out on the sofa under a throw with Fred curled up on her feet. Daylight had faded while she'd been snoozing and it was now dark outside, the faint glow of the street lamps filtering through the window from the street below. She should really get up and close the curtains, but she was comfy, and she didn't want to disturb Fred.

It had been a strange week, a mixture of ups and downs. Her intention had been to take Fred to Battersea Dogs & Cats Home yesterday and start the process of finding him another home. She wouldn't leave him there; that would be cruel. Instead, she'd hoped the charity would allow her to hang on to him until he'd been matched with a new owner.

Whether she would have gone through with it, she'd never know. She wasn't enthusiastic at the idea of losing her companion; she'd grown accustomed to his furry face. So when Lucas and his nephews had turned up, it was the perfect excuse to change her plans.

Maybe it was her imagination, but she sensed Fred was relieved too. Almost as if he'd known what was coming and had been on his best behaviour all day.

Any plans to rehome Fred today also ended when Harper had shown up this morning and suggested a girly trip out. It had been a surprise when she'd opened the door to find Lucas's sister standing there, but not an unwelcome one. Harper was fun. She was also in need of company, and Sarah was glad of the distraction. Overthinking was an exhausting pastime.

They visited the hairdresser's first, where Sarah finally had her fringe trimmed. This was followed by a nail bar, and ended with a boozy lunch, where she'd eaten cheesy chips and drunk several glasses of Sauvignon Blanc. The result was a lot of laughing, a fuzzy head and the need for an afternoon nap when she'd arrived home. That was two hours ago; she'd been asleep ever since.

'Maybe I'll take you to the dogs' home tomorrow,' she said lazily to Fred, reaching down to stroke his ears. 'Don't look at me like that. Some lucky family will snap you up. You're a catch, Fred Bassett.'

Fred sighed and let his tongue hang loose, making his feelings on the subject known. Was it crazy that she'd started thinking about moving flat so she wouldn't have to give him up? He looked at home on her sofa, all relaxed and sleepy; it seemed cruel to be contemplating rehoming him.

Their relaxed state disappeared in a flurry of discarded blankets and flying cushions when someone knocked loudly on her front door. The noise sent Fred into a frenzy of barking, and they almost fell off the sofa as they scrambled to their feet.

'Shush!' she said, chasing after him into the hallway. 'Stop barking, you daft animal, it's probably just Lucas.'

Was it wrong that she hoped it was Lucas? Her pulse quickened at the idea of a visit from her neighbour, and

she stopped to check her appearance in the hall mirror…
and then wished she hadn't. Her face was creased and her
hair was matted from falling asleep.

'Coming!' She frantically wiped away smudged
mascara and flattened her hair, realising she was minus one
sock.

It took her brain a moment to compute that it wasn't
Lucas standing on the other side of the door, but Stephen
Stokes. Her instinct was to slam the door in his annoying
face, but Fred had shot between her legs and was growling
at the new medical director in a slightly aggressive manner.
It was a side of Fred she hadn't witnessed before. He didn't
like the man, either. Fred was a smart individual.

'Stephen?' she said, failing to hide her shock, and
embarrassed at being caught off-guard. 'What on earth
are you doing here?'

He tried to move closer, but Fred blocked his path. 'I
wanted to see if you were okay? You haven't been at work
this week.'

'I've taken leave,' she said, knowing she should pull
Fred away, but she was reluctant to do so; he was acting
as her protector.

'So I heard.' Stephen's eyes narrowed. He was dressed
in one of his power suits. Pin-striped, designer. Navy,
with a bold red tie. 'It's rather short notice to book time
off? Company policy requires at least a week's notice for
annual leave requests.'

He was quoting the staff handbook at her? Was the
man for real? 'I'm aware of the policy, Stephen. The
directive also allows for the notice period to be waived
for emergencies.' She reached down to grab Fred's collar
– partly for her own comfort, but also to stop him biting
her boss. Fred had teeth.

'What's so urgent that you had to take a week off?'

Sarah couldn't make out Stephen's expression. It didn't look natural, like he'd had Botox and was forcing himself to appear polite, when really he was annoyed. Dealing with him at work was challenging enough, but being confronted at her home was decidedly unnerving. 'I had a fall last Friday evening and felt I needed some time off to recover.'

'What kind of fall? Are you injured?' His eyes ran the length of her, intrusive and lingering. She hadn't injured her breasts, she felt like telling him, but that would only invite further glances at her chest area, and she was feeling exposed enough as it was in her thin wrap top.

'Nothing you need to concern yourself about. I'm fine.'

His gaze landed on her strapped wrist. 'You don't look fine.'

'Well, I am. Now, if you'll excuse me—'

Stephen's foot filled the gap before she could drag Fred away and shut the door. 'Aren't you going to invite me in?'

Fred was now barking and growling simultaneously, making his feelings on Stephen abundantly clear. 'No, Stephen, I'm not.'

Stephen's hand gripped the doorframe. 'Why not?'

She tried to maintain eye contact, which was impossible when Fred was trying to escape her grasp. 'Because that would be inappropriate.'

'Inappropriate? You mean like posting pictures on Instagram of you and Doctor Moore out and about when you're supposed to be off sick?'

'I'm not off sick,' she said, wondering if she should let go of Fred's collar. Only a fear of Stephen calling the police and having her precious dog put down for being aggressive prevented her. 'I'm on annual leave.'

'Which you requested as an emergency because you're supposedly sick.' He gave Fred a filthy look and lifted his foot as if he was about to kick him.

What Sarah would have done next, she had no idea. Although she suspected it involved grabbing the hall lamp and lumping Stephen over the head with it. The sight of Lucas appearing up the stairs prevented her from committing ABH. The cavalry had arrived.

'Stephen...? What are you doing here?' His expression conveyed genuine shock as he crouched down and beckoned Fred over, dumping a bag of shopping on the floor.

Sarah caught Lucas's eye and he nodded for her to let go of Fred. Trusting he had a plan, she released Fred's collar and the dog raced over to him.

Stephen recoiled when Fred barked, but then tried to cover it with bluster. 'I'm here in an official work capacity checking on an employee. Not that it's any of your business.'

Lucas picked Fred up in his arms. 'Is it normal practice for the medical director to show up at an employee's home without warning?'

Stephen adjusted his tie. 'I was concerned for Sarah's welfare.'

Lucas raised an eyebrow. 'Why?'

'Well... because she's injured; she had a fall.' Pleased with his response, he gestured to Sarah's injured hand. 'She's hurt her wrist.'

'I know, I was the one who dealt with her injuries.' Lucas came over to her doorway, forcing Stephen to shift out of his way. 'My question is, how did you know she'd had a fall? She hasn't been in work since.'

Stephen looked momentarily thrown. 'She just told me.'

Lucas frowned. 'But you said you were here to check on her welfare because she'd had a fall... and yet you didn't know she'd had a fall until just now.'

Stephen clenched his jaw. 'I knew something must be wrong for her to be absent from work.'

Lucas leant against the wall, his gait casual, his eyes astute. 'So send her an email.'

'I prefer the personal touch.' Stephen was on the back foot. He rubbed his hands on his jacket, clearly sweaty from being challenged.

'You'd do the same for any employee off sick, would you?' Lucas gave him a questioning look. 'You make a regular habit of showing up at people's homes enquiring about their health?'

Stephen puffed out his chest. 'I don't have to explain myself to you.'

'See, I disagree.' Lucas pushed away from the wall. 'You showing up at my girlfriend's apartment uninvited isn't something I'm happy about.'

Stephen fixed Lucas with a threatening gaze. 'May I remind you I am your superior.'

'Not outside of work, you're not. This is Sarah's personal space, and you're intruding on her privacy. Mine too.'

Sarah held her breath, her eyes darting between the two men.

'Careful, Doctor Moore, or you'll find yourself out of employment.' He made a move towards Lucas, but backed off when Fred growled.

'Good boy, Fred.' Lucas patted his head. 'No skin off my nose. I finish this week anyhow.'

Sarah's stomach flipped at the reminder Lucas was leaving soon. She'd got so used to him being around.

Stephen straightened his shoulders. 'I'm sure you don't want a bad reference.'

'And I'm sure you don't want a lawsuit.' Lucas's voice was calm, and yet there was no denying the warning in his tone. 'Which is what will happen if you try to defame my name over a personal issue, when there's been no problem with my work performance.' Lucas stepped closer to Stephen, forcing the man's back against the far wall. 'A lawsuit that will include you showing up at Sarah's apartment and harassing her.'

Stephen looked outraged. 'I'm not harassing her.'

'Sending her flowers and buying her a dress? You don't call that harassment? 'Cause I sure as hell do.' Lucas handed Fred to Sarah, his eyes meeting hers briefly, before turning to the medical director. 'You have two options, Stephen. Leave of your own accord. Or I call the cops. Which is it to be?'

A weighty silence hung in the air.

Sarah watched Stephen's face, a range of emotions making his jaw twitch. He was clearly torn between wanting to punch Lucas, and backing down and retreating.

Eventually, he turned to Sarah. 'A fine way to treat your boss. Such disrespect won't be tolerated. I'm disappointed in you, Sarah. Expect repercussions.'

'Oh, there'll be repercussions,' Lucas said, pointing a finger in Stephen's face. 'You come here again and I won't be so polite next time.'

Enraged, Stephen pushed past him and headed for the stairs.

'You have a good night, sir!' Lucas called after him, as Stephen disappeared down the stairwell. 'Don't call again!' He turned to Sarah. 'You okay, honey?'

She shook her head.

'Come here.' Lucas moved so quickly that before she knew it, she and Fred were enveloped in his arms and being hugged.

Tears ran down her face. Angry tears. Aggrieved tears. The kind of tears that physically hurt. Her chest ached, her eyes stung and her throat was so constricted she could barely speak.

'I've got you,' Lucas whispered, his arms holding her tightly. 'He's gone. I have a feeling he won't be back.'

Sarah wasn't so sure. Logic dictated he'd got the message; he'd clearly been humiliated at Lucas challenging him. But Stephen wasn't a logical man. He couldn't be; no rational person would act in such a way. She had a horrible feeling they hadn't deterred Stephen at all. Instead they'd stoked the fire. They'd picked a fight with an angry bear and made him even more determined. The worst part was realising that this time next week Lucas would be back in the US and she'd be dealing with this alone.

Fred yelped and began wriggling in her arms. He was fed up of being squashed.

'Let's get you inside,' Lucas said, releasing her so she could lower Fred to the floor and he could fetch his shopping. Closing the door, he reached out and gently wiped away the tears from her cheeks. His expression was kind and trusting, and she wanted nothing more than to be held by him again. Which would not be a good development.

Self-preservation kicked in and she stepped away, rubbing brusquely at her wet cheeks. Falling apart wasn't going to solve anything. She needed to dig deep and muster her inner strength and fight this problem herself. She hadn't spent the last five years becoming independent only to collapse now. There was no way was she going to succumb to Stephen's bullying.

She searched for her sock on the sofa, lifting the throw and tossing cushions away.

She also wasn't going to succumb to her feelings for Lucas Moore. Because, like it or not, she did have feelings for him. Dangerous, destructive feelings. The kind of feelings that could undermine her determination to live a strong and independent life. She'd come too far to return to relying on a man for her happiness. She'd been fine before she'd met Lucas. She'd be fine after he'd left too.

Lucas located her sock. 'Yours, I believe.'

She looked into his smiling face. Okay, so perhaps she wouldn't be fine. Adequate, at best. The problem was, adequate had been good enough when she hadn't known what extraordinary had felt like. She had a horrible feeling there was no coming back from that.

She dropped to the sofa so she could wiggle her foot into her sock.

'I'm staying, by the way,' he said, heading into the kitchen with his grocery bag. 'No arguments. You can fight me and lose, or accept the situation and let me cook you dinner.' His face appeared around the door. 'Where will I find a food blender?'

She pushed Fred away, who had decided it was play time and was trying to eat her sock. 'Why do you need a food blender?'

'We're having curry. Chicken tikka masala.'

She joined him in the kitchen. 'Wouldn't it be easier to order in takeaway?'

'Yes, but where's the fun in that?' He emptied the contents of the carrier bag onto the counter. 'We don't have Indian takeaways in the US, not like the ones over here.' He reached for a knife. 'Mind you, I haven't researched food options in Houston, so maybe they do. I'm not taking any chances. I need to know how to make curry, just in case.' He began chopping onions.

'Curry takes ages,' she said, searching the cupboards for the blender she'd never used. 'You have to cook off all the spices first and then marinate the chicken. Anything you make tonight won't be ready for hours.'

'Ah, that's where you're wrong.' He glanced over. 'Where shall I put the food waste?'

'Caddy under the sink.' She pulled out various baking tins, searching the cupboards.

Lucas continued chopping. 'This recipe was given to me by this amazing Indian woman called Meera who served me today in a grocery store in Brick Lane. She said it's the easiest curry recipe there is. You throw all the raw ingredients into a blender and then cook the sauce on a stove for an hour. While that's cooking, you season the chicken pieces and grill them. Add everything together and there you have it. Chicken tikka masala.'

Sarah located the blender. 'There has to be a catch.'

'I guess we'll find out. How was my sister today?'

'Exuberant.'

'Ah, yeah, I should've warned you. She gets a little crazy at times. I hope she wasn't too full-on?'

Sarah focused on unpacking the blender, unwilling to divulge the true extent of their girly shopping trip, which had included visiting the Ann Summers shop in

Kensington. An experience that had left Sarah hot and flustered. She had no idea who invented such bizarre stuff, but they had a vivid imagination, that was for sure. Even buying a fruity body lotion had felt slightly scandalous. Harper had no such inhibitions and had bought a selection of toys and gadgets specifically designed for the newly single woman.

'Harper was fine,' she said, getting to her feet. 'I think she enjoyed the outing.'

'Was it okay me suggesting she come over? I didn't want you feeling alone today.'

'It was fine; I had fun too.' Sarah plugged in the blender. 'She's good company. But you really don't have to worry about me. I have Fred.'

'Who you can't keep.'

'I managed before without him, I'll cope after.' She switched on the blender. 'Hey, it works.'

'You sound surprised.'

'It's new.' She returned to the floor and replaced the other utensils back in the cupboard. 'A wedding gift the giver didn't want back.' She ignored the fact that his chopping had slowed. 'You can find all sorts of guides to wedding etiquette on the internet, from best man's speeches to seating arrangements for divorced parents, but funnily enough, there's no instructions for being jilted.'

A beat passed. 'So, write one.'

She looked up. 'Excuse me?'

'Write a blog. Put your shitty experience to good use for someone else. Sadly, you won't be the last person whose partner turns out to be a dick. It might help. Both for you and them.' He returned to peeling a lump of ginger. 'Although, maybe leave out the bit about being off men for five years; that might prove a bit—'

'Extreme?' She climbed to her feet.

'Negative. People like to believe that life will get better and even though they're hurting in that moment, love still awaits them further down the line. You could become a shinning hope for all lost souls.'

She opened a tin of coconut cream. 'I'd forgotten you were such an old romantic.'

'Less of the "old", thanks.' He added the ginger and garlic to the blender. 'Pass the tomatoes… Returning to the subject of Fred, I wish you didn't have to rehome him. It makes me sad to think of you being here without him. You make a good team.'

'It makes me sad too.' She opened the garam masala. 'He really didn't like Stephen, did he?'

Lucas laughed. 'He really didn't. He's a smart dog. Stephen isn't a likeable man.'

'He's certainly deluded.' She took the limes from him. 'Let me help with that.'

'He's also dangerous; he doesn't accept boundaries. I doubt he understands the concept of informed consent. He crossed a line tonight. Several. You need to report him.'

She refused to meet his gaze. 'I know.'

'Seriously, Sarah. He wasn't taking no for an answer. I hate to think what he'd have done if I hadn't shown up.'

She sliced the limes. 'Lucky you did— *Ouch.*' She went over to the sink. 'You distracted me. I sliced my finger.'

'Nothing lucky about it,' he said, coming over and inspecting her finger. 'I asked Mrs Kelsey to keep watch and call me if a silver Merc showed up outside. She spotted him when he arrived and called me straight away; I'd just arrived back from the shops.' He washed her finger under the tap. 'Mrs K would make an excellent spy. The FBI should hire her.'

She looked into his kind blue eyes. 'I think you'll find it's MI5 in the UK.'

'Oh, right. Whoever they are, she missed her calling. Hold that.' He pressed a paper towel against her finger. 'Where will I find Band-Aids?'

'On top of the fridge.' She watched him fetch the first aid box. 'Who knew our neighbour's nosiness would come in so handy. How's she doing, by the way?'

'Better. Her health's improving and she's allowed me to refer her for support.'

'Crikey, how have you managed that?'

'Charm, perseverance and blackmail.' When he smiled at her, her insides flipped. He was standing so close she could feel the heat radiating off him and see all the contours of his face in high definition. It was like being tipsy all over again.

'You're an annoyingly nice bloke, do you know that?'

He grinned. 'What have I been trying to tell you? I am a nice guy. No games. No agenda. Just a good ole country boy from Duluth, Minnesota.' He pretended to tip his hat. 'At your service, ma'am.'

'Idiot. Give me that plaster. I'm not incapable of taking care of myself.'

'I know, but it makes me feel useful. You know, all macho and manly.' He flexed his biceps. 'Me man, you woman.'

She couldn't help laughing.

Grinning, he emptied all the ingredients into the blender and whizzed them into a pulp. While he poured the sauce into a pan and lit the hob, Sarah went into the lounge to light the festive candles. By the time she'd lit them, switched on the lantern and closed the curtains, Lucas had put the chicken on to marinate and had joined her in the lounge with a bottle of wine.

'Wow, look at you,' he said, picking up discarded cushions from the floor. 'There's no holding you back now. It's full-on Christmas festivities.' He opened the wine. 'Visiting Santa Claus. Feeding reindeer. Cuddling up with my nephews to watch a Christmas movie. You'd best be careful: your aversion might be lifting.'

'It might be.' She accepted a glass of wine. 'I'm going to my brother's house on Christmas Day to celebrate with my family. I haven't done that since before... well, you know... so it's well overdue.' She took a sip of wine.

Lucas stopped pouring. 'For real?'

She slumped onto the sofa. 'Spending the day with your nephews yesterday reminded me I'm missing out by not seeing my family at Christmas. Worse than that, I'm punishing them for something that isn't their fault, and that's not fair. They deserve better.'

'Well, would you believe it.' Lucas sat beside her. 'I'm proud of you.'

Embarrassed, she stared at her wine. 'It's no big deal.'

'Are you kidding me? It's a huge deal.' He nudged her foot. 'I bet they're excited to see you?'

'Ridiculously so. Mum cried when I told her.'

'I'm not surprised. I'm crying too.'

'No, you're not,' she said, laughing.

He leant closer. 'Look... tears. Genuine tears.'

Good grief, he did have tears in his eyes. 'You daft thing. You're worse than Fred. He's a soppy thing too.' She took a slug of wine, trying to dampen the effect of seeing him wiping his eyes. She cleared her throat. 'Are you spending Christmas with Harper and the boys?'

'That's the plan. I went shopping for gifts today.' He ran a hand through his hair. 'I may have spoilt them.'

'I can imagine,' she said, wondering what his hair felt like. Was it as soft as his hands? Did he use conditioner? He probably didn't have to; he was naturally blessed. Of course he was. Infuriating man. 'You're a very loving uncle.'

'It's a practice run for when I have kids of my own.' His smile was big and open and she nearly spluttered on her wine.

'You want kids?'

'Sure.' He shrugged. 'Kids. Wife. A dog. Maybe even a goldfish. I want it all.'

Fred jumped onto his lap and was rewarded with a tummy rub.

She had a sudden vision of him playing with mini versions of himself, cute blonde kids with their dad's infectious laugh and positive can-do attitude. Good at sports, popular at school. She could see it: the all-American family. Wholesome. Pillars of the community.

In contrast, all she could see when she tried to imagine herself in the picture was the Addams Family. Sullen kids with pale expressions and a passion for beheading rats.

The alcohol was making her morose. She took another slug. 'I can see you as a family man,' she said, her vision decidedly dizzy. 'You're great with Max and Elliot.'

'You too,' he said, placing his glass on the coffee table, dislodging Fred from the sofa. 'I could hardly believe it yesterday. Ms Anti-Christmas was all of a sudden *Ooh, let's go see Santa! Look at the reindeer! Who wants a candy cane?*' He reached over and tickled her ribs.

'Stop that!' She edged away, trying not to spill her wine. 'I was doing it for the boys. They've had a rough time lately.'

'I think you needed it as much as they did.' He patted his lap. 'Feet up.'

She pinned him with a confused look. 'Excuse me?'

'Put your feet up.' When she didn't respond, his picked up her feet and swung them onto his lap.

'Hey!' She fell backwards, slurping her wine. 'What are you doing?'

'You've had a shock. You need to relax.'

'The only shock I've had is you upending me.'

'Want me to stop?' His fingers sank into the arches of her feet, sending a fizz up to her thighs. Crikey, this was certainly better than the wine.

'Yes.'

He raised an eyebrow. 'Sure?' His fingers dug deeper.

'No.'

It was hard to think straight with his warm hands circling her feet and kneading the knots out of her toes. It was nice. More than nice. Exquisite. Bone-meltingly good. Her eyes drifted shut. Five minutes and then she'd get him to stop. There was no rush. Other than it felt like her resistance was ebbing away with each stroke of his hand. No wonder Fred liked being petted if this was what it felt like.

Lucas continued massaging her feet. 'I got a glimpse of the real you yesterday. The person you were before shit-face did his disappearing act. I liked her. She's fun.' When Sarah opened her eyes, she found him watching her, his expression tentative. 'Is she here to stay?'

Her head flopped against the cushions. 'Not while I have Stephen to deal with.'

'Every good Christmas story needs a bad guy. Think of him as the Grinch. Only don't let him steal your Christmas. You hear me?'

'I hear you.' Her ears were the only thing that appeared to be working. Every other part of her body had melted into a puddle of useless fluid. Who knew a foot massage could be quite so... unravelling.

And then he said, 'So where's the fruity body lotion you bought yesterday?'

It was like being doused in cold water and electrocuted at the same time. Her wine shot in the air, she sat bolt upright and her cheeks flamed hot. 'Harper told you? I can't believe she told you!'

'Told me what? That you bought some body lotion? Yeah, why? Is it a big deal?'

She searched his face, looking for signs of trouble, but he appeared innocent enough. She wasn't fooled, though. He was up to mischief.

'I thought you might like me to massage some lotion into your feet?' His lips twitched... and there it was. The smile. A wicked glint in his eye and she knew that he *knew*.

She dislodged her feet from his grasp. 'I need the loo. I've spilt my wine.'

She ran for the bathroom, his teasing laughter ringing in her ears, mortified that Harper had told him about their shopping trip. What was the woman thinking? She was his *sister*, for crying out loud. Did she have no boundaries?

Sarah screeched to a halt in front of the mirror. Her cheeks were flushed, her pupils were dilated and her hair was loose and messy. She looked like she felt: completely unravelled.

Boy, was she in trouble.

Chapter Fourteen

Thursday, 22nd December

Lucas finished his last shift at the Queen Adelaide Hospital with mixed emotions. He'd enjoyed working as a locum GP; it had been relatively stress-free, and certainly less demanding than his previous medical positions. He'd miss Carla and her insights into his love life and Americanisms, and he'd miss dealing with the patients. What he wouldn't miss was Stephen Stokes.

There had been a tense moment today in the canteen where they'd stared at each other like competing lions in the wild, fighting over territory. With narrowed eyes and threatening looks, they'd stood their ground, neither one prepared to back down and walk away. It was only when people had started to notice that Carla had intervened and invented a medical emergency that required his immediate attention and given him a good excuse to escape.

It had taken the edge off his leaving do. Instead of feeling sad, he'd mostly felt relieved to be out of there.

'How was your last day at the hospital?' Sarah asked, bringing him back to the present, almost as if she'd read his mind. They were heading out of the crowded Tube station and making their way towards the Hyde Park Winter Wonderland event. The crowds were out in force tonight, the pubs and restaurants full of festive parties.

'Uneventful.' He didn't want to upset her by telling her about his standoff with Stephen. 'Except for Carla hanging a good luck banner in the consulting room, and insisting I eat her homemade zucchini cake. What do you call it again?'

'Courgette.' Sarah smiled as she pressed the button on the crosswalk. 'I wouldn't have thought it was a suitable cake ingredient.'

'It wasn't. But I appreciated the gesture.' The traffic lights changed and they crossed the busy road along with all the other people heading for the park entrance. It was a relatively mild night compared to the low temperatures of last week, helped by a lack of wind.

Sarah pointed ahead. 'Oh, wow! Look at that car.'

Parked by the entrance was an old green car with a stack of wrapped gifts piled on top. There was a lit wreath on the front fender and the whole thing was wrapped in a gold ribbon and shimmering fairy lights. 'What kind of car is that?'

'A Morris Minor, I think. They were very popular in the fifties and sixties. I think my gran had one. Cute, isn't it? Perhaps not as robust as the Bentley.' She laughed, and he was relieved to see her enjoying herself. Especially after last night.

They'd gone from the trauma of dealing with Stephen's unexpected visit, to making curry, to messing around on the sofa. A situation that had abruptly ended when he'd mentioned fruity body lotion. The memory made him smile. It was fun to tease her. If nothing else, he had a great curry recipe to take home with him to the US.

Despite the chill lifting, Sarah was kitted out in her woollen hat and scarf, looking snug in her winter coat and walking boots. She looked relaxed and comfortable, less rigid than when she was dressed in her formal workwear.

'What car do you have back home?' she asked, removing her hat and stuffing it into her coat pocket. 'I imagine something big and flashy, like a fancy powder-blue Cadillac with chrome bumpers and tinted windows.'

'You mean, like a pimp?'

She laughed. 'I watch American movies.'

'Exactly. The movies. Not real life.' He gave her a gentle nudge. 'I had a Chevy Silverado pick-up. Good for off-roading.'

'A Chevy?' She nudged him back. 'That's more of a cliché than a Cadillac.'

It was her turn to tease him. Payback for last night, no doubt. 'So what car do you own? I can imagine you driving one of those Morris Minors. I bet it has fluffy dice in the window and a nodding toy dog on the rear shelf.'

She laughed. 'Sorry to disappoint, but I don't have a car. No need when you live in London. It's easier to use public transport. Besides, I've never actually learnt to drive.'

He stopped walking, nearly causing the family behind to bump into him.

By the time he'd caught her up, she'd paid for their tickets and had entered the park, where they were immediately engulfed by a wave of colour, lights and music. The skyline was filled with numerous fairground attractions, pulsating with strobe lighting.

'How come you never learnt to drive?' he asked, as they walked past stalls selling candyfloss, toffee apples and popcorn.

'I kept meaning to, but it was never the right time. I didn't need a car at uni, and then I went straight into a job in London. I've always lived close to where I work, so I've never had the incentive to learn. I will one day, I guess.' She headed over to the carousel.

'You'd struggle to survive in the US without a car; everywhere is so spread out.'

Her head bobbed along as she watched the wooden horses circle past. 'That settles it. If I ever move to the US, I'll learn to drive.'

He leant on the fencing, imagining her in the States. It wasn't an unpleasant thought. 'You have a reason to visit there now. I'd love you to come over.'

'Maybe I will someday.' She gestured to the carousel. 'Fancy a ride? Even I can manage a static horse.'

'Wow, a few weeks ago changing boroughs gave you the jitters, now look at you! We'll make an adventurer of you yet.'

'Stranger things have happened,' she said, laughing. They shuffled through the gate and climbed onto the carousel, selecting two horses on the outside. 'I'll be glad when the Stephen situation is sorted. It's like waiting for an operation you know you need, but don't want to have. Painful, but necessary.'

'Have you thought about reporting him?'

She settled onto a pink steed, leaving him with the slightly garish purple one. 'Yes, but I've decided to get tomorrow night out of the way first. I don't want to cause any issues for the fundraising ball; the event is too important to risk ruining it. After the Christmas break, I'm going to lodge a formal complaint. You're right, I can't allow his behaviour to continue. He needs to know his actions are unacceptable.'

The music grew louder and they started to move. Sarah gripped hold of the pole.

'It's the right thing to do,' he shouted over the music. 'I just wish I'd still be around to support you.'

She frowned. 'When are you leaving?'

'I have a flight booked from Heathrow on Tuesday.'

'That soon?' Her smiled faded and for a moment she looked sad… but then her expression brightened. 'Nice horse!' she shouted, patting the animal's wooden mane. 'Are they all this well-behaved?'

'Sadly not!' he shouted back.

For the next few minutes, they bobbed up and down, drowned out by the fairground music and the sound of kids screaming, until eventually the ride slowed.

'Are you flying straight to Houston?' she asked, as the carousel ground to a halt.

'I'm flying to Minneapolis to spend a few days back home sorting things out, and then I'll fly to Houston later in the week.' He climbed off the horse and offered Sarah his hand.

'Are you excited about your new job?'

'Not as much as I should be,' he admitted, catching a waft of her fruity body lotion. It reminded him of massaging her feet last night. For all his talk about it being for her sake and helping her unwind, in truth, he'd just wanted to touch her. He still wanted to touch her. 'I guess I'm feeling sad about leaving. I wasn't expecting that.'

Her eyes met his. 'With everything that's going on with Harper, it's understandable. It's always tough saying goodbye to family. You'll miss her, the boys too.'

His gaze dropped to her lips. 'Not just them.'

She blinked, and then shook her head. 'You won't miss me… or if you do, it'll be fleeting.' She broke away and climbed off the carousel.

He followed her, waiting until they were back on the main walkway before asking, 'Why do you think I won't miss you?'

'We've only known each other a few weeks. Hardly enough time to get attached. Give it a month, and you'll be like… *Sarah who?*' She was trying to make light of it, he could tell.

'You underestimate yourself.'

She stopped by the ice-skating rink. 'I'm a realist. I'm nothing special; I'm not delusional.'

'If you can't see how special you are, then you *are* delusional.' He manoeuvred her towards the entrance. 'Can you skate?'

'It's been a while.' She pulled a face. 'And you would say that; you're a nice polite man.'

'Now you're underestimating me.' He headed for the boot rack. 'What size are you?'

'Five.' She took the boots from him. 'How am I underestimating you?'

'You assume because I look on the positive side of things I'm shallow, and that's all there is to me, but you're wrong.' He sat on a bench and removed his trainers.

She sat next to him and laced up her boots. 'Have I offended you?'

'A bit.' With his boots secured, he stood up and offered her his hand.

She took his hand and stood up. 'I didn't mean to.' She looked puzzled, as if she couldn't work out what she'd said wrong.

'Don't worry about it. Ready?'

'To fall flat on my face? Sounds like fun.' When he rolled his eyes and turned away, she caught his arm. 'Sorry, that was me being negative again. I *believe* I can ice skate, and I *will* be good at this. How's that? Torvill and Dean have nothing on me.'

'Who?'

'You've never heard of—?' She waved her hand about. 'Oh, never mind. Come on, let's go.'

They stepped onto the ice and tried to find their footing. She gave him a filthy look when he skated around her, getting a feel for his boots.

'Of course you're good at this,' she said, placing her hands on her hips. 'Why am I even surprised. Let me guess, you played ice hockey in college?'

He nodded. 'For a while, yeah.'

'Whereas my ice-skating experience comes from shuffling around Streatham ice rink with my brother once a year when we visited my grandparents.' Her arms were now stuck out to the sides and she moved tentatively around the edge of the rink.

'Move your feet. Bend your knees.'

She shot him a look. 'Helpful.'

'Here… take my hand.' He positioned himself behind her right shoulder, one arm around her waist, the other holding her hand so he had control. 'Better?'

'Much.' They skated off, slowly at first, gradually building speed as she relaxed.

'You're not half bad,' he said, even though they were being overtaken by kids that barely reached his kneecaps. Eventually, he was able to let go of her waist as she found her balance.

'I'm sorry about what I said earlier,' she said, giving him a quick glance. 'It's just that you're so confident and assured all the time. Life's about moving forwards for you. You see endless possibilities for the future. You want to build your career and have a family one day.' She tightened her grip on his hand. 'I'm not knocking that. I think it's great, and I'm absolutely certain those things will happen for you. You deserve it more than anyone I know.'

He pulled her away from a woman flailing about and looking like she was about to hit the ice.

'I only meant that once you're settled in your new job, and making friends and building a life in Houston, this little... interlude, for want of a better word, will be a distant memory. It'll be superseded by far more exciting and adventurous things. And quite rightly too.'

He swerved her around the woman who was now face down on the ice. 'You're an infuriating woman, you know that? You have no trouble seeing what's good and positive about another person, but when it comes to assessing your own qualities, all you see are the negatives. You're incredibly blinkered.'

She toe-picked the ice and shot forwards. He skated in front of her and caught her before she fell. When she smacked against his chest, he had to hold her steady until she'd found her feet.

She looked up at him with concerned brown eyes. 'Are we arguing?'

He kissed her cold cheek. 'Never. An argument is where two people disagree with equal and valid points. On this occasion, I'm entirely right, and you're entirely wrong. No argument required. Had enough yet?'

'God, yes.' She let him lead her over to the side. 'I'm glad we cleared that up. I'd hate to think we'd fallen out. Especially as we have so much still to see. How do you feel about big wheels?'

'I'm a fan. You?'

'Never been on one. I'm willing to give it a go. In the spirit of being adventurous, and all that.' Her expression was sheepish and he wondered if he'd been a bit blunt with her. It just infuriated him that she couldn't see how special she was. Maybe he was also upset because she wasn't going to miss him anywhere near as much as he was going to miss her, and that stung.

They made their way over to the big wheel, passing a parade of dancers dressed in ice-white gowns and twirling batons. A man on stilts breathed plumes of fire into the night sky, and a woman in a white carriage followed behind, waving, pulled along by men dressed as horses.

Sarah stopped walking. 'Okay, so can you please just say it.'

He gave her a puzzled look. 'Say what?'

'Whatever it is you're itching to say. Your jaw's twitching. It's a tell of yours. It means you're agitated, so just come out and say it. I can take it.'

He waited until they were climbing into a pod and the bar had settled over their laps before replying. 'You really want me to tell you?'

She gripped hold of the bar. 'I do. Give it to me straight.'

'Even though it risks making things awkward between us?'

She turned to him, her expression incredulous. 'Things are already awkward. We're fake dating, for heaven's sake. We're dealing with a stalker, your divorced sister, a rude elderly neighbour and my aversion to Christmas and men. How much more awkward can it get?'

She had a point. The pod began to swing and with a clunk they moved off, lifting into the night sky. The London landmarks came into view the higher they ascended, the vast sprawl of the city below.

'Okay, here goes,' he said, wondering if he was about to make a colossal mistake in airing his feelings. 'I like you. A lot. And the more I get to know you, the more I like you. It's not logical; I get it. We're very different. But despite your negativity, your issues and your resistance to anyone being kind to you, I find you interesting and attractive and fun to be with. And it irritates me when you put yourself down and play up to this wounded woman routine, when in reality you're strong and capable and beautiful.'

'I'm not—'

'And if you dare contradict me, we really will fall out.' He pinned her with a look, ignoring the way her hair blew gently in the breeze as the pod swung back and forth. 'You're beautiful. And smart, and adorable. And yes, it offends me when you dismiss my feelings and tell me I'm not going to miss you, because I am. So do me a favour, now you've got over your aversion to Christmas, start thinking about dating again. Get therapy, or something. Do whatever it takes, because you're missing out. You have so much to offer and you could be so much happier than you are. And some lucky bloke is also missing out, because you, Sarah Haynes, as annoying as you are, are a catch. Now can we please enjoy the ride before I embarrass myself any further.'

She was completely silent next to him.

See? He knew he shouldn't have opened up. Why hadn't he kept his mouth shut? Five more days and he was out of here. All he had to do was keep his feelings to himself and they could have enjoyed their last few days together. Now she probably wasn't going to talk to him again.

'Lucas?'

Here it came. Her voice was soft and shaky, which didn't bode well. The rejection speech. She only saw him as a friend, and all that. 'Yes?'

'Please can I hold your hand?'

He hadn't expected that. 'Of course.'

She grabbed his hand, hard.

When he looked at her, she was white as a sheet. 'Ah, shit, you're not enjoying the ride, are you?'

'I absolutely hate... hate... it,' she said, visibly shaking. Then she started laughing. 'You are so right, though. I am such a catch. I mean, who wouldn't want this? The epitome of a strong, independent woman, who's so scared she's worried she might throw up.'

He slid his arm around her. 'You're doing it again. Using self-deprecation as a way of avoiding accepting a compliment.'

She was simultaneously laughing and shaking. 'Busted.'

'I know you better than you think.' He pulled her close and relented with a smile. He couldn't stay mad with her. Especially when she was smiling at him, her head resting on his shoulder... and trying not to throw up. 'Glad to know you haven't lost your sense of humour.'

'Sorry I've been such a pain.' She squeezed his hand. 'It's just hard for me to believe someone as lovely as you likes me, that's all.'

'Jeez, Sarah, like that's gonna help.' He dropped his forehead against hers. 'I want you even more now.'

Luckily, the big wheel ground to a halt and they could escape the growing tension building between them. It was an odd mixture of agitation and animal attraction. He wasn't sure whether to shake her, or kiss her. Both, probably.

The rest of the evening sped by in a blur. They steered clear of talking about their feelings, and instead ate buttery crêpes, drank mulled wine and let the surrounding music and chatter entertain them.

The Tube journey home was quiet, filled with furtive glances and awkward touches. She did a lot of frowning, followed by looking at him with a questioning gaze. It didn't take a genius to work out she was conflicted. As to what, he didn't know. Did she like him? Had he come on too strong? It was giving him a headache.

By the time they'd walked home from the station and reached their building, he was feeling as though tonight would be the last time they'd be alone together. Tomorrow was the fundraising ball, and they were spending Christmas Day with their respective families. By Tuesday he'd be gone and she'd forget all about him. He doubted he'd recover as quickly.

'Thanks for a lovely evening,' he said, as they reached the steps. It was time to put his feelings aside and ensure they parted on friendly terms. There was no need for things to end awkwardly.

She looked up at him, her gorgeous face creased into a concerned frown, and he couldn't make out what she was thinking. How to let him down gently? Was she about to remind him they weren't really dating and it was just pretend? That she only saw him as a friend? He steeled himself for what he knew was coming.

But she didn't say anything. Instead, she reached up on tiptoes and kissed him. His first instinct was to assume it was a fleeting goodbye kiss... or a kiss intended for his cheek that had accidentally landed on his lips. It was soft, tentative, and her lips were cold. Strangely, when she broke the kiss, she didn't move away. She continued looking at him, as if asking him a question.

Figuring he had nothing to lose, he cupped her face in his hands and kissed her back. He wasn't about to take things any further; he wasn't stupid. She wasn't ready, and he couldn't risk falling for her any harder than he had. It would, and should, have stopped there.

But when he pulled away, she blinked up at him, and said, 'I like you too,' and kissed him again.

It was different this time. Urgent. More primal. Her hands slid around his waist, pulling him close. She moaned and deepened the kiss. His hands laced into her hair and he was lost. This was what he wanted. She was who he wanted. This prickly, slightly barmy woman, who seemed to have left her insecurities behind and was kissing him like someone who didn't want to stop. Neither did he.

This wasn't a good-night kiss. This was a prequel to stumbling up the stairs, clothes being ripped off, falling onto the bed hot and sweaty, and spending the night, kind of kiss.

And he was helpless to stop himself. Forget logic. Ignore the awkwardness of tomorrow morning... because she was bound to regret it. And maybe he should be checking to ensure this was what she really wanted? But he'd lost any ability to speak. Or stop. It was too hot. Too enticing. He wanted her. And she wanted him. There was nothing tentative about her now.

In hindsight, he might thank Mrs Kelsey for breaking the moment, but when she shouted, '*Oi*, what's going on out there? Filthy bloody kids!', he couldn't profess to being happy about the interruption.

They broke away from each other, both dazed and unwilling to let go.

'Oh, it's you two,' Diana said, waving her fist about. 'Like that, is it? Well, sorry to interrupt your canoodling, but my nebuliser ain't working and me breathing's not so good. I need you in here, Doctor.'

Lucas stared down into Sarah's flushed face. 'I'd better help her.'

Sarah swallowed awkwardly. 'Of course. No problem. She needs you. I understand.' She seemed unsteady on her feet.

'You okay?'

'Absolutely peachy. See you tomorrow.'

'Night, Sarah.'

He kissed her again, and for a moment things threatened to reignite, until Mrs Kelsey shouted, 'Are you going to leave me standing out here in the cold all night?'

Sarah stepped away. 'You'd better go. Thanks for tonight.'

He watched her disappear up the steps and into the building.

With a heavy sigh, he headed down the steps in the opposite direction towards his neighbour. 'Coming, Diana.'

It wasn't the ending to the evening he'd hoped for.

Chapter Fifteen

Friday, 23rd December

When Lucas knocked on her door promptly at seven p.m., she knew the time for avoiding him was over. He'd been dealing with Mrs Kelsey today, so she'd gone to visit Harper this morning and they'd taken the boys out for a long walk with Fred. When she'd returned to the flat, she'd played loud music, indulged in a long hot bath and pretended not to hear the numerous knocks on her door throughout the day. It wasn't very mature, but she'd needed time to recover from last night.

Slipping her feet into a pair of black court shoes, she checked her appearance one last time and headed into the hallway. The fundraising ball was listed as a black tie event, but she hadn't felt much like dressing up. Still bruised from her fall and her horrible encounter with Stephen, she didn't want to draw any unwanted attention to herself. That said, she'd stand out more if she didn't make the effort, so she'd opted for a knee-length, dark green dress, and jazzed it up with dangly gold earrings. With her hair loosely pinned up, she felt suitably dressed up for a night out.

Drawing in a deep breath, she opened the door, unsurprised to find Lucas standing on the other side smiling at her. If she'd briefly panicked that Stephen might show up, as he'd threatened to, her fears had vanished when Fred hadn't started barking. The clever animal now knew when it was her friendly neighbour at the door.

'Hi there.' He looked suave and ridiculously good-looking in his evening suit, complete with black tie and silver cufflinks. 'You look amazing,' he said, leaning closer to kiss her cheek. 'Nice perfume. What is it?'

'Can't remember. It's a sample I picked up when I went shopping with Harper.'

'It suits you.' His gaze was appreciative and her nerves subsided a fraction. He had a way of complimenting her that didn't freak her out. Unlike when Stephen checked her out and she felt violated.

'Glad you like it.' He smelt good too. His blonde hair was fashionably styled and she'd never known a man with such neat fingernails. 'You look nice too.'

'Thanks.' He crouched down and rubbed Fred's ears. 'Ready to go?'

She picked up her clutch bag and coat. 'I'd be lying if I said I was looking forward to tonight.'

'It'd be a shame if you didn't enjoy yourself. Think of me as your wingman. Fake date. Protector of your honour, and fetcher of drinks.' He offered her his arm. 'At your service, ma'am.'

Smiling, she closed the door behind her. 'Stay close, okay?'

'That's the plan.'

Accepting the offer of his arm, they headed down to the waiting taxi outside.

'You booked a black cab?'

He opened the door for her. 'I didn't want to go home without experiencing one last taxi ride.'

They climbed in the back seat together and settled in for the ride. Lucas slid closer and reached for her hand.

She let him, for a number of reasons. It was a cold night and she was grateful for his warmth. She needed the comfort to steady her nerves. They were on a 'date' so it was necessary to keep up the illusion they were a couple, and... well... because she wanted to.

The last reason was the real kicker. She'd stopped fighting her attraction towards Lucas – as demonstrated last night when she'd kissed him. Maybe her aversion to men, like her aversion to Christmas, was finally lifting. More likely, the security of knowing he was leaving on Tuesday had enabled her barriers to lower temporarily. Nothing could develop between them, so it was safe to indulge in a brief moment of pleasure.

She glanced over, to find him watching her.

He gently caressed her hand. 'Do you want to talk about last night?'

'Absolutely not.' What was he, a sadist?

'Fair enough. You're okay, though? We're all good?'

She nodded. 'We're fine.'

'That's all I need to know.'

She was far from fine, but she had no idea what fine even was these days. Her quiet, carefully controlled life that she'd crafted for herself had been blown sky-high these last few weeks. First Fred had bundled into her life, then Stephen, and then Lucas. And people wondered why she avoided men.

The journey through London was quiet, with them both seemingly content to hold hands and watch the sights blur past as they headed into town. Feeling Lucas's body next to hers no longer felt strange. His warmth and scent were a familiar comfort. Her body had stopped stiffening at his touch. She now welcomed his presence. A little too much at times, as demonstrated last night when she couldn't get enough of him. Kissing Lucas had been like discovering water after forty nights in the desert. She'd been left craving more... a lot more.

The taxi pulled up behind a line of other taxis snaking along Cromwell Road dropping off their fares for the event. Scores of dressed-to-impress people swarmed the pavements, chattering and making their way towards the grand entrance.

Lucas exited the taxi. 'So, this is the famous Victoria and Albert Museum?'

'Wait until you see inside; you'll be blown away.'

He took her hand. 'Game face on.'

'Let's do this.' She straightened her shoulders. 'And what I really mean is: let's get this over and done with.'

'Focus on the positives,' he said, as they entered the huge lobby. 'Like that tree.' He nodded to the giant Christmas tree standing centre-stage, glistening with baby-pink lights, glass ornaments and ribbons. 'And that ceiling?' His eyes grew wide as he took in the tall marble-white domed ceiling, with leaded skylights leading down to a series of carved sculptures on huge plinths. 'This is incredible.'

His awe at the place helped to distract her, and she tried to look at the place anew. He was right, it was an impressive venue.

Depositing Sarah's coat in the cloakroom, they were directed through to the courtyard, where a giant marquee had been erected. Sparkling chandeliers hung down from the ceiling, interspersed with large spinning glitter balls, casting the space in flickering light.

Tables filled the outer areas, each one decorated with gold tablecloths and elaborate centrepieces. A wooden floor filled the middle, creating a dancefloor, and a stage had been erected where a quartet of musicians played. Behind the musicians was a disco set up ready for when the evening switched from formal and classy to drunken and raucous.

Hundreds of people were gathered, a wash of long sparkling dresses and formal evening attire. Some people had opted for Christmas-themed outfits and were dressed in Santa-red and elf-green. Others had embraced the excuse to gown up, like Georgia, who raced towards Sarah, who was wearing a full-length silver foil dress, so tight she had to lift the hem off the ground so she could walk properly.

'Sarah! You're here!' Georgia's hug was so forceful Sarah was knocked backwards. 'And with the lovely Doctor Moore too.' Her eyes darted between them. 'So, is it official? Are you back on the horse? Or should I say, back on the cowboy? I hope you're riding him good.' Georgia's loud laughter caused heads to turn.

'Honestly, Georgia. Have some discretion.' Sarah gave Lucas an apologetic look. He didn't seem bothered. In fact, he smiled and put his arm around her.

'Oh my God! You are soooo hooking up.' In Georgia's exuberance, she bumped into Jafrina, who had just arrived with Tyler.

'What have I missed?' Jafrina looked unbelievably elegant in her red and gold salwar kameez with her dark hair tied into a sleek bun and large hoop earrings.

'It's official, Sarah has bagged herself Doctor Moreish. They're dating,' she said, loud enough to turn heads.

Georgia flicked Sarah's dangly earring. 'You lucked out, girl.'

As cringey as it was to be the subject of such scrutiny, Sarah also knew a public declaration of their 'relationship' was necessary if they were to permanently deter Stephen's advances.

Lucas gave her a loving look. 'I'm the lucky one.'

Jaſrina sighed. 'That's so romantic. I'm delighted for you both.'

Tyler was grinning. He looked very dashing in his dinner suit, his dreadlocks tied into a plait down his back. 'We missed you at work this week. Have you had a good break?'

Knowing it wasn't the time or place to mention her issues with Stephen, she nodded. 'I've had a lovely week, thanks. Lucas and I have been sightseeing.'

'We went to the Winter Wonderland event at Hyde Park last night,' he said, hugging Sarah close. 'It was great.'

Georgia looked shocked. 'You went to a Christmas event?'

'It would appear my aversion to all things festive might be lifting.' Sarah gave Lucas a shy smile.

'Dating *and* celebrating Christmas? Blimey, he must be good in bed.' Georgia saluted Lucas. 'You're a talented man, sir. You have succeeded where other mortals have failed.'

Their attention was drawn to the main stage, where the string quartet were taking their bows and exiting to polite applause.

The clapping faded as Stephen Stokes walked up to the microphone and tapped the end.

Sarah tried to maintain a neutral expression. Booing him and giving him a thumbs-down wouldn't be very mature, however tempting.

'Ladies and gentlemen, welcome to tonight's fundraising ball. Please show your appreciation for this evening's entertainment, provided by members of the London Philharmonic Orchestra.' He started clapping, encouraging everyone to join in with the applause.

Sarah was grateful for Lucas's arm still being around her. Even the sound of Stephen's voice unsettled her.

Stephen waited until the clapping has subsided before continuing. 'Tonight's event is in aid of a number of charities supported by the Queen Adelaide Hospital. There'll be various auctions throughout the evening and opportunities to part with your cash. I'd like to encourage everyone to give generously and enable these worthwhile organisations to continue making a difference to people's lives.'

'He almost sounds sincere,' Lucas whispered. 'He's still a creep in sheep's clothing.'

Sarah smiled. 'Wolf.'

Lucas shrugged. 'That too.'

'There are a number of people I'd like to thank for making tonight possible.' Stephen smoothed down the front of his shiny red cummerbund. 'The fundraising team who you can see standing behind me.' He made a point of clapping in their direction. 'And TaylorMade Events for their sponsorship and for hosting tonight's event.'

More clapping, with a couple of people at the side of the stage looking pleased at being singled out.

Georgia turned to Sarah. 'Stephen's been asking about you this week. He wanted to check you were okay. Wasn't that nice of him? You're clearly in with the boss.'

Sarah feigned a smile. If only Georgia knew the real Stephen.

Watching him on stage, full of confidence and swagger and commanding the audience's attention, he was in his element. Master of ceremonies. No one knew what lurked beneath.

Stephen rested his hand on the microphone. 'Finally, I'd like to thank the staff team at the Queen Adelaide Hospital for making me feel so welcome as their new medical director.' He nodded in appreciation when a few people cheered. 'In particular, I'd like to single out Sarah Haynes.'

Sarah felt Lucas's arm tighten around her.

'Where is Sarah; can anyone see her?' Stephen searched the crowd.

'Here! She's over here!' An excited Georgia jumped up and down, gesturing to where Sarah was standing.

'Ah, there she is!' Stephen pointed in her direction, causing a mass of heads to turn and look at her.

Only Lucas holding on to her prevented her from kicking off her shoes and running. She wanted the ground to open up and swallow her whole.

'Keep smiling,' Lucas whispered, his smile as forced as hers. 'Don't let him rattle you.'

Too late. She was about as rattled as a rattlesnake who had another rattle attached to its already rattly rattle tail.

Stephen's smile was big and filled with veneers – false like him. 'I'd like to thank Sarah for her tireless commitment in ensuring a safe and inclusive working environment for all the staff team at the Queen Adelaide and helping us provide the best service for our patients.' He started clapping. 'Great work, Sarah. You're an asset to the hospital. A round of applause for Sarah Haynes.'

It was torture. The sound of clapping was like an assault on her ears. She hadn't done anything to warrant being singled out. No more than any other staff member. There was only one reason why Stephen would make such a public show of support, and that was to undermine any complaint she might make against him. He was getting in first. Landing the first blow. And it was a first-class strike.

To do anything other than smile and accept the applause, however sick it made her feel, would only make her look ungrateful and churlish. So she did her best to ride out the attention, praying it would end soon and she could escape.

Stephen continued talking for a few minutes, detailing the auction items and providing timings for the evening's activities.

Throughout it all, Sarah stood rigid, held up by Lucas, trying to stem the shake in her body.

When Stephen finally wrapped up his speech and left the stage, she made to leave, but Lucas stopped her.

'Hold fire,' he whispered, pulling here close. 'Don't let him win. If you leave now, you'll lose the upper hand.'

'He did that on purpose. If I make a complaint now, it'll look like I'm lying.'

'I know, but if you leave, you'll only draw further attention to yourself. Take a deep breath and look at me.' His face was inches away from hers, handsome and kind. 'Nothing's going to happen tonight. Hang in there a little longer and then we'll get out of here, okay?'

'Aw, would you look at these two, all loved up!' In her excitement, Georgia nearly spilt her champagne over Jafrina. 'Get a room, will you. You're making the rest of us jealous.'

'Leave them alone,' Jafrina said, moving away from Georgia's wayward champagne flute. 'It's lovely to see. And I'm glad the new medical director recognises your talents, Sarah. You've been overlooked for too long. It was about time someone noticed how tirelessly you work. Good for you.' She raised her own glass, and Sarah wanted to cry.

She felt like such a fraud. Pretending to be dating Lucas, covering up Stephen's harassment and harbouring an illegal pet. For someone who was such a stickler for the rules, she sure had fallen off the wagon lately.

'Excuse us,' Lucas said, taking Sarah's hand. 'I'd like to dance with my girlfriend.'

Sarah allowed him to lead her onto the dancefloor, a welcome escape from her colleagues with their smiling faces and oblivion to her torment.

Lucas took her in his arms and held her tight, before slowly moving to the music. The string quartet were playing a waltz from Tchaikovsky's *Sleeping Beauty* ballet, and several couples were dancing, filling the dancefloor. It took a while for her to relax and allow herself to be led. The exhaustion of it all helped. Lucas was the only thing holding her up.

'I know this is hard, but Stephen's made his play now,' Lucas said, as they gently swayed to the music. 'Forget about him for now; focus on me instead.' He grinned at her and kissed the end of her nose. 'Hi, I'm Lucas Moore. I live downstairs from you, and I think you're really cute.'

She almost smiled. 'I seem to remember seeing you around.'

'I made an impression, huh?'

'You're a hard man to ignore.'

His expression turned serious. 'Then don't.'

His face was so close she could feel his breath on her cheek. With his arm around her waist, and the other pressing her hand to his chest, something inside her melted a little.

'I'm going to miss you,' she whispered, almost to herself.

He seemed momentarily stunned. His dancing faltered ever so slightly, and he took a beat to recover. 'That's some admission. I might have expected a little thawing after a few glasses of champagne, but this early in the evening? Consider me surprised.' His eyes were fixed on hers and it was quite intoxicating. No alcohol needed.

'You were right, what you said last night. I have been unfair to you. I've been holding back and expecting you to deal with my insecurities, and that wasn't fair of me.'

His expression softened. 'You're worth the effort.'

'No, I'm not. You deserve so much better. But I realised something last night when I was lying in bed thinking about you.'

Both his eyebrows raised. 'Okay, this is getting interesting.'

'I shouldn't be afraid of admitting I like you. You're leaving on Tuesday. I'll never see you again. It's not like I've anything to lose by telling you how I feel.'

'Right.' He seemed to swallow awkwardly. 'And how do you feel?'

'Safe... Scared... Happy... Sad... Turned on... Mostly confused.'

He seemed to process this. 'I'm going to come back to the "turned on" remark, but why scared?'

With the music acting as a mask, and the lights dimmed and atmospheric, it seemed the right moment to open up. 'I'm scared of how I feel. I've managed very successfully to avoid feeling anything for five years. It hasn't exactly been difficult. There's been nothing to resist. No feelings to deny. I wanted nothing more than to be alone. You've made me realise that it's easy to diet when you only have carrots in the fridge, but it's a whole other ball game when someone brings you doughnuts.'

His face split into a grin. 'You're comparing me to a doughnut?'

'The worst kind,' she said, staring at his lips, and remembering how they felt pressed against hers. 'Filled with cream *and* jam, covered in sticky sweet icing, and with added sprinkles on top. Eating one would trigger a massive sugar addiction. Diet over.'

His pupils were starting to dilate. 'It had to happen sometime. No one can live on carrots their whole life.'

'I guess. But I thought there'd be something in the interim, you know? Like a gradual slipping. Testing the water before diving in. With you it feels full-on, no holds barred, binge-eating an entire fridge in one go.' She blinked up at him. 'You're a hard man to resist.'

His eyes locked on hers. 'So don't.'

'You're leaving. Which is the confusing part.'

'How so?'

Her mouth was suddenly dry. 'Well, part of me thinks: you're leaving, so I can indulge in the safe knowledge it can't go anywhere. I can return to being alone and pathetic after you've gone, no permanent damage done. But the other part of me is like: why torture yourself by eating a whole box of doughnuts when after Tuesday sugar will be off the menu. The crash could be fatal.' She shook her head, confusing herself with thoughts of doughnuts and sugar rushes. 'But then I think: will it make any difference? I like you regardless. I'm not going to miss you any less whether I've eaten doughnuts or not. Are you following any of this?'

'It's a lot, I'll admit. Can we go back to the "turned on" bit?' He must have clocked her expression, because he said, 'Oh, right, that *was* the "turned on" bit. I'm with you now. Does it help if I tell you last night was incredible? And that I could've cursed Mrs Kelsey for interrupting us?'

'It's just as well she did. If I'm being honest, I don't think I would've stopped otherwise.'

He let out a low moan. 'Can you warn me next time you're going to be this honest? I need to prepare myself.' His smile turned playful. 'So tell me what would've happened next?'

'I'm not going to indulge you by spelling it out.'

'Not even a little? Did it involve fruity body lotion?' The wanting in his eyes grew, and they may well have picked up where they left off last night, if it hadn't been for Carla interrupting them.

'Lucas! You made it! You must come and meet Vince,' she said, jostling her way through the dancers. 'He's just transferred from the same hospital you'll be working at in Houston. How's that for a coincidence? I told him you'd want to pick his brains. You don't mind if I borrow him for a moment, do you, Sarah?'

Still a little unsteady from the heat building between them, she shook her head. 'No, it's fine.'

Lucas still had hold of her hand. 'Now's not a great time, Carla.'

'It's fine, really.' Sarah reassured him. 'I need to use the ladies' room anyway. You go with Carla.'

Lucas lowered his voice. 'You sure? I said I wouldn't leave you.'

'Absolutely.' A break from him was probably for the best. Her tongue had loosened past the point of propriety. 'You can hardly come into the loo with me.'

He kissed her hand before letting go. 'Come and find me straight afterwards.'

'Sure.' Sarah waved as Carla dragged him away, and then she went in search of the ladies'.

There was a long queue for the toilets close by, so she followed the signs for the loos inside the museum. There was a display of African fashion in the main area and Sarah stopped to admire the outfits, colourful and bold. It was nice to be away from the noise for a while. The quiet of the exhibition hall was a welcome respite.

She studied the animal prints and mismatch of geometric patterns. She should wear more colour, she decided. Her wardrobe had dampened like her mood over the years and she now favoured muted tones. It seemed everything in her life needed a kickstart, not just her love life.

'Admiring the exhibition?' She turned to see Stephen Stokes standing behind her.

Panic raced through her veins. 'I was looking for the ladies'… Excuse me.' She attempted to stride past, but he blocked her escape.

'I'm glad I caught you. You owe me an apology.'

The gap he'd left wasn't big enough for her to get through. 'An apology? What for?'

He placed a hand on the wall, creating a barrier. 'The accusations you made the other night.'

'The night you showed up at my flat, you mean?' She tried to sound authoritative, but the shake in her voice gave her away.

'I've tried my best to be supportive, Sarah, but you seemed determined to wilfully misunderstand me. I don't appreciate having my good intentions being labelled as inappropriate. And I certainly don't appreciate being threatened.'

She backed up a step; she didn't like his menacing tone. 'In what way did I threaten you?'

'All that nonsense about lawsuits and complaints, when I've done absolutely nothing wrong.' He moved towards her, forcing her backwards. 'All I've done is be supportive and accommodating, and instead of thanking me for taking an interest in your career, you've shown nothing but ingratitude and insubordination. If anyone has the right to make a complaint, it's me.'

Her head was whirling with panic. 'What grounds do you have for making a complaint, Stephen? My work is satisfactory, I was given an excellent rating at my last annual appraisal and my conduct in the workplace is professional at all times.'

'You call kissing Doctor Moore in the car park professional conduct?'

She recoiled at the force in his voice. 'No less so than sending an employee flowers… or buying her a dress to wear… or showing up at her home uninvited.'

He pointed a finger at her. 'I've already explained myself. I was concerned about you.'

She bumped into the wall behind. 'How… how did you even get my address?'

'You gave it to me.'

'No, I didn't.' She was full on trembling now. 'You're lying.'

'Lying?' Before she knew what was happening, he'd grabbed her arm. 'You're accusing me of lying? That only adds more weight to my complaint about your conduct.'

She tried to dislodge his hand. 'I also know you've been hanging around outside my flat. I've seen you.'

His eyes narrowed. 'Another accusation you can't back up with any evidence.' His body was pressed against hers, pinning her against the wall.

'That's where you're wrong, Stephen. I have enough evidence to submit a claim for sexual harassment in the workplace. Now let go of my arm.'

'Evidence like what? Your boyfriend backing up your story? No one's going to believe him. His contract has been terminated with the hospital. He's no longer a member of staff. His testimony will count for nothing.'

'What about the dress you sent me? The emails? The flowers? And my neighbour saw your car the other night.'

He laughed, a bitter sound. 'That batty old lady? How old is she? I'm sure her eyesight excludes her as being a reliable witness. As for the flowers and emails, they were simply an expression of my gratitude for all your hard work. As demonstrated this evening when I publicly thanked you.'

She tried to push him away. 'I still have the dress.'

'No, you don't.' His hand came up and grabbed her by the throat. 'Lucas returned it, remember? So there's no evidence and no witnesses to back up your claim. You have nothing. I'm warning you, if you dare breathe a word of complaint against me, I'll sue you for defamation of character. But only after you've been fired for gross misconduct, with no notice, and no reference. Do I make myself clear?'

'You're hurting me.'

He increased his grip. 'I said, do I make myself clear?'

'Let go of me, or I'll start screaming.'

'There's no one around to hear.'

She screamed.

And screamed some more.

And when he released his hand and tried to cover her mouth, she brought her knee up hard between his legs.

Chapter Sixteen

The ball was in full swing. The champagne was spilling over, the music had switched from classical to power ballads and the dancefloor was packed with people waving their arms about. As interesting as it was to hear about Vince's experience working in Houston, Lucas wanted to check on Sarah. She'd been gone a while and he'd promised to stay with her tonight; her absence was making him edgy. He searched the crowds, but he couldn't see her. The place was packed; he worried they might never find each other again.

He was at the point of politely excusing himself from the conversation and going off in search of her, when someone tugged on his jacket sleeve.

He turned to find Sarah's work colleague Georgia looking kind of buzzed and unsteady on her heels. Her red lipstick was smudged and she reeked of alcohol. Standing beside her was another of Sarah's colleagues, Jafrina. She shared her friend's anxious expression, although without the effects of too much champagne.

'You have to come quickly,' Georgia said, tugging his arm. 'It's Sarah – she's in trouble.' Without waiting for a response, she turned and dragged him through the crowd.

Looking alarmed, Carla followed them. 'It's not Stephen, is it?'

Jafrina seemed taken aback. 'Why would you think that?'

Lucas hadn't said much to his nursing assistant about Sarah's issues with Stephen; he hadn't needed to. Carla was an astute woman. She knew 'trouble' when she saw it, as she'd aptly put it.

'I've no idea what's happened,' Georgia shouted over the alcohol-fuelled laughter. 'I just got a text from Tyler saying to fetch Lucas quick.'

The four of them made their way across the courtyard, bumping into people as they tried to navigate the crowds, and apologising for spilling drinks and treading on toes.

Lucas's mind was whirling; he knew he shouldn't have left Sarah alone. If anything had happened to her, it would be his fault. He was a bad boyfriend, fake or otherwise. 'Where is she, do you know?'

'Somewhere inside the main building. Near the loos, apparently.'

The noise level faded as they left the revelry behind and moved from the party area and into the quiet exhibition space. They were running now, their heavy breathing and footsteps hitting the marble flooring and echoing off the high ceiling. Georgia was struggling to keep up, hindered by a tight dress and blood-alcohol levels. To be fair, he'd be struggling to run in four-inch heels too. He wanted to sprint ahead, but he had no idea where they were going.

In the dim lighting, Tyler appeared, frantically spinning the wheels of his chair like a competing athlete. 'Over here!' he called, sliding his wheelchair to a halt and turning with the grace of a ballerina, before leading them back the way he'd come. 'I've called security. They're on their way.'

That didn't sound good. Lucas prayed Sarah wasn't hurt.

Lucas heard Sarah before they rounded the bend and came across the most bizarre sight he'd ever seen. Stephen was on his knees, clutching his groin, and Sarah was standing over him, yelling.

'I will not be silenced!' she screamed, stamping her foot. 'You will not bully me! Harass me! And threaten me! Do you hear me? I've had enough.' She shook a fist at him, causing the burly security man who had appeared from the opposite direction to assume she was the aggressor and pull her away.

'Arrest this woman!' Stephen was red-faced and sweating. 'She assaulted me. I want her charged.'

Sarah tried to shake off the security man, but he held firm. 'Come over here, miss.' He dragged her away, but she continued fighting him.

'Let go of me!' She stumbled as she was forcibly removed from the altercation. She was minus a shoe and an earring, and there was blood on her ear. Her hair had slipped from its clasp and long strands were falling onto her face.

'And in case you're in any doubt… you're fired!' Stephen shouted, sounding like a poor imitation of Lord Sugar. 'You'll never set foot in a hospital again. You hear me? Your career is over!'

Lucas raced over to Sarah. 'It's okay, Officer. I've got her.'

The security guard looked relieved as he handed Sarah over to Lucas. 'She can't go anywhere. The police are on their way.'

'Good!' Stephen had recovered enough to get to his feet. 'I want her charged with assault.' He tried to move towards Sarah, but Carla and Georgia blocked his path.

'Get out of my way. This has nothing to do with you. Do you want to lose your jobs too?'

Georgia hesitated, but Carla wasn't one to succumb to a threat. 'Don't waste your breath threatening me, Stephen. I've no idea what's happened here, but if you think I'm going to let you near Sarah in this state, you're mistaken. Now calm down.'

'It's not me who needs to calm down, it's her. Look at her! She's out of control.' Stephen rested his hands on his knees, wincing.

Sarah wasn't out of control, but she was fired up. Her jaw was clenched and her hands were shaking, although Lucas suspected from rage rather than fear. He wanted to touch her, but he knew it wouldn't help.

'Everyone needs to calm down,' Carla said, using the soothing tone she saved for agitated patients. 'Shouting's not going to help anyone. Let's keep things civil until the police arrive.'

Lucas desperately wanted to assess Sarah's injuries and discover the cause of the bleeding, but she was too wired to stand still. She was like a wounded tiger pacing its cage, unbalanced on one shoe. He touched her arm, hoping it wouldn't alarm her. 'Are you okay? What happened?'

'He… he cornered me,' she said, pointing a finger at Stephen. 'And then he threatened me… and grabbed me—'

'I did no such thing!' Stephen tried to stand, still visibly in pain. 'I'm the victim here.' He glared at Carla and Georgia as though they were restraining him, but they weren't doing anything. He looked like one of those soccer players whose teammates had to hold him back from thumping another player, even though it was just showboating. An act for the baying crowd.

Jafrina was standing to one side, her hands covering her mouth.

Tyler was checking something on his phone.

Lucas looked to the security guard for help. 'How long until the police get here?'

'I'll find out.' He mumbled something into his walkie-talkie.

Lucas moved in front of Sarah, blocking her sightline of Stephen. 'It's okay, honey, I'm here. You're bleeding. Where are you hurt?'

She shook her head. 'I'm fine.' She swiped at her ear, frowning when she saw the blood on her hand. 'My earring must've got pulled out in the scuffle.'

Scuffle? Lucas swallowed. 'Okay, anything else?'

'A bruised arm from where he grabbed me, and my throat is sore. Other than that, I'm okay.' When her hand came up to touch her neck, he could see red marks forming on her skin.

'Did Stephen do that?'

When Sarah nodded, Lucas was filled with such rage he thought he might explode. Only the fear of making matters worse and strengthening Stephen's claims that he was the victim prevented him from grabbing Stephen by the throat to see how he liked it. Getting violent might not be the answer, but that didn't mean Stephen should go unchallenged.

Lucas turned to the medical director and walked slowly towards him. 'How did Sarah get these marks on her neck?'

All heads turned to look at Sarah, who'd removed her remaining shoe and was holding it like a weapon in front of her, ready to defend herself.

'No idea.' Stephen leant against the wall. 'She probably did it herself. A proper little drama queen.'

Lucas bunched his fists. 'You're saying Sarah tried to strangle herself?'

Jafrina gasped.

Stephen glanced between Carla and Georgia, as if to say, *Aren't you going to stop him?* But they parted ways like the Red Sea and let Lucas through. 'She's unhinged. Unstable. She's been spreading lies about me.'

Lucas decided to change tactics. As much as he wanted to throttle Stephen, no one other than Carla knew what had been happening, and even Carla didn't know the extent of the problem. It was time to enlighten them.

'Since joining the hospital, Stephen has been making a nuisance of himself and harassing Sarah at work.'

Stephen looked outraged. 'That's not true.'

'He started out sending her emails and inviting her for lunches. He then invented meetings for no good reason. Any excuse to get her alone.'

Stephen pushed away from the wall. 'I did no such thing. Don't listen to this nonsense. He's lying.'

'When that didn't work, he sent her flowers.' Lucas stood his ground, a warning sign he wasn't someone Stephen wanted to upset. 'Then he followed her home. He's been hanging around outside her apartment, *stalking* her.'

'Utter rubbish.' Stephen limped over to the security guard. 'I want him charged with slander. Why aren't you writing this down?'

The security guard shook his head. 'Not up to me, mate. I'm waiting on the police.'

Lucas glanced at Sarah. Her anger was subsiding and she looked small and fragile in her bare feet. He headed over. 'Stephen hand-delivered an invite for tonight's ball to Sarah's apartment, and included a dress for her to wear, and instructions for picking her up tonight.'

Georgia pulled a face. 'Creepy.'

Stephen waved his arms about. 'All lies!'

The security guard shrugged when Lucas looked at him. 'No good telling me, mate. Save it for the authorities.'

'Don't worry, I intend to tell them everything.' Lucas glanced at Sarah, hating what this man had done to her. 'But Sarah's colleagues need to know what the real Stephen is like. The kind of man who won't take no for an answer. Who thinks it's his given right to have any woman he wants. And when he doesn't get his own way, he resorts to violence.'

Stephen threw his arms in the air. 'She attacked me!'

'It was self-defence!' Sarah waved her shoe at him, finding her voice. 'I hit you because you were choking me and refusing to let go. I had no choice.'

Georgia gasped. 'Bastard!'

Jafrina clutched hold of Tyler's shoulder.

'The only person who's struck anyone is you.' Stephen's sudden move towards Sarah made her recoil. 'And these people were witness to that. I was on my knees. You can't deny it.'

Lucas shot in front of Sarah, instinctively protecting her. What he would have done if the police hadn't shown up at that moment, he wasn't sure. He was glad he didn't have to find out.

'Oh, thank goodness.' Jafrina sounded relieved as the two uniformed officers approached.

'Arrest this woman for assault!' Stephen pointed at Sarah and then down at his groin. 'She attacked me! She struck me in the groin with her knee.'

'Calm down, sir.' The female cop took a moment to look around, taking in the scene. 'Let us do our job.'

Stephen jabbed a finger at her. 'Your job is to do as I say and arrest that woman.'

The policewoman raised her eyebrows. 'Is that so?'

'What I mean is, I'm the medical director of the Queen Adelaide Hospital. My word can be trusted. I'm telling you this woman physically assaulted me.'

The female cop looked between Sarah and Stephen. 'And why did she do that?'

'Why? Well, because she's unhinged!'

'So, no reason?' The female cop removed a notebook from her pocket. 'She just kneed you in the bollocks for the fun of it?'

'Are you doubting my story?' Stephen's jaw twitched. 'We were talking, she became hysterical, she struck me with her knee and started yelling abuse. Perhaps I should talk to your senior colleague. You're clearly not impartial. You would take the woman's side.'

Stephen turned to the male cop, who raised his hand. 'I'd advise you not to talk to my colleague like that, or we'll be having words. And for the record, she's the senior.'

Stephen growled and pointed at Tyler. 'Ask him. He witnessed the attack.'

The female cop turned to Tyler. 'Did you see this woman strike this man?'

Tyler nodded. 'I did.'

'Thank you!' Stephen looked triumphant. 'Now arrest her.'

'I also saw what happened before that.' Tyler rolled forwards in his chair.

The female cop nodded. 'Go on.'

'When I exited the disabled toilet, I heard a man's raised voice.' He pointed to Stephen. 'He was saying something about there being no evidence to back up her claim. When I came around the bend, I saw Stephen holding Sarah against the wall. His hand was against her throat. He said: "I'm warning you, if you dare breath a word of complaint against me, I'll sue you for defamation of character, and fire you for gross misconduct."'

'That's a complete lie—'

'Not now.' The female cop raised her hand, cutting Stephen off. She gestured for Tyler to continue.

'Sarah was struggling to breathe and begging Stephen to let her go, but he wouldn't. That's when she hit him.'

'That's not how it happened.' Stephen looked flustered; his shirt had become untucked. 'This man works for Sarah; he would side with her. He's not an impartial witness. It won't stand up in court. If you know what's good for you, officers, you'll do the sensible thing and support my claim against this woman. I have very expensive lawyers who don't like to lose.'

The female cop noted something down. 'Don't threaten us, sir. We don't take kindly to being told what to do. Our job is to find out the truth.'

Stephen shook a fist. 'The truth is this woman assaulted me. How many times do I have to repeat the same information before it gets through?' He was losing control.

'It's all on video.' Tyler's statement caused a collective intake of breath.

Everyone turned to look at him.

He pressed his finger against the screen, unlocking his phone. 'I wanted to intervene, but this chair doesn't allow me to do much physically. I decided to record the incident instead. It's all here.' He pressed the play button and held the phone up for everyone to see.

The image wobbled initially before coming into focus. It showed Stephen pinning Sarah against the wall, his hand on her throat, and repeating the words as Tyler had described.

Jafrina started crying.

Carla glared at Stephen and called him an arsehole.

Georgia went over and enveloped Sarah in a hug.

As for Lucas... he had no idea what he felt. Mostly numb.

Tyler waited until the video had stopped playing. 'I was about to call for help, but then Sarah managed to break free. I stopped the recording and called security.'

The male cop addressed Stephen. 'You're required to accompany us to the station for questioning, sir.'

Stephen wasn't having it. 'I will do no such thing. He's fabricated the video, doctored it. It's not what happened.'

'I'm sure we'll get to the bottom of it once we're at the station. This way.' The cop took Stephen by the arm. 'You do not have to say anything, but it may harm your defence...'

Leaving her colleague to read Stephen his rights, the female cop came over to Sarah. 'Do you need medical attention before making a statement?'

Sarah shook her head. 'I'm okay. But I need my other shoe.'

Georgia sprang into action. 'Don't worry, I'll find it.'

'I'm coming with her to the station.' Lucas was prepared to argue with the cop if he had to. 'I'm her boyfriend. I need to be with her.'

'That's fine.' The cop turned to Tyler. 'You too, sir. We'll need you to make a statement, and I'll need to take your phone as evidence.' She unfolded a plastic bag from her pocket. Tyler dropped the phone inside.

Having located her shoe, Sarah wiped her hands on her dress and indicated she was ready to go.

Leaving Carla, Georgia and Jafrina looking collectively distressed, the rest of them headed towards the exit with the two cops.

Sarah was unsteady on her feet, so Lucas held her up, relieved when she didn't object. She offered him a weak smile as they made it outside. 'Thanks.'

'No problem, honey.' He could feel her whole body shaking as they walked towards the cop car parked on the walkway. 'Stay strong,' he whispered. 'Stephen can't argue his way out of this one. We have proof.'

'Thank goodness for Tyler,' she said, her fingers gripping his.

'He's a smart man.' He kissed the side of her head, wanting to take away her pain and protect her from all this trauma. She'd been through enough in her life. She deserved so much more.

'Don't leave me,' she said shakily.

'I won't,' he said, lowering her into the cop car. 'I love you.'

Chapter Seventeen

Saturday, 24th December

It had been an odd night, to say the least. Sarah wasn't sure she'd slept at all. It was gone three a.m. by the time they'd arrived home from the police station having made their statements. The officers had been very kind and assured her she was doing the right thing in making a formal complaint. Stephen had been charged with assault and harassment, and had been instructed to refrain from making any contact with her. She wondered how that would play out at work. Would the board of directors suspend him? Maybe they'd side with Stephen and sack her instead. Somehow she doubted Stephen would pay for his crimes. He was too wily, with a set of expensive lawyers who would spin the whole thing on its head and make it look like a misunderstanding. Was it any wonder she hadn't slept?

Stirring, she rolled over to discover two males sharing her bed.

'Morning.' Lucas was petting Fred; the cheeky dog had wiggled his way in between them.

When Lucas had suggested staying the night, she hadn't had the energy to argue with him. Besides, she'd been glad of the company. Her nerves were still on edge, triggered by recollections of Stephen grabbing her, pushing her against the wall and his hand squeezing the air from her throat.

She shuffled into a seated position against the head-board. 'Did you get any sleep?'

'Not really. You?' He'd propped himself onto one elbow. He was bare-chested and wearing nothing but a pair of boxer shorts. He made quite an impact lying in her narrow bed, his masculinity at odds with her Cath Kidston floral bedsheets. Having Lucas stay over hadn't been an issue last night; she'd been too traumatised to worry about her hormones getting the better of her. In the cold light of day, it was a different matter entirely.

She pulled the duvet higher, checking she was still wearing her winter pyjamas. 'I didn't sleep much, no.'

'Understandable in the circumstances. Can I get you a cup of tea?'

It was such a minor gesture in the scheme of things, and yet part of her still wanted to refuse. She was becoming too reliant on this man. She needed to return to being self-sufficient and taking care of herself. Letting him look after her gave out the wrong signals, and that wasn't fair. But then, refusing his offer would be self-harming too. She had a bitch of a sore throat and a cup of tea was desperately needed.

'Yes, please,' she said, grateful for his thoughtfulness. 'That would be lovely.'

He climbed off the bed and went to open the curtains, letting in a wintery shaft of sunlight. The sight almost made her groan. Bathed in sunlight, and wearing only his shorts, she was subjected to the full force of Lucas Moore. Tall, wide, smooth. He was too big and too masculine for her dainty room, with its period furniture and satin cushion covers. The sight of him yawning and stretching out his back sent a wave of longing coursing through her and she had to look away. Her resistance had been weakened by recent events and she needed to tread carefully. One false move and she'd be dragging him back to bed. She focused on petting Fred instead.

'Back soon.' Lucas left the room and she almost felt the warmth leave with him.

Sarah rubbed her eyes. 'What am I going to do, Fred?'

Fred tilted his head, his tail thumping against the bedcovers.

In among the images flickering through her mind from last night's ordeal was a faint recollection of Lucas telling her he loved her. It had been fleeting. A brief comment that had disappeared on the breeze, drowned out by police sirens and traffic noise, to the point where she wondered if she'd imagined it.

Even if she hadn't, he couldn't have meant it. It was a throwaway remark. A flippant comment people used without true thought or meaning: *See ya. Bye. Love ya.* It was something she overheard all the time, especially on the phone. It seemed to be people's default way of ending a call these days.

There was no point getting in a flap about it, or overthinking its meaning. It was Christmas Eve, after all. Lucas was leaving on Tuesday. Dwelling over an isolated comment he may or may not have said was a waste of time. She had bigger issues to focus on.

Lucas returned with a mug of tea and handed it to her. She tried not to look at his bare chest and held her breath so she wouldn't breathe in his musky scent.

'I added sugar. I figured you'd need the energy.'

'Thanks.' She appreciated the gesture.

'There was an envelope pushed under the door,' he said, waiting until she'd drunk a few mouthfuls before handing it to her. 'It looks official.'

'Surely it's not from the police already,' she said, placing her mug on the bedside cabinet. 'We've only been home a few hours.' She tore open the envelope and read the short letter. Her head began to thump as the words sank in. 'And I didn't think anything could be worse than last night.' She handed the letter to Lucas. 'It's from the landlord. He knows about Fred. I've been given seventy-two hours to rehome him. There'll be an inspection on Wednesday to ensure he's gone.'

Fred's ears pricked up, as if he knew they were talking about him.

Sarah couldn't face looking at him. 'I'm guessing this is Stephen's doing. He certainly knows how to land a blow.'

'Oh, honey, I'm sorry.' Lucas sounded genuinely upset.

Whether it was Lucas calling her 'honey', or the real-isation that her time with Fred was over, she wasn't sure, but she needed to be alone.

'Excuse me,' she said, climbing out of bed and heading into the bathroom.

Turning on the shower taps, she used the sound of the noisy pump to drown out her tears. There was no point trying to hold back. She'd learnt enough about grief to know sometimes you just had to succumb, and she had a lot to be sad about. The Stephen situation, losing Fred, her career being put in jeopardy. Not to mention falling for a man she couldn't have. That was the real icing on the cake. She'd tried so hard to protect herself from further heartbreak, and it had all been for nothing. Here she was sobbing over the exact thing she'd been so careful to avoid.

She had no idea how long she stood under the shower crying, but it was long enough for the water to have run cold.

Dousing her eyes with eyedrops in an effort to reduce the redness, she wrapped her hair in a towel and fastened her dressing robe. Exiting the steamed-up bathroom, she padded into her bedroom, noticing that Lucas was in her lounge opening curtains and lighting Christmas candles.

'Let me know when you're ready and I'll make a fresh cup of tea. The previous one's gone cold,' he said, striking a match. 'I've taken Fred out to do his business, so he's all sorted.'

'Er... thanks.'

'Happy to help.' He smiled and the ache in her heart pinched a little tighter.

He was dressed in jeans and his green sports hoodie, his hair was damp and his skin fresh. It was as though he'd had twelve hours' uninterrupted sleep, not a fitful few minutes. He must have gone down to his flat to shower and change.

She closed the bedroom door so she could get dressed in privacy. She was about to unearth her leggings, when she remembered she was off to her brother's later today to spend Christmas with her family. She chose smart jeans and a red wrap top instead – another purchase from her shopping trip with Harper – adding some much-needed colour to her wardrobe.

'Very festive,' Lucas said, as she came into the lounge.

He was smiling, but she suspected he felt as awkward as she did. She hadn't noticed it before as she'd been too preoccupied with her own troubles, but he wasn't his usual attentive self. He looked uncomfortable and was keeping his distance. Was he worried about freaking her out after her encounter with Stephen last night? Or maybe he was regretting telling her he loved her? A far more likely scenario. He'd blurted out the words in the heat of the moment. His brain had been distorted from heightened adrenaline and fear, but sanity had returned this morning, and he was retreating at a rapid rate.

A knock on the door startled them both – especially when Fred started barking and raced into the hallway.

'It won't be Stephen,' Lucas said, trying to cover his uncertainty. 'He wouldn't be that stupid.'

'Maybe it's the landlord checking I received his letter?'

'Stay here; I'll find out who it is.' Lucas disappeared into the hallway, leaving Sarah feeling like her carefully constructed world was crumbling around her.

Any fears it was an unwelcome visitor vanished when she heard excited voices in the hallway. With Fred jumping at their heels, Max and Elliot raced into the lounge, and Sarah was nearly knocked off her feet as they bundled into her. She hugged them and breathed in their chocolatey scent.

'Merry Christmas!' they shouted, bouncing up and down and making her laugh. It was enough to lift her spirits.

'Merry Christmas,' she said, and kissed them both. 'This is a nice surprise.'

'We came to fetch Uncle Lucas.' Max wiped his cheek where she'd kissed him. 'He's spending Christmas with us.'

'Are you coming too?' Elliot looked up at her, wide-eyed and adorably cute.

'I'm spending Christmas with my family,' she said, smoothing back his hair. 'But I have got you both presents.

I'll give them to you before you leave. They're not to be opened before Christmas Day, okay?'

Max nodded. 'Okay. We got you a gift too.'

Sarah was taken aback. 'You did?'

'We made it,' Elliot said excitedly. 'It's a tree.'

'Don't tell her!' Max shoved his younger brother. 'It's supposed to be a surprise.'

Sarah laughed. 'A tree? Will it fit in my flat?'

'It's a small tree.' Max pointed to her fireplace. 'To go on your thingy.'

'My mantelpiece?'

He nodded. 'So the robins can perch on it.'

'Oh, that's lovely. Thank you.' She hugged them again.

'I'll fetch it.' Elliot went racing into the hallway. 'Muuuummy!'

Elliot reappeared moments later carrying a wrapped gift, followed by Lucas and Harper.

Lucas's sister was wearing a cream sparkly jumper and heeled boots. With her make-up and nails done, she looked confident and gorgeous.

'Here it is!' Elliot handed her the mini tree modelled in plasticine.

'Aw, thank you. I love it. Can you put it up for me?'

He ran over to the fireplace, joined by his brother.

'Lucas told me what happened last night,' Harper said, coming over and hugging her. 'How awful. I'm glad that S.O.B. has been arrested.'

'Who's been arrested?' Max looked shocked.

'Oh, no one important, darling. Just a nasty man Sarah works with. Carry on with what you're doing.' Harper rubbed Sarah's shoulder. 'How you holding up? You doing okay?'

'I'm not sure.' Sarah gave a half-shrug. 'I've no idea what the fallout will be, but I'm glad it's over. I've resigned myself to looking for another job. Knowing Stephen, he'll manage to persuade the board of directors of his innocence. There's no way I can stay if he continues working there.'

'Don't rush into any decisions,' Lucas said, lifting Elliot so he could reach the mantelpiece. 'If the charges stick then he won't keep his job. The hospital wouldn't want the bad publicity, and with Tyler's video evidence I can't see any court dismissing the charges. At the very least they'll suspend him in the short term, pending the investigation.'

'Maybe.' Sarah hoped he was right. She really didn't want to leave her job.

Harper dropped onto the sofa and patted the seat next to her. 'What did the police say when you told them what's been happening?'

'Not much.' Sarah joined Harper on the sofa. 'They took down all the details and said there'd be an investigation. It helps that Mrs Kelsey downstairs can corroborate Stephen turning up here last week. There's a record of the phone call to Lucas, and hopefully she'll cooperate with the police.'

'Diana might be difficult, but she has a strong sense of justice,' Lucas said, moving Elliot away from the lit candles. 'She won't want Stephen getting away with this.'

'I hope you're right.' Sarah watched the boys place the robins either side of the tree.

'Done!' Max stood back to admire their work. 'Do you like it?'

Sarah smiled. 'I love it. Thank you. The robins look very at home there.'

Lucas ruffled Elliot's hair. 'Clever kids.' He pulled them in for a hug and Sarah's insides turned to mush. He was such a good uncle.

Harper squeezed Sarah's hand. 'I hope it was all right us turning up like this?'

'Of course, it's lovely to see you.' Sarah lowered her voice so the boys wouldn't hear. 'Did Lucas tell you about Fred?'

'He messaged me this morning,' Harper whispered back, checking Max and Elliot weren't listening in. 'That's partly why we've come over.' She turned to her sons. 'Boys, I need a private moment with Sarah.'

'That's my cue.' Lucas ushered them into the kitchen. 'Be good and you might get Oreos.'

Harper waited until the door had closed before turning back to Sarah. 'How would you feel about us taking Fred?'

Sarah was shocked. She certainly hadn't seen that coming. 'Goodness… is that something you want? I mean, I'd hate for you to think you had to take him to help me out. I'm sure I can get him rehomed elsewhere.'

Harper shook her head, making her earrings sway. 'I promise that's not why I'm offering to take him. Things have been rotten for the boys lately, and I feel guilty about that. Paul and I have behaved shamefully, but we've had a breakthrough at counselling this week, and he's agreed to let me stay in the house until the boys start secondary school.'

'Thank goodness for that.'

'It's a relief, I can tell you.' Harper picked up one of Fred's squeaky toys from the floor. 'They miss their dad, dreadfully, but I think having a dog will really help them. It'll restore the balance; we'll be a family of four again. They adore Fred – he's all they talk about.' She checked the door was still closed. 'I haven't said anything in case you didn't think it was a good idea, but if you're willing, then we'd love to have him. You'd be doing us a favour.'

Sarah swallowed past the lump in her throat. 'I'd love for you to take him.'

Harper seemed to hold her breath. 'Are you sure?'

'Absolutely. I can't think of a better home for him.' She reached forwards and hugged Harper, mainly so her anguish would be hidden from view. It was the perfect solution, however much it hurt.

'And it's not like you won't see him,' Harper said, hugging her hard. 'Aside from my brother's feelings for you, we're friends now. You're stuck with me. Sorry about that.'

Sarah laughed, and tried to ignore the comment about Lucas. 'Lucky me.'

Harper drew back. 'Shall we tell the boys?'

Sarah nodded. This was the best possible outcome: Fred was getting his forever home. She should be pleased. She *was* pleased; she was just a little bit heartbroken too.

'Boys! Get in here!' Harper let out a loud whistle.

The kitchen door opened with a bang and two blonde heads appeared. They came rushing into the lounge, traces of chocolate around their mouths.

'I have a Christmas surprise for you.' Harper stood up. 'We're going to be Fred's new family.'

Max froze. 'For real?'

'But he's Sarah's dog.' Elliot looked at Sarah with a worried expression.

Sarah knew she had to be convincing. 'I can't keep him, sadly. I'm not supposed to have a pet here. I only took him in because he was homeless and needed a temporary home. I've been looking for somewhere he can live permanently, and your mum thinks he'd fit well with your family. What do you think? Would you like to adopt Fred?'

Max fist-pumped the air. 'Yes!'

Elliot copied his brother. 'I would too!'

What followed was a chaos of crying and cuddling, with children and adults alike hugging and kissing, and poor Fred looking utterly confused as so many people fussed over him.

Lucas stood in the kitchen doorway, his sad smile a reflection of his understanding. He'd know Sarah's heart was breaking. Giving away Fred wasn't what she wanted. But he'd also know rehoming him to a loving family who would adore him was the next best solution.

Harper clapped her hands. 'Right, we've interrupted Sarah's Christmas Eve enough. Let's get Fred's things packed into the car and then we'll take him for a walk around the block before the journey home.' Harper caught Sarah's arm. 'I assume it's okay to take his things? Sorry, I should've checked first.'

Sarah waved away her concerns. 'Of course, the stuff's no use to me.'

Besides, she didn't need the reminder. The loss was going to be tough enough without seeing his lead or empty bed lying on the floor.

'I should warn you, he's supposed to sleep in his own bed, but he has a habit of climbing onto mine in the middle of the night when he thinks I'm asleep.'

'I would love that!' Max hugged Fred.

Elliot jumped about. 'Me too! He can sleep on my bed.'

'Well, not mine,' Harper said, rolling her eyes. 'Anything else I should know about?'

Sarah shook her head. 'I'll message you if I think of anything. He's an angel, really. No trouble at all. The perfect family dog.' She clenched her jaw so she wouldn't cry. 'Remember to give him lots of cuddles.'

'And treats,' Elliot said, as Fred licked his fingers.

'Thank you for taking care of him, boys.' Sarah turned to Harper and lowered her voice. 'I don't think I can cope saying goodbye to him, so just take him. Leave as if you were coming back. I can't deal with anything more today.'

'I get it.' Harper hugged Sarah tightly. 'You come over soon, okay? Don't be a stranger.'

Sarah stayed behind in the flat while Lucas helped Harper and the boys collect Fred's things together and load up the car. They left in a flurry of laughter and shouts of 'Merry Christmas!' and thanking her for their presents. It was chaos, accompanied by barking, dropping toys and bumping into furniture.

The real killer was when Fred paused by the front door and looked back at her. It was like he knew, and Sarah felt her heart split in two.

'Bye bye, Fred. I love you,' she whispered, turning away so he wouldn't see her cry. This was what she'd tried so hard to avoid. The torment of being left. Again. Her heart wasn't strong enough to cope.

It was only when she heard the door shut and the flat descend into a deathly silence that she sank to her knees and buried her face in the sofa cushions.

Having indulged in another good cry, she got up and went into the bathroom to wash her face. She couldn't show up at her brother's in such a state; she needed to pull herself together. Reapplying her tinted moisturiser, she decided to focus on packing an overnight bag as a way of stopping herself from dwelling.

It wasn't just saying goodbye to Fred that hurt; she was upset about the situation with Lucas too. He'd barely been able to look at her this morning, and he'd left without so much as a peck on the cheek.

'Merry Christmas to you too,' she said mournfully, stuffing her pyjamas into her travel bag.

A knock on the door surprised her – not least because it wasn't immediately followed by barking. The silence was going to take some getting used to.

Pausing when she reached the door, she realised with no Fred or Lucas to protect her, she needed to be more cautious. She'd buy a chain after Christmas. And maybe get a spyhole fitted. She'd definitely be requesting additional security for the main door downstairs. 'Who is it?'

'It's me.' The sound of Lucas's voice made her nerves twitch.

'Forget something?' she asked, opening the door.

He looked sheepish. 'I didn't want to say goodbye with an audience. They're walking Fred around the block. Can I come in?'

'Sure.' She went through to the lounge. 'Quite the morning, huh?'

'Exhausting.' He didn't look exhausted; he looked amazing. 'How y'doing?'

She folded her arms across her chest, needing a barrier. 'It's a lot to process. I'm mostly relieved, but also a little raw.'

'Understandable.' He hesitated. 'Did I do the right thing telling Harper about Fred?'

'Absolutely. It's the perfect outcome.'

He reached out and touched her arm as if he didn't believe her, but admired her fortitude. 'I hated the idea of leaving on Tuesday without things being resolved for you.'

'And now they have been. Stephen's been charged, and Fred has a new home. It's all good. You can leave with a clear conscience. I'll be fine.' She didn't want him feeling bad for her; he'd helped her enough.

'Will you?' His eyes softened. 'I'm not sure I will be. Did you hear me last night? I love you.'

Okay, so they were going there. She tried to rally her inner strength, what was left of it, anyhow. 'I wasn't certain that's what you'd said.'

'Surely you already knew?' He seemed embarrassed, which was unlike him. He was normally so confident about everything.

'Why would I? It came out of the blue.'

'Really?' He ran a hand through his wavy hair and let out a breath. 'I know we've been play-acting these last few weeks, but you must've felt something building between us. You said as much last night.'

'And that's true, but I don't see how that changes anything.' She sounded a bit harsh, and she wished she could moderate her tone, but she felt on the back foot, thrown by his confession.

'Admitting I love you doesn't change anything?'

She stepped away from him. 'How can it? You're leaving. And I'm still not ready to get involved with anyone.' She was feeling warm. Too warm. Was the heating playing up?

'I don't believe that. I think you're just scared.'

'I'm also practical.' She flexed her fingers, trying to hide the shake in them. 'You'll be on the other side of the world doing a full-on job. There's no way this could work, even if we wanted it to.'

256

He paused. 'What if I stayed in the UK?'

Was he serious? 'Don't be daft.' She wanted to escape somewhere, but her flat was too small to hide anywhere.

'Why's it daft? I love you.' Why did he have to keep saying that? 'My sister and nephews live here. I've enjoyed working here. I'm at a turning point in my life, and about to embark on another adventure. Why not do that here in the UK?'

'That's… crazy. You have a job lined up.' She picked up a discarded cushion from the floor.

He edged towards her, a pleading expression on his far-too-handsome face. 'A job I can do anywhere. They have plenty of medical roles advertised over here.'

She moved behind the sofa. 'But your life is over there, in the States.'

'My life's where I want it to be, and I want it to be with you.'

Oh, heavens. She plumped up the cushion, fluffing it so hard she feared it might split. 'You cannot possibly move country because of me.'

'Why not?'

'Why not? Because… it's… it's…' She threw her hands in the air, forgetting she was holding the cushion and it flew across the room, knocking over one of the candles.

'Crazy? Yeah, so you said.' He went over and righted the candle. 'It's not crazy to me. I'm thirty-five years old and I've never loved anyone as much as I love you. So much so, I'm prepared to take a huge leap of faith and settle here to give us a fighting chance.'

She scanned the rug for spilt candle wax. It seemed odd to be concerned about furnishings, but focusing on normality was all she had as a defence – like passengers collecting their luggage before exiting a burning plane, reverting to habit as a coping strategy.

'It's taken me by surprise too,' he said, watching her fussing with the furnishings. 'I didn't see it coming, I'll admit that. And I know it's a gamble, but it's one I'm prepared to take.'

'Well, I'm not.' She fanned her face; it was definitely too hot in here. 'Lucas, you're asking too much of me. I've barely come to terms with celebrating Christmas, let alone getting involved with anyone, and you expect me to jump all in.'

'Not straight away. I get that you need time. I can wait.'

'And supposing it doesn't work out? You've given up everything on a whim. How could I live with myself knowing you stayed because of me and then we split up?'

'I'm not staying because of you,' he said, moving towards her. 'I'm staying because of *me*. This is what *I* want. You're the person I want to be with. It's my gamble, not yours. And you're so focused on it not working out – suppose it *does* work out? Suppose we're great together? What if this thing between us grows into something amazing? Isn't that worth the risk?'

'No.' A searing pain shot through her, as if she'd been zapped with electricity.

'No?' Lucas lifted his hands. 'That's it? No. That's all you have to say?'

Seeing the hurt look on his face was awful. He deserved so much better than her, and knowing that was the only thing keeping her on track. He'd be much better off without her messing up his life.

'Lucas, I'm more grateful to you than I can express; you've been amazing. You've helped me so much over these last few weeks. You've given me the push I needed to start living my life again, and I'll always be grateful for that. But this is only the beginning of my recovery. I'm still finding my feet. I can't deal with the pressure of you relocating your life for me; it's too much.' How could she convince him she was doing him a favour? 'This was never real, remember? It was fake dating. Pretend. Things have become blurred because of everything that's happened. It's fooled us into thinking this is something real, when it's not. It can't be.'

'It could be, if you let it. But you're too scared to even try.'

He'd got that right. 'Scared? I'm bloody petrified.'

Both his hands were gripping his hair. 'There's nothing I can do, or say, to change your mind?'

Sarah shook her head. 'It wouldn't be fair on either of us.'

'Right.' His jaw twitched. 'Okay then. Thanks for letting me know where I stand. Good to know.' He headed into the hallway. 'Merry Christmas, Sarah. I hope you have a fun time with your family. Take care.' The door slammed behind him, making the mirror on the wall rattle.

The flat descended into silence, and once again Sarah found herself collapsed in a heap on the rug and crying. It was all too much. She had to protect herself. If this was how she was after a few weeks with Lucas in her life, what would she be like if she let herself fall in love with him? She'd never recover.

Using the coffee table to steady herself, she noticed a small wrapped gift with her name written on the side. Ripping away the paper, she discovered a bottle of the perfume she'd sampled the other day. The one Lucas had said suited her.

There was a note attached.

I tracked down the perfume you liked.
You deserve the world, Sarah.
Love always, Lucas x

And she'd thought she was done crying.

Chapter Eighteen

Monday, 26th December

It was early evening by the time Lucas arrived back from his sister's house, having spent an exhausting couple of days entertaining the boys and playing with Fred – who had adapted to his new home surprisingly quickly. It was reassuring to see his nephews smiling and running around the garden, getting muddy and squealing with delight without a care in the world. Fred's presence seemed to have had a positive impact on his sister too. Harper pretended to be infuriated by the dog's mischievous antics, but Lucas could tell she secretly loved it. Fred matched her energy. He was a welcome distraction and just what the family needed. Lucas was sad to be leaving it all behind.

Tired from a lack of sleep, and having drunk far more wine than was good for him, he exited the cab and paused to look up at Sarah's window, before heading down to say a final goodbye to Mrs Kelsey.

He regretted the ways things had ended with Sarah on Saturday. He needed to make amends before leaving tomorrow.

Mrs Kelsey answered the door in her usual gruff manner and ushered him inside, sporting a pair of new floral slippers. 'And close the door behind you; I'm not paying to heat the entire street,' she said, shuffling down the hallway. 'Make yourself useful and put the kettle on; I'm parched.'

With a rueful smile, he headed into the kitchen, glad to note gleaming work surfaces and a lack of washing-up. She obviously hadn't kicked the help out as yet. 'How was your Christmas, Diana?'

'Started out terribly. Ended a bit better.' She lowered herself into the armchair and reached for the Quality Street. She had chocolate stains down the front of her red kaftan. 'Both my kids phoned last night for a chat. Can't tell you how surprised I was. I'd only spoken to them in the week. They don't normally call so often.'

Lucas opened the fridge door, glad to see plenty of food staring back at him. 'Nice that they did.'

'I suppose. My daughter, Keeley, is planning to visit next month.'

Lucas stuck his head around the lounge door. 'That's great news. You must be thrilled?'

'No need to rub it in. You were right. They needed to know about my health problems. They told me off for not telling them I was struggling.' She pulled a face. 'Where's my tea – you gone to China to fetch it?'

With an eyeroll, he returned to the kitchen. 'Coming right up.'

As Lucas finished making the tea, he read through the chart attached to the fridge door, listing all the times her liaison worker, Kath, would be visiting this week. He could imagine Diana's disgruntlement at being checked up on so often. Hopefully, she'd get used to it. It was a weight off his mind knowing she had a support package in place.

'Why did yesterday start off badly?' he asked, returning to the lounge with her cup of tea. He hoped the reduction in the smell of cigarette smoke meant she was cutting back.

'Nurse Ratched showed up and dragged me off to the local church hall for lunch.' Diana grimaced when she sipped her tea. 'Not enough sugar.'

Lucas fetched the sugar. 'I assume you're referring to Kath?'

'Who else?'

'Why was being taken out for lunch so bad? It sounds great.'

She pursed her lips. 'Sitting around with a load of old cronies wearing stupid hats is not my idea of fun.'

He spooned in some more sugar in her tea. 'Did you have Christmas dinner there?'

'Stop stirring, you'll wear the mug out.' She moved her cup with a tut. 'I'll admit the food was nice. It's been years since I've had Christmas pudding. Didn't get the silver sixpence, mind you.'

He had no idea what that was, but thought better of asking. 'Did you play any games?'

'Scrabble, and a card game called Sevens.'

'Did you win?'

'Course I did.' She looked so indignant he couldn't help smiling.

'So not such a bad day then? Better than spending it alone?'

'Debatable.' Her attempted indifference didn't work on him any more; he could tell she'd had a nice day, despite her grumblings.

He looked around the room, his gaze landing on a selection of puzzle books and a few Christmas cards on the shelf. 'How are you getting on with Kath?'

'She's all right.' Diana sniffed. 'A bit too bouncy for my liking.'

Lucas raised an eyebrow. 'Bouncy?'

'You know, all chirpy and enthusiastic. She's almost as bad as you.'

Lucas grinned. 'That bad, huh? Poor you.' He noticed a fresh prescription on the table and read through the items. 'And what about Doctor Khan? How did you get on with him when he called around this morning?'

'He'll do. At least his hands are warm.' High praise indeed. 'He'll probably bugger off when he's had enough too.'

Lucas turned to her. 'I'm not leaving because of you, Diana.' If he had his way, he'd be staying for good.

'So you say.' She ate another chocolate. 'Didn't she want you, then?'

He frowned. 'Who?'

Diana pointed upwards. 'The woman upstairs? The do-gooder.'

'Ah, you mean Sarah.' Lucas lowered his gaze. 'No, she didn't want me.'

Diana wiped her chocolatey fingers down her front. 'Even after you saved her from that stalker fella?'

'I didn't do much,' he said, with a shrug. 'Not really.'

Diana slurped her tea. 'Her loss.'

Lucas smiled, despite his sadness. 'Is that a compliment?'

'Don't let it go to your head.' She pushed herself to her feet. 'Right, bugger off then. I don't want none of your sentimental slush. You've done your job; you can go now.'

He held out his hand. 'It's been a pleasure getting to know you, Diana.'

She looked in disgust at his hand. 'Liar.'

No one could say he hadn't tried.

With a sigh, he headed for the hallway. 'You take care of yourself. And do what Doctor Khan tells you, okay?'

'Still bossing me around,' she mumbled, loud enough to ensure he heard. He'd almost reached the door when she added, 'I suppose I should thank you for... well, you know.'

He turned to her. 'Interfering?'

'Too bloody right. Now go find someone else to annoy. Preferably in another country.' She shut the door, although not before winking at him.

Figuring that was as much as he was going to get, he left Mrs Kelsey's apartment and headed up the steps to say goodbye to his other feisty neighbour.

Nerves were racing through him as he neared her apartment, and he braced himself for another emotionally draining encounter. It had to be done; he'd hate himself if he didn't make things right with Sarah before he left.

The climb felt heavy on his legs and he had to swallow hard to stop the tears surfacing. This would be the last time he'd come up here. The last time he'd knock on her door, and the last time he'd feel his pulse quicken when she opened the door and he saw her standing there.

Now he was here, it was even harder than he'd imagined. He tried for a smile when she opened the door, but she looked drawn and tired.

Worse, she visibly flinched when she saw it was him, and his already shattered heart splintered into a million pieces.

'Can I come in?' he asked, his cracked voice betraying him. He'd wanted to appear so composed, and he was failing at the first test. 'I don't want to leave things how they ended on Saturday.'

She stood back to allow him inside. She was dressed for bed, her hair loose and damp, and she tightened her dressing robe self-consciously around her. 'How was your Christmas?'

'Great, thanks.' He followed her into the lounge. 'The boys loved their presents. Thanks for doing that – it was thoughtful of you.' He'd nearly blubbed when they'd opened their craft kits and started professing how much they loved Sarah. He knew the feeling.

She headed for the armchair. 'How's Fred settling in?'

'It's like he's always been there. He has them running around after him, especially Harper. She's still finding things difficult with Paul, but she's in a much better place than she was.' He hesitated when they reached the couch, not sure what to do with himself. Should he sit? Stay standing?

Sarah snatched a tissue from the side table and dabbed her nose. 'I'm relieved he's okay.'

'I think having a dog will be good for Harper,' he said, wanting to hug her, but knowing it was off-limits. 'Fred needs his routine, and Harper needs a purpose in life to help her get back on track. It was funny to see her laughing when Fred stole one of Elliot's mini sausages from his plate. You know the ones I mean, wrapped in bacon?'

Sarah smiled. 'Pigs in blankets.'

'That's them. Weird, but strangely appetising.'

'It's nice to know things are working out.' She perched on the edge of the armchair and gestured to the couch. 'You can sit down.'

'Thanks.' The apartment seemed odd without Fred's presence. It was too quiet, almost as if the energy had been sucked out of it. 'How was Christmas with your family?'

'Okay,' she said, with a shrug. 'A bit awkward to start with. Everyone was walking on eggshells and not sure how to behave around me, but after a few glasses of bubbly everyone relaxed. It was a nice day. Draining, but nice.'

'Have you heard from the police?'

'Nothing as yet, but it's a bank holiday, so it's not surprising.'

He watched her face, depressed by the sadness etched on it. 'Will you let me know the outcome?'

'Of course.' She fiddled with the tie of her dressing robe. 'What time is your flight tomorrow?'

It was an unwelcome reminder he was leaving. 'Early afternoon. My sister's picking me up at ten.'

'Right.' An awkward pause followed. 'All packed?'

'Not even started. Last-minute job for the morning.' He tried for a self-deprecating shrug, but he could see he was making her uncomfortable. He needed to bite the bullet and do what he'd come for. 'I wanted to say goodbye properly... but also apologise for how I behaved on Saturday. I was out of line, and I'm really sorry.'

Her eyes lowered to her lap. 'It's fine.'

'No, it's not. It was only later that night when I was replaying everything in my head I realised how unfair I'd been to you. You never wanted a relationship, you made that crystal clear from day one, and yet it didn't stop me pursuing you. I told you I understood why you didn't want to get involved, and I was happy staying friends, but then I acted the opposite.'

She looked up. 'To be fair, I kissed you first.'

'Yeah, but only to deter a creepy bloke from stalking you. Not because you were into me. I knew that, and yet it didn't stop me pestering you.'

She looked alarmed. 'You never pestered me. What on earth makes you think that?'

'Sure I did. That's exactly what I was doing on Saturday. I was pressurising you into agreeing to something you didn't want to do, and not listening properly when you said no. I'm no better than Stephen.'

'You're nothing like Stephen.' Her cheeks flushed red as she clutched the arm of the chair. 'How can you even think that?'

'I'm not so sure.' He rubbed the back of his neck. 'Instead of accepting your decision, I focused on what *I* wanted instead. I was so consumed by my own feelings, I ignored yours. That's exactly what Stephen did. It's what men have been doing to women throughout history, not listening to what they truly want. We talk about equality and respect, and yet we still act like entitled Neanderthals and think we can win over a woman by ignoring her wishes, like she's something to be conquered. A game to be won.'

Sarah shook her head. 'You're being too harsh on yourself.'

'Am I? Isn't that how your ex behaved? Didn't you say he only wanted you when he thought he couldn't have you? And when you relented, he returned to being mean to you.'

Sarah flinched.

'Sorry, I'm making things worse. That wasn't my intention.' He rubbed his face. 'My point is, you've had three men in succession who haven't listened to your wishes, or respected your decisions, and I'm mortified that I'm one of them. You deserve so much better, Sarah. And if I've added to your aversion towards men and relationships then I'm truly sorry. I'll never forgive myself.'

She got up and came over to the couch. 'You need to stop beating yourself up, Lucas. You've done nothing wrong. The opposite, in fact.' She perched beside him, close enough that he could smell her fruity body lotion, but not so close that they were touching. 'You've been an amazing friend and support to me over these last few weeks. I wouldn't have got through all this without you.' Her hand rested on his arm. 'I might be a bit bruised, but I'm not so damaged I can't stick up for myself. There's been nothing coercive about this relationship. Challenging, yes. But only because you had my best interests at heart. You were encouraging me to embrace life again. And you've achieved that. Look around you. I have candles.'

He smiled at her efforts to allay his concerns. 'I still shouldn't have pressurised you on Saturday with all that talk about relocating. It was too much. I get that now. I'm sorry.'

'Stop apologising.' Her hand squeezed his arm. 'It was just a reaction to everything that's happened recently. All that emotion was bound to spill over at some point.' She met his gaze. 'And you make it sound like it was one-sided, like somehow you've been chasing me and it wasn't reciprocated. Well, that's not true. I've enjoyed your company; I've welcomed it. Crikey, I've even invited it.' The colour in her cheeks deepened. 'I'm not going to pretend I haven't fallen for you, Lucas, because I have. And I think that's been evident in my behaviour. You haven't misread the signals. I've been flirting with you just as much as you've been flirting with me. And it's been great. So great.' She smiled shyly. 'This is not a reflection on your behaviour. You've been the perfect gentleman at all times. Please never think otherwise.'

He felt the tears welling up. 'You're just saying that because you're a nice person.'

'You know me better than that. Have I ever held back from telling you the truth?'

He thought for a moment. 'I guess not.'

'Trust me, if you'd behaved like a dick, I'd have told you. You haven't. My reaction on Saturday was entirely down to my own hang-ups and my unwillingness to start dating again. Nothing more. Okay?'

He wanted to believe her. 'Okay.'

'I'm going to miss you so much,' she said, her voice quivering. 'You have no idea how much I wish things were different. *You deserve the world*, you wrote on my gift card. Well, you do too, Lucas Moore. You're the best man I've ever known.' She blinked and a tear trickled down her cheek. 'It's just not meant to be.'

'Another time and place, huh?'

'We're the modern-day Rick and Ilsa. *Casablanca* has nothing on us.' And then her eyes flickered down to his mouth, and he felt the air leave his lungs.

All her defensiveness disappeared, and she was back to being the Sarah he knew, looking at him with wanting and heat, as if he was the answer to her prayers, and he wanted so much to be that. If only she'd let him, he was up for the challenge; he wouldn't stop trying to make her happy until his last breath. But like she said, it wasn't meant to be, and he was heartbroken.

She cleared her throat, as if coming to her senses. '"You'd better hurry, or you'll miss that plane",' she said, her attempt at an American accent woeful. 'I think that was Ilsa's last line to Rick in the film… Apt, really.'

He took her hand and held it to his chest. 'Do me a favour?'

'What's that?'

'Allow yourself to be happy again. When the time's right and someone comes along who deserves you, find the courage to let them love you.'

She met his eyes. 'I'll try.'

'Please. Because I'd hate for you to miss out on something wonderful.'

Nodding, she got up and rushed into the hallway, waiting until he'd joined her by the front door. 'Good luck in Houston.'

'Thanks.' He hugged her close, holding the moment for as long as he could, and trying to commit everything about her to memory. Her smell, the feel of her soft skin against his cheek, the way her long hair brushed his face. He never wanted to forget a single thing.

She hugged him just as tightly.

'Take care, honey,' he whispered, escaping out the door before he blubbed and embarrassed himself further.

I love you.

Chapter Nineteen

To say Sarah had woken up out of sorts would imply she'd actually been asleep. Something had been niggling at her all night, keeping her awake and annoying the hell out of her. As to what was wrong, she had no idea. Maybe she was coming down with a cold?

It was also eerily quiet in the flat. She missed Fred. Lucas too, and he hadn't even left yet. She'd always relished the peace and quiet; coming home from a busy day and shutting the door on the world had been a relief, a pleasure even. But it no longer provided her with any comfort. Silence hung in the air like the grey fog outside, hovering above the wet murky pavements, and making the view from her flat window mournful and depressing.

Despite the miserable weather, she kept gravitating towards the window, waiting and watching for Lucas to leave, and hoping the sick feeling in her stomach would lift when he did. While he remained downstairs, she couldn't shake him off. He was like a virus – while he was still in the vicinity, she was susceptible to another infection.

Once he was gone and back home in the States, she could return to how things were before. Safe. Quiet. Calm. Organised. She'd settle into her routine, focus on her career and regain control. Lucas had disrupted her equilibrium, that was all. She needed to recover her stability.

If she hadn't been staring morosely out of the window, she wouldn't have spotted two women climbing off a bright orange Lambretta scooter. It was only when they removed their crash helmets and shook out their hair that she realised it was Georgia and Jafrina. She couldn't have been more shocked if Fred had been riding the bike.

Pushing open the window, she waved at them as they searched the road, no doubt looking for her flat. 'Hey, up here!'

Georgia spotted her and shoved Jafrina, before pointing up to the window and waving.

Sarah beckoned them up and ran to the door to wait for them.

She heard heavy footsteps approaching and Georgia swearing about the number of steps. 'Bloody hell, I feel like I've climbed Mount Everest,' she said, panting as she reached the top. 'Haven't they heard of lifts?'

'In a Victorian building?' Sarah rolled her eyes. 'Where's Jafrina?'

'She was right behind me.' Georgia turned and yelled down the stairs. 'Jafrina!'

Jafrina appeared a few seconds later. 'Sorry, I stopped to say goodbye to Lucas. He's heading off to the airport.'

Sarah inwardly cursed. 'Come in and make yourself at home,' she said, ushering them inside. 'Excuse me a moment.' She ran over to the window, arriving in time to watch Lucas carrying his two suitcases down the steps.

Harper had pulled up in the road and had climbed out to help him. He was wearing a blue hoodie and jeans. He might have worn his favourite green hoodie if she hadn't pinched it. He'd left it here the other day, and instead of returning it, she'd hung on to it. Why she'd put it on this morning, she had no idea. Especially as she hadn't washed it yet. Subjecting herself to his scent couldn't be good for her efforts to restore her equilibrium; it just prolonged the agony. And yet despite this reasoning she couldn't bring herself to take it off.

It was only after he'd loaded the cases into the boot and walked around to the passenger door that he looked up at her window. He did a double take when he saw her staring at him, no doubt surprised to find her palms pressed against the glass, like a child staring through a confectioner's window. For a long moment, they just stared at each other.

Eventually, his face broke into a smile, but it wasn't a happy one. He looked incredibly forlorn.

'Goodbye,' he mouthed, blowing her a kiss, before disappearing inside the car.

Sarah dropped her forehead against the glass as she watched them drive away, the sick feeling in her stomach increasing. So much for feeling relieved. The lump in her throat was so acute it felt like she had tonsillitis.

'Why aren't you going with him to the airport?' Jafrina asked, snapping Sarah from her thoughts. She'd almost forgotten Georgia and Jafrina were in the room.

'And why's he going to the airport anyway?' Georgia sounded confused.

'His visit's over; he's returning to the States.' Sarah came away from the window. 'This is a nice surprise, I wasn't expecting you. And certainly not on a scooter.'

'It's my brother's,' Georgia said, slumping onto the sofa. 'I borrow it when he's away.'

Jafrina joined Georgia on the sofa, daintily lowering herself onto it, in contrast to her friend, who was sprawled out taking up most of the space. 'After what happened on Friday, we wanted to check you were okay.'

'That's kind of you.' Sarah went over to sit on the armchair. 'I'm doing okay, thanks. Dreading going into work tomorrow in case Stephen's there.'

'Oh, he won't be. He's been removed from his position.' Georgia made a slicing motion across her neck. 'He's had the chop.'

Sarah was shocked. 'He has? How do you know?'

'Tyler told me. He knows one of the board of directors, a solicitor who specialises in employment law. She insisted Stephen was dismissed with immediate effect.'

Sarah couldn't believe what she was hearing. 'How did she know Stephen had been arrested? I didn't think anything would happen over the Christmas break.'

Georgia kicked off her boots and curled her feet under her. 'Tyler emailed her on Saturday with a signed petition from dozens of staff members stating that unless Stephen was sacked they'd all resign. Once word got out about what'd happened, it was evident whose side people were on. I told you people liked you. You're very popular among the staff team; no one wanted you to leave.'

Sarah rubbed her temples, trying to compute what Georgia was saying. 'I can't believe it. Stephen's really not going to be there any more?'

'Nope, you can relax.' Georgia's expression turned inquisitive. 'So, returning to the issue of Lucas... I sense gossip... is he going back to the US for good?'

Sarah nodded. 'He starts a new job in Houston next week.'

Georgia flicked her messy hair, nearly catching Jafrina in the eye. 'But I thought you were an item now? I'm confused.'

Truth time. Sarah knew she had to come clean. 'We were never an item.'

'Excuse me, but you most certainly were an item.' Georgia's expression turned suggestive. 'Who're you trying to kid?'

'It was make-believe. The truth is, we pretended to be a couple in the hope it would deter Stephen from harassing me. Lucas thought Stephen might back off if he thought I already had a boyfriend.'

Georgia shook her head. 'Sorry, don't believe it.'

Sarah felt horribly guilty for deceiving her friends. 'I'm really sorry I lied to you, but I didn't want anyone to know I was having problems with Stephen.'

'No, I mean I don't believe it.' Georgia waved her hand. 'As in, I don't believe you were pretending.'

'Well, we were. Fake dating, I think it's called.' Sarah gave a shrug.

'Bollocks. There was nothing fake about the way you two looked at each other Friday night. Nobody's that good an actor. Even Dame Judi Dench couldn't have pulled that one off. Say what you like, but I know when two people are into each other, and you two have more chemistry than Marie Curie discovering radioactivity.'

Jafrina nodded. 'She has a point.'

Sarah shook her head. 'I'm not saying we didn't like each other; we became good friends. But it wasn't a real relationship.'

Georgia pouted. 'It looked real to me.'

'And me.' Jafrina nodded in agreement. 'I've never seen a man look at a woman the way Lucas looked at you. Pretending or otherwise, he's in love with you, Sarah. I'm certain of it.'

Sarah fiddled self-consciously with the cuffs of Lucas's hoodie. 'He'll get over it.'

Georgia exchanged a look with Jafrina. 'So he *is* in love with you? He told you that?'

'It doesn't matter any more.' Sarah pulled the sleeves down over her hands and hugged herself. 'His life is in the US and mine's over here.'

Jafrina edged forwards. 'One of you could always move.'

Sarah shook her head. 'I told him I didn't want him to move – it's too much.'

Georgia sat upright. 'You mean, he actually offered to move?'

Sarah shifted uncomfortably. 'He suggested staying here in the UK so we could... you know, date... but I told him that was ridiculous.'

Georgia slapped her forehead. 'Let me get this straight. He fancies you; that much is obvious, he pretended to date you to protect you from Stephen, he rushed to your aid on Friday night at the ball, he told you he loved you and he wanted to relocate to be with you... and you told him he was ridiculous? Bloody hell, that's harsh, Sarah. And that's coming from someone who eats men for lunch.'

Sarah flinched; she hadn't thought of it like that.

'How do you feel about *him*?' Jafrina's tone was kinder than Georgia's.

'I've no idea,' Sarah answered honestly, slumping back in the chair. 'Anyway, it's not relevant. I've no intention of getting involved with anyone, so what does it matter how I feel?'

Jafrina stood and brushed the creases from her top. 'It matters, because falling in love doesn't happen every day. I get why you've steered clear of relationships; it was understandable, and dating for the sake of it would be pointless, I agree. But turning away from a real chance of happiness on nothing more than principle is self-sabotage… and that's something you might come to deeply regret.' She came over and knelt next to Sarah. 'You need to be sure you're rejecting Lucas because he's not the right man for you, and not because you think you're not ready to start dating again. So I'll ask the question again: how do you feel about him?' Her hand rested on Sarah's arm. 'Do you like him?'

Well, that was a no-brainer. 'Of course I do.'

'Does he make you laugh?'

Like no one before. 'Yes.'

Georgia rolled off the sofa and shuffled over on her knees. 'Do you want to remove his clothes with your teeth and lick his—'

Jafrina slapped a hand over Georgia's mouth. 'What she means is… are you physically attracted to him?'

Sarah felt nodding an affirmative was safer than audibly moaning.

Jafrina squeezed Sarah's arm. 'Do you feel happier when he's around?'

'Yes.'

'Do you miss him when you're not with him?'

Sarah's throat was getting lumpier by the second. 'Yes.'

Georgia removed Jafrina's hand from her mouth. 'And what do you feel right at this moment, having just watched him drive away?'

Sarah closed her eyes. 'Sick to my stomach.'

'You see!' Georgia smacked the arm of the chair.

Jafrina shook Sarah's arm, forcing her to open her eyes. 'I hate to break it to you, Sarah. But you're in love with him, too.'

Georgia shoved Jafrina. 'Uh, duh, well of course she is. Any dummy can see that.'

Sarah blinked. 'I am?'

'You are,' they said in unison.

'The question is… what are you going to do about it?' Georgia rested her elbows on the arm of the chair. 'The way I see it, you have two options. Stay here, and slowly shrivel away until you turn into Miss Havisham and become a sad bitter old lady whose only companion is a dead cat—'

It was Jafrina's turn to shove Georgia. 'Or… you become the leading lady in your own romcom and race after him to the airport and tell him you love him and you want him to stay.'

Sarah felt overwhelmed with them both crowding her. She got up and stepped over them. 'Oh, crikey. I don't know what to do.'

Georgia scrabbled to her feet. 'It's easy… Miss Havisham or Julia Roberts?'

Jafrina was up on her feet too. 'Living alone… or living happily ever after?'

Georgia tripped over her boots as she advanced on Sarah. 'Dead cat… or kissing a hottie doctor?'

Jafrina swerved around the coffee table. 'Remaining heartbroken… or seizing the opportunity for love?'

They were backing her across the lounge at a rapid rate, firing interrogation questions at her.

Sarah smacked into the dresser behind. 'Okay… okay, I'll do it!' she said, mostly to end the onslaught. 'Call me an Uber.'

'No need.' Georgia grabbed her hand. 'Your taxi awaits. I'll take you.'

Sarah pulled away. 'Are you mad? I can't go on that thing. And what about Jafrina? How will she get home?'

Jafrina dug out her phone. 'I'll take the Uber; you take the scooter.'

Sarah couldn't think straight. 'I should really think this through – this is a big decision.'

Georgia shoved her feet into her boots. 'You don't have time, woman. HE'S LEAVING NOW!'

'Right, yes. Okay.' Sarah ran towards her bedroom, but skidded to a halt. 'And you're absolutely certain I'm in love with him?'

'YES!' Georgia threw a cushion at her.

'Oh, crikey, I'm really doing this, aren't I?' Sarah ran into the bedroom to fetch her trainers.

When she returned, Jafrina was scrolling through her phone. 'It's Terminal Five you need.'

Sarah grabbed her flat keys. 'Terminal Five. Okay, got it.'

They bundled her out of the flat and down the stairs.

'I'm so proud of you,' Jafrina said when they reached the street. 'This is just what Julia Roberts would do. Now go get him!'

If anyone had told Sarah that morning she'd be perched on the back of a noisy Lambretta, hurtling down the A4, with her eyes streaming, her hair wrapped around her neck and nearly strangling her, and clinging hold of Georgia's midriff for dear life, she'd have called them crazy. Although, no more crazy than realising she was in love with Lucas Moore. How had she been so clueless?

It had to be love, right? Why else would she be enduring thirty minutes of riding down a busy main road with cars splashing up dirty rainwater, lorries rocking them off balance each time they whizzed by, and seeing her life flash before her several times. At this rate, she'd never make it there alive; she'd be squashed under an artic lorry before getting the opportunity to tell Lucas she loved him. Now that she'd realised how she felt, she couldn't snuff it before telling him. How unfair would that be?

Jafrina might have compared this mad dash in pursuit of love as a scene from a romcom, but she doubted Julia Roberts ever had to contend with temporary traffic lights, a climate change protestor glued to the tarmac or having to circle a roundabout three times because of conflicting road signs. Hollywood had clearly never visited the London Borough of Hillingdon.

The final obstacle was discovering the slip road leading up to the drop-off zone was so steep the scooter lost speed and they were in danger of rolling backwards like a bizarre snakes and ladders game and ending up back where they'd started. A warning sign announcing charges for drop-offs at the airport was enough to convince them completing the final section on foot would be in both their best interests.

Bringing the scooter to a halt, Georgia gave Sarah a thumbs up as she climbed off the bike. 'Good luck!' she shouted, struggling to be heard above the deafening shudder of planes taking off above them.

Sarah handed Georgia her crash helmet. 'Thanks for the ride!'

Ignoring the sight of Georgia swerving into the traffic and nearly colliding with an ambulance, Sarah ran up the slope towards the terminal. A run that started out spritely, but gradually slowed to a shuffle as fatigue kicked in, and ending in a walk as the slope increased and her lack of sleep drained her remaining stamina.

By the time she'd reached the entrance, she was soaked through from the rain and boiling hot. If this was a romcom then she'd look like Andie MacDowell in *Four Weddings and a Funeral* when she declares her love for Hugh Grant in the pouring rain. Instead, Sarah suspected she looked more like a survivor from the *Titanic*, shipwrecked and clinging hold of a lifeboat.

Terminal Five was heaving with people. Queues of travellers were snaking their way towards the endless rows of check-in desks. Where to even start?

Shrugging off her jacket and tying it around her middle, she looked up at the flight board, checking for flights to Minneapolis, and trying to remember what Lucas had said about timings.

There was an American Airlines flight leaving at 1:25 p.m. That had to be it.

Sarah raced towards the check-in desks, hopping over abandoned suitcases and swerving around passengers like an Olympic downhill skier. She was a woman on a mission.

There were two long queues for the flight and Sarah scanned both of them, running up and down the lines in search of Lucas, and attracting odd looks from everyone patiently waiting. Her panic levels increased with each face she glanced at and then discarded. Lucas was nowhere to be found. He must have checked in already.

She was too late. He was gone.

Lacing her hands into her hair, Sarah let out an anguished sob. This was not how things were supposed to conclude. Romcoms had happy endings. They worked out. They weren't supposed to end in disappointment.

If only she'd got her act together earlier. But until forty-five minutes ago, she'd had no idea whether her friends were right, or whether she was making a monumental mistake. She'd realised too late she loved Lucas. Talk about rotten timing.

Walking over to a bench, she kicked a metal post, annoyed that her stupid brain had taken so long to figure it out. Why couldn't she have come to this conclusion last night? Or even this morning before he'd left? But no, it was only when she couldn't have him that she'd realised she really, really wanted him. Talk about dumb.

She slumped onto the bench and dropped her head in her hands.

Above her, a loud ding-dong echoed from the speaker on the wall, alerting the travellers to an announcement.

'*We have reports of a missing child. She's ten years old, with long dark hair, and wearing a man's green hoodie. Would Sarah Haynes please head for the information desk to be reunited with her father. Sarah Haynes. Please report to the information desk immediately.*'

Sarah sat up. Was it a coincidence? There was another Sarah Haynes? A child? And then she stared down at Lucas's green hoodie. What were the chances of another Sarah Haynes being in possession of a man's hoodie? They must have got the age details wrong.

Scurrying to her feet, she searched for the information desk, trying to fathom who could be looking for her.

And then she saw him.

Lucas was standing by the information desk with a burly security officer next to him, his suitcases on the ground. Her belly flipped at the sight of him. It spun into cartwheels when he spotted her and smiled. Her happy ending was back on.

Swamped with love and relief, she raced over to him, fully intending to throw herself into his arms and kiss him

– just like they do in romcoms – except an arm swung out in front of her, cutting off her approach.

'Not so fast, lady.' The burly security man stopped her.

'It's okay, this is Sarah… my *daughter*.' Lucas gave her a strained look. 'Sweetie, you found Daddy.'

Sarah ground to a halt. What the heck?

The security man kept his arm out. 'This is your daughter?'

Lucas nodded. 'Uh-huh.'

The man's eyes narrowed. 'Your ten-year-old daughter?'

Lucas shrugged. 'She's big for her age.'

The security man turned to Sarah. 'Do you know this man?'

Sarah wondered what on earth was going on. 'Er… yes.'

'This man told me he'd lost his daughter and asked for an alert to be put out. This was *after* I'd explained that we didn't make announcements for non-emergencies. It was only then he mentioned the missing person was a *child*. So you'll forgive me if I'm a little sceptical.' There was a warning note in the security man's tone.

Sarah tried for a young voice – although shaving twenty-five years off was a tall order. 'That's right… he's my dad.' She glanced at Lucas. 'Hi, *Dad*. I've been looking for you everywhere.'

The security man wasn't fooled. 'You do know I can have you fined for this? Announcements are only permitted for emergencies, like a genuine lost child. She is clearly not your child.'

Lucas looked sheepish. 'No, but it was an emergency. I only said that so you'd help me.'

The security man pinned Lucas with a disgruntled look. 'Mislaying a travelling companion is not an emergency.'

Lucas shook his head. 'I didn't mislay her. I didn't even know she was here until her friend Jafrina messaged me.'

Ah, so that's how he knew she was here. 'I had to stop him getting on his flight, officer. It was vital I reached him in time.'

The security man turned to her. 'And why was that? Was there a medical emergency?' He was clearly running out of patience.

'Er… kind of… it was heart-related.'

'Lord give me strength.' The security man rubbed his chin. 'I should report you for wasting airport resources.'

Lucas grinned at Sarah, softening the anguish of being 'told off' like naughty teenagers. 'Why didn't you want me getting on my flight?'

Sarah knew she had to be brave and admit how she felt – even though a six-foot man mountain was standing in between them looking highly pissed off. 'Because… well, it's come to my attention that… perhaps I *do* love you. No, scrap that. There's nothing "perhaps" about it, I *definitely* love you. I absolutely one hundred per cent… love you.'

The security man flushed red. 'Are you for real, lady? That's your emergency?'

'You don't know what I've been through to get here,' she said, backing up when he glared at her. 'For me, it *is* an emergency. If he'd left, I'd have missed my opportunity.'

Lucas smiled at her. 'You love me?'

'You stay put,' the security man said, blocking Lucas's path. 'I haven't decided what I'm doing with you yet.'

Sarah needed to get in quick in case the security man dragged Lucas away and locked him up. Or worse, forced him to get on his flight. 'So… you know, having admitted how I feel… I was wondering… hoping, maybe… that you might want to stay… you know, here in the UK with me… and not go home to the States.'

Lucas seemed to swallow awkwardly, before turning to the security man. 'I appreciate you might not be the most romantic man in the world, and I'll pay whatever fine you want to administer, but can I please get past so I can kiss my girl, because she's just told me she loves me, and it's kind of a big deal.'

The security man folded his arms. 'I take issue with that. I am very romantic, I'll have you know. You ask my wife.'

Lucas raised his hands. 'My mistake. So as one romantic man to another, can I please get past?'

The security man harrumphed. 'Go on, then. Don't do it again. It's more than my job's worth.'

Lucas rushed forwards and swept Sarah off her feet, spinning her around and making her dizzy. 'Tell me again,' he said, her feet still off the ground. 'I need to hear it.'

She looked into his blue eyes. 'I love you.'

His expression softened. 'And you're sure you want me to stay?'

'More than I've ever wanted anything. Sorry it's taken me so long.'

'That's okay… although you sure cut it fine.' He smiled. One of his loving, cheeky, adorable smiles that made her insides turn to mush. 'Let's go home, honey.' He hugged her close, vanishing any doubts she had. 'By the way, nice hoodie.'

'It belongs to my fake boyfriend.'

'You don't say?' He pulled back to look at her. 'Well, you'd better brace yourself, Sarah Haynes, because there's nothing fake about the way I feel about you. This is the real deal. All that fake stuff was child's play; you won't know what's hit you when we do this for real.'

'Bring it on.' Smiling, Sarah kissed him. And didn't stop kissing him despite the security man clearing his throat several times, and a few people gasping, and even when an electric cart drove past and a man said, 'Get a room, will you. This is a ruddy airport!' She still didn't stop kissing him.

She may never stop kissing him. She had a lot of time to make up for.

Julia Roberts… eat your heart out.

Epilogue

One Year Later

Ignoring frantic shouts from her bridesmaids that if they didn't leave the hotel right at that moment they'd be late, Sarah raced into the bathroom and threw up for the second time that morning. She doubted she was the first bride to be hit by a wave of nausea on her wedding day. Her only real concern was ensuring she didn't throw up on her dress.

Georgia banged on the bathroom door. 'Sarah? You okay in there?'

'All good!' Sarah gripped the basin, waiting for the nausea to pass. 'Nothing to worry about... just a last-minute pee.'

'You're not having second thoughts, are you?' Jafrina's tentative voice was muffled through the closed door.

'Just pre-wedding nerves,' Sarah lied, regretting eating scrambled eggs for breakfast. 'Give me a moment and I'll be out.'

'He will be there,' Georgia said, rattling the door handle. 'I promise. I've already checked with Tyler and Lucas is already at the venue. You can stop worrying.'

'I'm not worrying,' she said, getting to her feet so she could clean her teeth for the umpteenth time. 'I know he'll be there. I trust him.'

Some people might say that fixing her second wedding attempt on Christmas Eve was inviting trouble. Like a bad omen, but Sarah felt it was a necessary risk. One last-ditch attempt to reclaim her love of Christmas. The final step on her road to recovery.

Besides, it was different this time. She was marrying Lucas Moore. A man who had proved himself over the last year to be loyal and trustworthy and unbelievably attentive. Boy, was he attentive. Whether it was sharing household duties, cooking for her, making her late for work by coercing her back to bed or massaging her with fruity body lotion, she'd been thoroughly spoilt. The memories made her blush. Ann Summers had a lot to answer for.

There had been no game-playing with Lucas, no blowing hot and cold, and no withdrawing of affection – even after a fight. And they did fight. But it never felt like anything was at risk. Lucas was a straight shooter. He said what was on his mind, but he never held a grudge. Once an argument was over, it was over, and they were back to snuggling on the sofa. It was a blessing not to spend her days trying to second guess what someone was feeling. Thank goodness she'd come to her senses and hadn't let him board that plane.

Opening the bathroom cabinet door, she smiled when she saw another Post-it note stuck to the inside.

Hey there, future wife. Fancy getting married today?

She'd been finding Post-it notes all morning, stuck to the pillows, the dressing table mirror, even inside the loo seat. When Lucas had gained access to the room to hide them, she had no idea. Each note reassured her of his love, his devotion, and with the promise of being there today – something she already knew. Lucas was a man she could believe in. More importantly, she could believe in herself now. She was a woman in control of her life... Well, mostly. This latest development had shaken her, but she knew deep down everything would turn out okay.

Having reapplied her lipstick, she checked her appearance in the cabinet mirror and exited the bathroom to calls of 'Finally!' and 'Sarah, we need to go!'

The room was in mayhem; her bridal party had certainly left their mark. Discarded shoes created hazards on the plush carpet, make-up paraphernalia stained the dressing table, and hair products obscured the walnut surfaces. The air reeked of clashing perfumes, and the bed was covered in so many items of clothing it masked the large tartan comforter.

Sarah smiled at her bridesmaids, wondering how three identical dresses could look so different. Jafrina looked classy and elegant in her mulberry shift dress. Harper looked sexy and edgy, and Georgia looked positively scandalous – helped by the dress being two sizes too small so it 'emphasised' her cleavage.

Jafrina was holding the four bridal bouquets. 'Are you ready to go?'

'I'm ready.' Sarah slipped her feet into a pair of satin stilettos, the champagne colour a match for her dress.

She'd opted for a knee-length fitted dress, with a lace bodice that hugged her curves. A Highland wedding in December was never going to be warm. And besides, she'd wanted something more sophisticated this time around. Less romantic, and more 'badass', as Georgia had referred to it. Gaining Georgia's approval that she looked 'hot' in the dress was all the incentive she'd needed to choose something less conventional – although she might have opted for something slightly stretchier if she'd known her waistline would be expanding at a rapid rate.

'Sunglasses on,' Georgia instructed, handing each of them a pair of tinted Ray-Bans.

Harper opened the bedroom door. 'Let's go, girls!'

Donning their sunglasses and furry boleros, they exited the bedroom as if they were the Pink Ladies strutting into Rydell High on a mission to take over the school. Several hotel guests did a double take as they sauntered past and exited through the grand foyer, where a huge Christmas tree twinkled away.

The car Sarah had hired was parked out front, waiting for them. She couldn't help smiling when she saw the convertible metallic blue Cadillac, with chrome bumpers, and the hood already down. It was a real statement piece, just as she'd intended.

'I really hope it doesn't rain,' Jafrina said, shivering as they walked towards the car.

'And I hope we don't crash,' Georgia said, peering over the top of her sunglasses.

Sarah opened the driver's door. 'I've passed my test, haven't I?'

'*Yesterday*,' Georgia said pointedly, rolling her heavily made-up eyes. 'And in a Ford Focus, not a bleedin' space wagon. And not in the Highlands of Scotland. And not in a left-hand drive.'

'You worry too much.' Sarah lowered herself onto the sumptuous cream leather seat. 'The venue is less than a mile away; what could possibly go wrong?'

'We end up face down in the loch?' Georgia squeezed herself into the backseat. 'You know, there are times when

I miss the old Sarah. Doctor Moreish has a lot to answer for. This is his doing. He's turned you into an intrepid.'

Sarah adjusted her sunglasses. 'You can't blame Lucas for this one; he's got no idea I've even been taking lessons.' She started the engine, sending a deep rumbling noise across Loch Duich. 'Buckle up, everyone!'

Harper checked her lipstick in the visor mirror. 'I can't wait to see the look on his face. He won't believe his eyes.'

That was the plan. Lucas had spent the entire year arranging surprises for her, from booking trips away, to sending her gifts and messages. He'd even surprised her with a dog when they'd moved into their new 'pets allowed' rental. Bless him.

It was her turn to surprise him.

'Everyone ready?' Sarah looked around the car, smiling at the sight of her bridal party wearing sunglasses, each resting one arm on the door frame like Fifties film stars.

Harper punched the air. 'Wagons roll.'

It was fair to say Sarah's one practice session earlier that morning driving the Cadillac hadn't totally prepared her for negotiating her way down the narrow winding roads of the Wester Ross region of Scotland. Thankfully, Eilean Donan Castle was close enough that she could manage the short drive without encountering too many other vehicles. By the time the castle came into view she was quite enjoying herself – unlike her passengers, who looked relieved to be arriving in one piece.

Sarah could argue it was the stunning views of the centuries-old castle standing proud against the steel-grey loch that took her breath away. In truth, it was the sight of Lucas standing by the entrance of the walkway that almost caused her to crash the Cadillac. He was wearing a dark green suit, with a mulberry-coloured shirt and tie. By his side was their recently acquired dog, Tank, a squat British bulldog rescued by Lucas from Battersea Dogs & Cats Home as a surprise for her birthday. On Lucas's other side were his adorable nephews, Max and Elliot, both dressed in the same outfits as Lucas. His mini groomsmen.

Lucas's face when he saw the Cadillac approaching and realised who was driving was priceless. It was a mixture of shock, confusion and then hilarity as he burst out laughing. Even Tank raised an eyebrow, worried for his owner's sanity as she slowed the car to a halt.

Laughing, Lucas skipped forwards and opened the driver's door. 'I'm guessing this explains the secret Thursday appointments?'

'Busted,' she said, taking his hand and removing her sunglasses. 'Surprised?'

'Astounded,' he said, pulling her out of the car and looking at her in such a way it made her insides flip. 'You look amazing.' He kissed her cheek. 'Absolutely beautiful.'

'You scrub up quite well yourself,' she said, touching his face and loving the feel of his clean-shaven skin. It made a change from the close-cut beard. While they waited for the others to exit the car, Sarah bent down to stroke Tank, or as much as her tight dress would allow. 'You be a good boy for Harper and the boys while we're away,' she said, ruffling his ears. 'And play nicely with Fred. No bullying, you hear?'

Lucas helped her up. 'When do I find out where we're going on honeymoon? My sister's refusing to tell me. You've got me intrigued.'

Sarah mentally crossed her fingers, praying he'd like the trip she had planned. 'Well, I've booked us a cabin in Cedar River on the shores of Green Bay in Door County, not too far from where you holidayed as a kid.'

His eyes grew wide. 'For real?'

Sarah nodded. 'Harper helped me book it. And then we fly to Honolulu for two weeks in Hawaii.'

He looked thrilled. 'Wow, you really went all out. It sounds amazing.' His expression softened as he snuggled closer and whispered in her ear, 'You're turning into quite the adventurer.'

He smelt divine and her insides did another flip. 'It's nice to surprise *you* for a change.'

'Consider me surprised.' He kissed her cheek again and pulled away to look at her. 'Any more surprises I need to know about?'

'Just the one.'

His eyebrows raised. 'Come on then, hit me with it.'

She linked her fingers through his. 'Let's just say it's lucky we moved to a bigger place... we're going to need the extra bedroom.'

'Come on, you two!' Georgia ushered them down the walkway. 'Everyone's waiting inside!'

Jafrina handed Sarah her bouquet and Harper took charge of Tank.

Lucas waited until the party were out of earshot before whispering, 'You're... pregnant?'

'It would appear so.' She smiled when he skidded to a halt, looking as stunned as she'd felt when she'd seen the test results. 'Well, come on,' she said, urging him on. 'Are we getting married today, or what?'

'We're definitely getting married.' Before she knew what was happening, he'd swept her up in his arms and was kissing her.

Max and Elliot made disapproving noises, and Harper shouted, 'No time for smooching! There's plenty of time for that *after* you're married.'

Lucas carefully lowered Sarah to the ground, but didn't let go. She thought she'd experienced all the love he had to offer, but the way he looked in that moment was another level entirely.

'I thought it was the bride who was supposed to cry?'

'I'm an equal opportunities crier,' he said, kissing her again, and setting off a flutter in her tummy.

Unable to delay things any further – mostly because Georgia and Harper were threatening to frogmarch them into the castle if they didn't get a move on – they walked under the portcullis and headed inside where their collective friends and family were waiting in the grand banqueting hall.

As the bagpipes played, and the lit torches flickered on the surrounding stone walls, Sarah scanned the faces of those gathered for their celebration. Among them were Mrs Kelsey, Carla and Tyler. Her family were seated at the front, and even Lucas's parents had made the trip over from the US. All the pain from the last six years finally melted away and she could relax and enjoy her special day.

Of course, this was no traditional wedding. Far from it. The moment Lucas and Sarah stepped through the arched doorway and made their way down the long red carpet towards the waiting officiant, the congregation burst into a spontaneous applause, accompanied by cheers, whistles and the stamping of feet. Their smiling faces were stained with tears of relief and happiness.

They weren't the only ones.

Sarah turned to Lucas. 'Something tells me they're glad you showed up.'

Lucas grinned at her. 'Wild horses wouldn't have kept me away.'

Acknowledgements

Thank you so much for reading *Only for Christmas*. It was hugely enjoyable to write and I really loved revisiting the historic streets of Putney for my research.

I'd especially like to thank my cousin Richard Markham and his wife, Laura, for helping me create a backstory for the character of Lucas. They live in Minnesota with their lovely family and it's such a beautiful and fascinating part of the US. If you get a chance to visit, I'd highly recommend it. It was fun to write an American character, and I rather fell for Lucas myself. I'd also like to thank Laura Doyle for sense-checking my stalker storyline and advising me on the likely criminal repercussions; her extensive career with the police service certainly came in handy.

As always, a huge thank you to my agent, Tina Betts, who is always encouraging and a huge supporter of my writing. And a big thank you to my lovely editor, Emily Bedford, who gives me such constructive and helpful feedback and makes editing a joyful part of the process. I'd also like to thank the rest of the Canelo team for supporting my books and helping to publicise them and make them the best they can be. It really is very much appreciated.

Finally, thank you to all the fabulous readers, bloggers and fellow authors for supporting my journey, sharing posts, posting reviews and generally being wonderful people. In particular, my wonderful family and drama friends, who are always the first to read my books, leave reviews and recommend them to their friends. It's incredibly humbling. Thank you!

If you'd like to follow me on social media or make contact, then I'd love to hear from you:

Twitter
@tracyacorbett

Facebook
@tracyacorbettauthor

Instagram
@tracyacorbett

Website
tracycorbettauthor.co.uk
tracycorbettauthor.com